Let Flowers Be Flowers

Let Flowers Be Flowers

Daniel Rehm

The characters and events portrayed in this book are fictitious. Any similarity to real persons, living or dead, is coincidental and not intended by the author.

Hardcover ISBN-13: 978-1-7375154-7-0
Paperback ISBN-13: 978-1-7375154-9-4
Digital e-book ISBN-13: 978-1-7375154-4-9
Audiobook ISBN-13: 978-1-7375154-5-6

Cover design by: Adam Rehm
Cover photography provided by: NataliAlba
Other photography provided by: Nosyrevy & enjoynz
Printed in the United States of America

Rudbeckia Productions, LLC
P.O. Box 336
North Branch, MN 55056
www.RudbeckiaProductions.com
www.DanRehm.com

For Mary Beth
My Whirlpool Muse

CHAPTER 1

"It doesn't have to be perfect, but this is ridiculous!" the Mother screamed.

For the next thirty seconds, all the way out to, let's say maybe five minutes, depending on the severity of the atrocity, her anger would grow. She would start to take "it" more and more personally, whatever the "it" du jour happened to be. Today, the design on my bed cover wasn't perfectly centered on the made bed. It was best to stay out of arm's reach, and I knew this, but today I stayed. I don't like pain, but I can take it. Whatever she wanted to send my way was going to be fine with me. It had been awhile since I took a slap to the face. A slap isn't solitaire, it's not something you can adequately deal to yourself. And of course, you shouldn't see it coming. That way you can get an accurate gauge, a baseline of pain and tolerance.

People had it worse. When I was little, I would go cry somewhere. Sometimes I'd pull out the trundle bed, climb under and roll it in behind me. Like most kids, I had a desire to make the parents feel bad, to be sorry for treating me like crap. I enjoyed my "rage inward" time after the initial pain of not feeling loved wore off. I planned a life without them, without any real knowledge of what living alone involved.

I would occasionally get lucky in my daydreams and they would die. I didn't much care for gore. Usually, I would skip right to the funeral, to the crying people. I wanted everyone to know they were dead otherwise what was the point? After the funeral I'd come home to an empty house. It would have appeared to be a sad moment if anyone else could have seen into my head, but it was the part I always looked forward to. Usually right after I was done crying it was quiet. There was no one else in the house for her to yell at.

Mikey was my older brother, but I wasn't really sure how much older. Whatever our age difference, it must have been equal to the amount of time it takes for you to think you're emotionally over your son's accidental death and you're ready to have another child. The "not really" is something you never realize.

It was important for the parents to escape in the summer time. A cabin rental on a lake up north is the perfect place to take a kid who can't swim and isolate him from all social activities and relationship building. It's a perfect place to die. It's beautiful there. I loved being in the woods, talking to him, exploring together. The water I swam in, it went through him, he breathed it until he couldn't anymore. Water is a part of all of us. Same with dirt, ashes to ashes and all of that. It took days for divers to find his body in the coldest water in the deepest part of the lake. Plenty of time for things to bite and nibble on him, to make him part of the food chain. I caught and ate fish out of that lake so in a way he became a part of me. Not like a cannibal. It was more like appreciating and participating in the circle of life. It is worth noting that I wouldn't have eaten the parents no matter how they were presented. They were responsible for my arrest, sentencing and incarceration in this glorious prison. At the time I was quite angry with them and I think they knew that about me.

It is thanks to the parents that I was able to establish a baseline for life. Not for my life but for the lives of all beings. Empathy be damned, and sympathy is reserved for all characters Disney. There was a real world of make-believe where people and personified nouns cared for one another.

The family dog came with the name Bennet. We called him Ben and he got used to it alright. He was going to be my substitute brother, my friend through thick and thin. My version of Lassie. Ben was a brilliant mutt who didn't care anything for me beyond the food I gave him and my ability to operate a door knob. Still I tried to bring him along wherever I went.

At first, I didn't use a leash because I thought it was mean, but Ben ran away from me too many times. Once he scared the neighbor lady carrying her groceries into her house so bad, she dropped everything all over the sidewalk which resulted in a huge mess.

She pitched a fit that I swear lasted for years. Every time I walked down the street in front of her house, whether there was a dog with me or not there she'd be at the window, giving me the stink eye. Even after I learned to drive, she would come to the window like a shitty old cat whenever she heard my car. Her husband was a Nazi anyway, hiding in a low rent American suburb after the war. She was a sympathizer, an accomplice to the Holocaust and her hatred toward me was on automatic return. I didn't even have to bother with it because there was no way she wasn't dying first.

Ben was awesome to explore with, a welcome member of the team. Me, Mikey, and Ben. Back in the woods on the other side of the road we could dip our feet into tens of thousands of acres of lumber company land that men had logged for a hundred years. We were free to roam and roam we did. Further and further each time, until we were either cut off by a swamp or just got out a little too far and were scared of getting lost.

I wanted to hunt even at my earliest recollection. Killing was important then, not death. We always explored as if we were hunting.

I was in my earliest of teens when we found it. Ben got there first, his front paws barely crossing the threshold of some sort of crude structure. At first, I thought it was an old Indian building because I didn't really know any better. It was low to the ground, no taller than a man at its peak. It was built of progressively-sized logs with the smallest and thinnest sticks on top, kind of like a beaver lodge. It was built around an old triangular-shaped, canvas tent like the kind issued to GI's in the great wars. The door wasn't attached and maybe never was, instead it was heavy enough for its own weight to keep it in place. The rot of time opened it up wide enough for Ben to stick his head inside.

"Ben, Bennet, come!" I whispered in a loud scream. I was pointing behind me but not looking that way as I approached trying to signal the dog. The closer I got the more I could see that this thing was old and decrepit. The canvas was stained gray and green from moss and time. The door was tipped to one side, the bottom more dirt than wood. The canvas flap was torn nearly completely off, exposing enough of the inside to see a shoe with a bone in it.

I used a stick to pull back enough of the material to see inside. My heart skipped like I had just looked over a high edge. I was afraid of heights. What I saw I was able to determine was a man by what was left of his plaid, red, wool coat. His grey beard grew from beef jerky flesh over a smiling jawbone on the ground next to the rest of his head. A head that still wore a matching hat.

I backed away and stood for a while with my hands on my knees, thinking maybe I should puke. But did I really feel like it or not? Once it became a decision, the feeling went away. There was more to see.

Indeed, there was another. And it was a "her". Her pink top, blue jeans and once-pretty shoes were not tattered and destroyed like his clothes were. They weren't because they were not on her. They were instead folded neatly and stacked to the side. That must have made it easier for scavengers to pull her apart. Her arms and legs, what was left of them, were bound with wire. Not one of the four appendages were attached to the body. The ribs all laid flat as if she was drawn in chalk onto the rotted canvas floor. Her skull was gone.

I found that fact particularly shameful. I was angry for her, laying there without a head. It didn't seem fair. So what if his was next to him, at least he had one. The right thing to do would be to find it for her. I think I fell in love with her right then and there. She was older than me and I knew that, but I also thought that maybe I could love her like a sister, or aunt. Anyone besides the Mother. She would be perfect for Mikey and I knew he knew that too but was too shy to say anything.

Anger overwhelmed me to the point of exhaustion. I backed-out and pouted on the ground for a minute. I was mad at what happened to them, to her. There was nobody to blame for me. I was caught-up in the moment, obvious evidence meant nothing. I was mad that I didn't know what to do. I was mad that Mikey wasn't there with me. I was mad that I allowed that door to be open if only for a few moments.

If my god-damned mother had been watching my brother instead of compiling a life list of reasons she sucked, her life sucked, and because of that her husband and kids' lives must suck, I wouldn't have had a dog for a brother and we would never have found those people in the woods that day.

CHAPTER 2

I had to go back to the cabin. I wasn't sure why. I justified going back without looking any further by telling myself I needed to know what time it was so that I knew how much time I had. I ignored Mikey. Sometimes I felt like I didn't have to listen to him at all. I could just shut him off like a valve. A lie that fits into place so well that you can convince yourself it's true is a thing of beauty.

Of course, I was scared. I was always scared. I couldn't very well tell myself that though. Who knew how I could react? I had to keep everything I feared to my conscious self.

The old man was snoring in his easy chair, I didn't know where the Mother was but that was as good as knowing because I didn't have to see her. If he was sleeping already that meant it was just after lunch, I could tell without even looking at the clock, but I had to look anyway. I should have appreciated the accuracy. Instead I scorned myself for my lack of trust in myself. I had to get back out into the woods as quick as I could without seeming too obvious to myself that I was in a hurry. Ah, but the excitement.

I could talk to Mikey about it again because now the stress was anticipatory. He seemed slightly disconnected, like he was thinking about something else. Probably her I guessed. Still, I could tell he was excited to get back as well. Ben was too but dogs are usually excited to go anywhere.

"We need a plan, we need a plan, we need a plan Mikey!" I chopped the air with a knife hand, pleading with him for an answer.

"Okay, okay, okay, okay. We need something, stuff. Like at least a bag, or you know, um, a camera," I said to Mikey. We didn't have a camera. There was 110 slide model with a slot on top for a flash-cube in the drawer but there was no film. I could never get the Mother's "good one".

I had to find what I needed in the garage, but I didn't know what I needed. An ax. There was no real reason that I needed an ax, but it seemed to be intense and I wanted it. Then there was the moldy, green, looked like it had been in WWI tool bag stuck in the corner on the floor ever since I could remember. I was saving that for a "someday".

I found my pocket knife. I got it for Christmas a few years earlier after I mentioned I wanted to be a boy scout. I quit in the middle of cub scouts. I recall the stupid hurricane lantern, or whatever it was called we had to make for a badge. A tuna can on a broom stick with a glass jar glued onto it and a little candle inside. Asking the Mother to help me gather up the pieces was an Asian ground war even though she had no less than a million candles lying around the house. The Mother was fond of candles. With just enough time for the glue to dry

I got it done. If it required effort I really wasn't interested, unless I was really interested.

The foul odor of the moldy, canvas bag and its clanking contents told the entire natural world that I was on my way. In the garage I found a flashlight, a pair of pliers, a razor knife, and a magic marker. I had the ax slung "Paul Bunyan" style on my right shoulder while I simply carried the stinky, green bag by its God-given handle. Ben was irritating me as he walked along my left side, constantly nosing the bag. He liked the stinkiness.

This time as we approached the scene, I had a television show mind-set. We came up slowly, trying to notice everything. Nothing was out of the ordinary as far as I knew. The Quincy M.E. show theme song played in my head. I needed it, to keep humming along with it silently because otherwise I was just so excited, I wanted to scream and for some reason I thought I needed to be quiet. Quiet out of respect for something I was sure, but for what or whom, I didn't even think to ask myself.

Cloth of some kind, a clue, a tatter was mixed into dead leaves under a small Christmas tree pine near the entrance. I picked it up and rubbed it between my fingers. I couldn't think as two different mosquitos, each with their own tone picked an ear to infest. Their buzzing was maddening. They chose that moment to mock me because I was stone cold serious, and I looked like I knew what I was doing. They were just little soldier bullies that knew nothing. They didn't live long enough to learn. I killed one of them for sure but the longer I stayed still in the shade the more of them there would be.

Gently I pulled back the edge of the tattered and torn tent flap. I waited there by the entrance, waiting to be asked to come inside. I wanted to burst-in and start asking questions but as I prepared my speech, I realized I didn't know what to say. I crawled in carefully. It was wetter than I remembered. An odor lingered although I couldn't say whether it was foul or enlightening. It reminded me of coloring Easter eggs. A beam of sun cut through the branches outside the tent illuminating the inside upper corner. It made a hot spot and a bunch of flies gathered there soaking in the heat.

I just sat there staring at his face sideways on the ground. I couldn't tell whether he was angry, happy, in pain or anything. I was sort of frozen. It was like I was staring at some horrific accident on the side of the road. You're sitting there hoping to see blood and guts and when you do, you're shocked. It stays with you, sometimes you cry the first time you see it but never again. Then there is the moment when you're sitting there staring at a long-dead man's face and you wonder if you should be crying.

Thank god, I saw the accident.

In fall the big trees in our city yard would predictably turn yellow and leaves would cascade to the ground like snowflakes. I was too little to handle a rake but not to play in the piles. The leaves had to get to the curb, where people normally park cars. A truck that was part elephant, part monster would come to clean them up every so often. You could hear it coming for blocks. When it got close enough to see me, I ran and hid around the back of the house. Once it was done and gone, I would come back to find a wet spot in the road and a few leaf crumbs. My perfect pile gone. That was the monster's job though, it seemed right.

People in cars were different monsters. Constantly clipping the piles, spreading the leaves around, mashing them into un-rakeable crumbs. How did they know I wasn't in there? I could have been burying myself, breathing the air through the leaves that smelled like autumn.

I dragged two concrete blocks from the retaining wall across the alley that was supposed to hold back the hill. I placed them one on top of the other like a capitol "T". Carefully I built up the leaves around it until it was completely invisible inside the pile.

I waited on the edge of my seat all through dinner. Waiting to hear the bang and the brakes but nothing happened. Later the pile stood stoic under the street light, also waiting. I guess from that moment forward we both forgot about it.

I never really saw the bottom of a car before besides matchbox toys. That was the first thing that crossed my mind as I walked up to the scene. More accurately, I ran up to the scene because it was right in front of my house and I could see the emergency vehicles from a block away as I was walking home from school.

It was a blue car, but the bottom was rusty brown. It was on its side, the roof firmly caved-in and pressed against the base of the big elm next to the street. Glass was everywhere. There was muffled wailing coming from the car, kind of a haunting moaning or screaming. Men rushed around the scene. Everything was happening very quickly. It was loud and frightening. One of the police officers saw me watching from my front lawn, hiding partially behind the big maple. The tree gave me comfort. Other neighbors started to trickle out.

"Go inside kid," the police officer said to me pointing towards the house as he rushed to render aid.

I ran around the back of the house, through the alley, crossed the street at the corner and came around the front side of the wreck. On the sidewalk next to the juniper bush near the corner, a stained, white sheet was laid over what I presumed to be a body. At the time I don't recall how I knew that, but I never thought it was anything else. The person making all the noise had black, long hair. The top of her head was stuck partially out of the windshield which had been broken in so many pieces that it looked white around the hole. It explained why the screams sounded off. The face must have been about the half-way point. That's where most of the blood was coming from. Firemen stepped in my line of sight trying to peel the windshield away from the top down. A broken half of a cinder block leaned up against the curb a stone's throw away from the crash scene on the other side of the street. I never knew what happened to the other one.

CHAPTER 3

He wore boots, the regular hiking kind the color of tanned leather with black, knobby rubber bottoms. Bone, shreds of clothing, leaves and pine needles were the choice ingredients of a decomposed stir fry where he laid. The head I wanted to pick up so badly, but I was afraid a bug would crawl out of it. What a waste. I felt like Mikey could have used it while it was still good.

She was a puzzle literally and figuratively.

"Geez," I said to Mikey as I picked up a hoop of wire wrapped around her ankle bones.

It went around six times and was twisted together like a bread tie. Even now it kept the bones from falling apart. How tight must they have been when there was actual meat? She must have been pretty skinny.

I unfolded her clothes reverently. They weren't full-length jeans after all but instead shorts. The tag said size zero, the pink shirt was a small. The tennis shoes had been pulled off without being untied, size six. I didn't understand girls' sizes and like any kid I didn't want to look stupid in front of my brother, so I nodded and searched for anything that would make it seem as if this were an important clue. Writing things down always makes the writer look important and I remembered I had the marker. I didn't bring paper, so I used the piece of cloth I found outside the tent. It was lightly-colored, leathery. Maybe it was leather, I didn't know. It would suffice if I wrote small.

Nothing inside seemed to be made of the same cloth anyway. His coat and hat I recognized as the same type the Father wore for hunting. His pants were dark gray, and the material was brittle and thin. Her clothes weren't even torn, and it wasn't part of the tent either. I looked in his pants for a wallet but there was nothing.

I felt like a genius for even thinking of this, that maybe it was leather from his wallet. That word was thrown around loosely when it came to my learning prowess, "genius". So much so that I believed it as well. The teachers moved me into the most advanced classes my grade level offered. I was supposed to find the work more challenging, even difficult. They didn't care, they just didn't want me disrupting their classes. Next year I was going to have to skip a grade. They were all phonies, the teachers, the kids, probably the parents too. Follow our little routine and grow up to be like mommy and daddy. Grow up to be maniacs. Grow up to be slave owners and make more of the same. Keep the ball rolling. Nobody stops the ball.

Sometimes, you don't see something that's right in front of you, even something that's a big deal. Something like a rusty, old gun.

CHAPTER 4

The Father liked to shoot his guns. Moving targets, stationary targets, shotguns, rifles, handguns, he had them all. In the grand unlikelihood of invasion I guess the family would have been able to hold-out for more minutes than the initial few it would have taken to expose his fear. Every single time when I watched him, I just couldn't prepare my body for the sound of the shot. If I turned my back and didn't watch, I was fine, it didn't bother me. It was the anticipation that killed me. As far as attempting to shoot things myself I gave it a fair go on many an occasion. Whatever was exhilarating about the experience was quickly wiped-out by the over-scrutiny the Father reaped upon my technique. Apparently, the invading armies wouldn't appreciate being shot by a person who didn't use perfect shooting form. Do it this way or that way or you'll miss, you'll never get that big buck. When target shooting, deer and invading armies are synonymous.

The cowboys in the movies on horseback didn't have perfect form yet they managed to kill thousands of Indians. Why wouldn't they? Indiscriminate killing comes easy to people with superior weapons. It's almost as if having a better weapon makes you a better person somehow. Maybe that's what the Father clung-to, my gun is better, so it doesn't matter how much I lie or steal. Who do you clap for at the end of a movie? Is it the guy who overcame the odds and persevered or is it the bully who couldn't lose? The guys with bows and arrows were the real heroes, but the symphony playing in the background won't let you feel that way.

What does a gun really do except throw something really hard? If I had a robot arm could I throw a rock faster than the speed of sound? Like a bullet? If I arm-wrestled you with my robot arm, I'd win even though I cheated. Why not make a film of cowboys fighting Indians on horseback but instead of guns the cowboys would have robotic arms? What sort of music would it take to make them the good guys then?

It was the sort of gun made popular in old westerns. It was a short rifle, with a wood stock and grip under the barrel. It had a lever for cocking, but it was rusted-closed. I would have to guess there were bullets still inside but there was really no way for me to check. I treated it like it was a live bomb, an old mine found floating in the ocean years after the war was over.

"Holy shit Mikey! Holy shit!" I yelled quietly.

Ben was behind me, sniffing like he really meant something by it. He put his ice-cold nose against the exposed area of my back above my beltline.

"Shit Ben! That's cold!" I shrieked. He crouched and crawled to my side begging forgiveness. It was a ruse. Bones are what he was after and a split second later he had one of the girl's and was off to the races.

"Ben! Bennet! Come!" I screamed at him to come back but his game was to taunt me, to force my hand and leave me no choice but to give chase.

I kept calling and calling. I didn't want to get too far away from the find for fear of getting lost. I was just far-enough away to activate the "I'm a kid lost in the grocery store" sort of pre-game panic when I managed somehow to get ahold of myself. It occurred to me that the dog may have gone back to the cabin. It the parents saw Ben chewing on a girl's bone would they notice?

"Would they Mike?" I asked.

CHAPTER 5

I had to head back, I had to know if Ben went back with the bone.

"Jesus Mikey, you should have been watching him."

Immediately after the words left my mouth, I was sorry, but I didn't want to tell him.

As I was getting close to the cabin, I slowed my gait. I didn't want to be seen hurrying, it would draw suspicion. Then there would be questions followed by lies, theirs and mine, and finally we would all end-up mired in some sort of meaningless conversation. I'd rather fall and not hurt myself enough to cry.

I passed by the garage and the Father was in there monkeying around with something. He glanced at me as I passed but we spoke no words. I passed through the house, back door to front and saw the Mother. Again, no words were necessary as she and I didn't care at all about what the other was up to.

Ben was nowhere to be found and I wasn't sure if that was a good thing or not. After conducting a thorough search of the property it was clear that Ben had not returned. I was mad that I wasted the trip. I was mad at Ben but only for a second. Really, I was mad at myself, for being panicky and stupid, for not having control. I controlled nothing in my life, nothing. The most prime of examples became apparent as I once again passed by the garage on my way back to the find.

"Hey, don't get too wrapped up in anything, we're going home tomorrow," the Father said standing over his work bench.

"Home? But we just got here!" I said. It wasn't exactly the words that left my mouth I couldn't believe, it was the tone.

I sounded whiney like I was complaining. Only a few hours ago I hated it here.

"I tell you what. You start making the money and you can make the decisions," he said, offended and angry for some reason. How dare anyone question the king.

I huffed onward down the dirt road in the forest holding back my tears. The stupid dog met me about half way.

"Idiot Ben!" I screamed, taking my frustration out on the dog.

"Screw him, it's his fault," I told Mikey, who was angry with me for kicking air at Ben.

Our family had been renting the cabin by the lake for as many years as I could remember. It belonged to a man named Warmler, a cranky, old German guy who every time I saw him would be hacking-up a lung. One time he invited me to go fishing with him, but he was creepy, and I was afraid only one of us might come back. Usually we stayed at least two weeks, give or take a few days. Today was only our second full day and we were leaving already. Finally, when I found something worthy of my time.

I arrived at the find with a happy Ben and a quiet Mikey. I didn't even want to go inside. I didn't want to have to tell them I had to leave the next day. I spent the next hour closing the structure up the best I could manage.

"Hopefully nobody finds it. That would be our luck, right?" I told Mikey as I scattered handfuls of forest duff over the top of the structure.

"Nobody is going to find it," I said quietly, re-assuring myself.

Packing up to go home was the normal hell. Rush around like crazy getting stressed-out, yell at anyone you can see until you're on the road and everybody is mad at each other. This time around I was foolish enough to open my mouth and question something I found odd.

"There's still stuff inside," I told them as we were getting ready to get into the car.

"Yeah? So? What if there's supposed to be stuff inside? I'm sorry son, if your mother and I don't offer every decision we make for your approval before we make up our minds."

Sarcastic dick.

"We're coming back in a few days, maybe a week or so. Oh just tell him," the Mother never gave him a chance. "Your father and I are buying this place, the cabin. Sooo, that's it."

That's it. That's all she had to say about it. They began to talk amongst themselves. Almost five hours in the car and I can't remember if I spoke another word to them or not.

The good news was I was coming back, back to the find, back to them. They were most definitely a "them" and not a "those" unless they were "those" people. You have a name if you're a "them". He had a name to be sure, as decrepit and foul as he was, he had a face. You can put a name to a face. Her on the other hand, well, how would I know she wasn't just a collection of parts?

"Those" refers to things. Things like those bones, those shoes, or even those remains. By default, if you are one of "those" people, then you are no better than any inanimate thing. What could be more insulting than to completely remove a person's humanity from the conversation? I had to believe she was whole, that together they weren't one of each. I needed her to have humanity so that I could care for her.

Ben was sitting on the seat next to me. He just kept staring at me with a confused dog face, like he was dumbfounded listening to my thoughts. As long as I had his attention I wanted to know where he put the bone. I couldn't ask out loud because of the parents but as long as he was receiving my thoughts it couldn't hurt to ask him in my head.

C'mon man, dogs and bones, bones and dogs, this is your thing.

He was never going to tell me where he put the bone, either because he didn't want to, or he couldn't. I was hoping he could give me a mental picture. That somehow, he could psychically implant one in my mind, or maybe I could pick it up by some sort of dog to human psychic translation. It would have been black and white, how he saw the world, but I was okay with that.

Stupid dog.

I wondered if he could find it again. Dogs are supposed to be good at that sort of thing, finding bones. I wondered because it wasn't the only bone we needed to find. If he could locate the bone he stole, then he could find any other. I needed her skull, her head. He could give me that joy, that closure, that

level of humanity that I would apply to her, even if her face
was bare bone.

Good boy.

CHAPTER 6

The next day I made the rare add to the shopping list, dog bones. Our local corner store was really just a butcher shop with amenities. The Mother could get a bag of bones from the butcher for pennies on the dollar so my request would not be met with the specter of major financial hardship.

For the first bone I dug a hole in the yard as far from the house as I could find dirt and still be on the property, next to the garbage can corral on the edge of the alley. The small patch of dirt between a rusty shed and the corral was large enough to park a few bikes you didn't mind being stolen and was the perfect breeding ground for noxious weeds and purposeful neglect. Past that space was a man-made perimeter of cracked concrete and crumbling patches of blacktop and tar. This was the far bone. I was sure at first it would be the last one Ben would find. I hated so much being wrong that I revised my prediction. Because I was so sure of the latter, it would probably be the first one he found. It was in that moment of doubt that deep down I knew he would never find it at all.

The second bone I pushed into the toe of an old shoe. It was a pair that at some point was supposed to fit me, but I never recalled seeing more than one of them at a time. Even when lining up shoes to meet the requirements of a certain excessively compulsive clutter organization zealot, it was forced to stand on line alone. Every so often, over the course of time there were moments when I might have noticed the other one, but it was always recognition after the fact and I never went back to retrieve it and potentially unite the pair. It lived alone for so long that it wouldn't have fit me anymore even if it tried. I put the shoe in an area no wider than it was long between the shed and the neighbor's garage. Only rotten and wet things lived there.

A third I tossed into the gutter on the roof of the house. I threw it up higher than I needed to, letting it roll down into an eventual thud. I spent countless hours alone with a tennis ball and a baseball glove, tossing the ball till it would barely reach the peak before gravity would send it back towards me. Occasionally it would go over the top and I would race to the other side in a failed effort to catch it before it hit the ground. Sometimes, I would never find it at all. The Father would eventually catch me and threaten me as loud as he could with paying for a new roof because in his world, the soft, stuffed animal skin of the tennis ball was destroying the shingles by blasting off all the tiny rocks. Hail, snow, ice, driving rain, branches, sticks and helicopter seeds from the surrounding maples were all preferred alternatives to me. I knew Ben would never be physically able to find it. I guess maybe I hoped he would get the scent and amaze me by staring straight up at the spot. Really, I wanted to clog the gutter and cause rain water to pour down the side of the house in order to cause as much damage and stress to the Father as possible.

Finally, the last bone I tossed into the deep window well that exposed a basement window on the north side of the house. It was the dark area between houses where even weeds wouldn't grow. It felt like an evil place, mostly because of the neighbor's house.

The neighbor's house, smaller than our own, was close, merely feet away. It was on slightly higher ground which gave it a metaphorical advantage. It had an evident life force, as many houses do. It was always looking down on us, peaking over the stockade fence, judging. The back door was the face. On most houses, the front door and maybe a few side windows make the face, but this house was different. The peeling paint of its shutters reminded me of the worn-out eye shadow of an old woman trying desperately to hang on to her youth. The occupants responsible for its bidding inadvertently steered its attention away from the road so that it could fixate on us, on me. When it opened its wooden mouth the rancid breath of their family smell would cascade down into our yard. Every family has their own distinct smell, but most don't realize it. Theirs consisted of cats and spoiled meat.

After my careful preparation, I finally let Ben out and watched him comb the yard. He sniffed around, ran zig zags, pissed in ten places and crapped in his designated crap area, but didn't initially lock-on to the scent of any bones.

As it would happen, I was right, at least as far as the first bone was concerned. At one point, Ben was pretty close to it, stopping long enough to lift his leg and pee on the garbage can corral. I thought about every spot I hid every bone for a long time after that day. The far bone may have been nothing more than me taking my turn at a piss on the fence post, marking my territory. For as long as that bone remained in the ground, I would always feel safe returning there. Whenever I came home through the alley, I entered the yard in a thin space between the corral fence and the neighbor's garage passing directly over the buried bone. Although as time passed and I forgot it was even there, it became my hidden totem, a secret harbinger protecting the gateway to sacred ground.

Bone two, the shoe bone, Ben never came closer to than his proximity to bone one. It's an area where the shoe needed to be, its own personal purgatory. It was alone so long that it had grown accustomed to solitude. It might as well live out the rest of its days in solitary confinement, saving its stark raving dinginess for near darkness. It was better than being temporarily enamored with the possibility that it could ever be reunited with its mate. The leaves of the next autumn would bury it forever, but not so deeply and soundly that it couldn't be tortured by the allure of the outside world. I often wondered what that shoe did to earn its fate.

The gutter bone eventually did what I had hoped it would do. The basement window beneath it also had a well, although much shallower than the deep well on the north side. They called it a hundred year flood. A deluge so powerful that it quickly filled the window well full of rain water. The old, wood window was never designed to hold back standing water. The water poured into the basement until everything that could float did float, and everything that could grow mold, grew mold. It was an absolutely perfect setting for dark things to take ahold and they got fat off the anger and discontent of the Father. They were another story.

The bone in the deep window well between the houses I never saw again. Ben was never even close to it, so I know he didn't find it. I didn't even go back to check on it that summer. Once I did, I looked up and accused the house next door of taking it in order to either tease me or simply cause me distress. I gave it the nod and grin of one who could always as a last resort strike a match. If it was going to do battle with me, it must know that I would stop at nothing.

I never did hide a bone for Ben. I needed help with his training. The next phase of the plan was all Mikey's idea. Ben needed stronger motivation than I had offered. He needed to appreciate what he was learning. For starters I would intercept and remove Ben's food. Hunger has always been a powerful motivator.

CHAPTER 7

I spent hours that afternoon combing through old magazines along with anything current there might have been in the house. I wanted pictures of the people in the find. I wanted Ben to see in them what I saw. One picture of a model wouldn't be enough because otherwise it would just be him or her, just as one picture of a madman would never adequately tell the tale of another.

Dozens of pictures large and small, from shiny to news copy laid scattered on the carpet before me. I daydreamed myself in professor garb, wielding a long stick, pointing to an easel adorned with my face-collage. The background was classic, lots of bookshelves and wooden walls, a small blackboard. I grew agitated knowing Ben would never understand in that way.

I cut every picture into tiny pieces individually. It took me the rest of the day but that was fine because Ben needed time to get hungry. I didn't want to cut through the eyes, those he needed to take-in whole. There's too much information in a person's eyes. Likewise for the lips and noses. A lip or nose can't tell what an eye can tell, but they can tell what a lip or a nose could tell.

I placed all the pieces into one bowl and added water. I didn't want so much water that I would have to strain the mix for fear of losing something valuable. If I needed the whole beast, what good is the beast without some of its blood? Carefully I kneaded the pieces of paper into a doughy mix. If only I had the power to bring it to life, as a brain, as a face. She could use it if only I had her skull to add to. I could use it for Mikey, he could use a new face, to touch, to hold. People that saw him wouldn't be afraid. Only we would know who he really was, and we would tell the Mother, to watch her freak-out, so she could suffer a bit for being who she was at the time.

I had to wait until the Mother was out doing whatever before hooking up the blender. Only then would she want to know what I was doing without any obvious ability to understand. I tossed in a handful of dry dog food. The mixture needed to have a base. For the girl, I added a few drops of the Mother's perfume. I knew she would have been pretty, she wore pretty girl's clothes. For him, a thin slice of deodorant stick and some cigar ashes from the ashtray at the Father's poker table in the basement. Still, I felt like he had the stench of old on him, so I added salt. I pictured him sweaty, and dirty, and foul. I remembered the taste of my own salty sweat mixed with summer dirt rolling down my face.

Tears are salty. I was addicted to the romantic idea of being a mountain man. Trapping for means and existence, trading my pelts for possibles. The city sewers were ripe with raccoons. They were in our trash cans nearly every night. I only needed a trap. Because I didn't have any, money was never an issue. I couldn't ask for money, I could never do enough.

Everything I did I had to do anyway. Cut grass, trim edges, shovel snow, dig holes, it didn't matter. I combed the alleys looking for miscellaneous junk. I would realize the proper materials when I saw them. Like so many other things in my life, I didn't know where I was going until I got there, and then I would realize that was where I was headed all along.

The old-growth lumber I found was closer to iron than wood. It was heavier than wood should have been. Hand-cutting the boards made me question the authenticity of the saw. Nails bent-over and sparks flew off the head of the hammer with every attempt. I was heart-broken with my crooked results. It didn't matter if it worked, but for the effort it looked like I never tried hard at all. I couldn't show anyone. My fear of ridicule lived on two levels, the basement, where the finished work belonged, and upstairs, where foolish ideas slept.

The trap's door hung-up more than half the time during testing. My frustration grew. The overhead garage door that faced the alley would have to remain closed, so I wouldn't have to interact with any neighbors. They would see me and wave, but their eyes spoke nefarious volumes. What is that kid up to now? Why even give them ammunition for their thoughts? Where did he steal that wood from? He can't afford nails, or tools. I kept the overhead door closed.

It's difficult to describe the sound of springs. They vibrate, twang, and fight like a snake you are trying to hold straight. These were long, made of heavy steel, and they lived over the top of the door on the garage across the alley. Our door had them too, but they never made such a racket, nobody's did. Even in the slightest wind, these springs battled hard against the shaft and wood header that kept them functioning and in place. I had never heard anything quite like it until that day.

I forget his German name, I only remembered it was German like every other surname in the neighborhood. The door was nearly down except for his head and one shoulder that it pinned to the concrete approach. The concrete was old and spalled, you could see smooth, colorful rocks imbedded in it next to his face. He struggled with the arm that was still inside to find any sort of purchase from which to lift. He banged it against the heavy wooden door. His outside arm was outstretched, palm down, pushing tiny stones into the concrete with such force that his hands bled. He couldn't speak, he couldn't scream, he couldn't turn his neck. His frightened eyes stared up at me like I was death itself, cloaked in a black robe wielding the scythe that would remove his panicked head.

I gave it my all. With my muscles already worn I grabbed the bottom of the door and lifted with all my might. His eyes looked away from me, telling me to go get help, that I was useless and if he died it was my fault. I tried even harder, involuntarily screaming from the strain. The fat cheeks of my sweaty face ground into the chalky-white door. His fingers splayed as his hand shook. I collapsed next to him. I was going to run for help, but it sounded for a second as if he was trying to speak. He gurgled as if the part of his body on the other side of the door was still breathing but forgot to tell his face. I sat there on the ground next to him, next to dead Mr. So and So, tasting my salty sweat. He wanted to blame me so bad. The last look in his eyes wasn't fear. Although they stared right at me, they looked beyond me. I turned to look for myself but saw nothing. I went to get the Mother. For the rest of my life in that house the springs on that garage made noise when the wind blew. It seemed to always be windy. I hid the trap in the shed.

On the windowsill, a dry plant died. I used a spoonful of its soil to make the flavor of salty, dirty sweat, and regret.

Finally, I added the paper paste I made earlier along with a few spoonfuls of sugar, just for flavor alone. I trickled in water as I blended the mix so that everything would stick together.

It was Mikey who stopped me. I knew there was something wrong, but I just couldn't put my finger on the issue. Everything seemed so antiseptic, so matter of fact. I felt like I had manufactured that elusive recipe that lacked the one thing that it needed to make it perfect. It was like a nice song meant for children at daycare that would never really rock. Mikey was hesitant to mention it because he knew I hated pain.

I couldn't cut myself, not on purpose. I decided to start doing risky things that may accidentally cause me to bleed. I flipped a large knife into the air, spinning and catching it like a professional juggler. Once it looked like I was definitely going to catch it by the blade I pulled my hand away like a coward.

Angry at myself once again I slapped the soup can with the lid partially attached, off the counter and onto the floor. Far from an accident, I knew the moment I hit it I would cut either my hand or my finger. I raged on purpose, faking it to myself so that I could use it as false courage to draw my own blood. The slice in my right ring finger was more than adequate. I could see white strands in the meat I assumed were nerves. Later that day the wound would result in a trip to the clinic for three stitches. I held my finger at the base where it met the palm and massaged my blood into the blended mix.

My intention was to give Ben more than food. I had hoped somehow the mixture I put together would turn him into a seeker of sorts. If he only knew them, if he only cared, he could find them, find the missing pieces. If it was me or Mikey out there, he could find either one of us. He would smell us. However he would find us is how he could find them. He could smell-out her skull, smell-out her soul. I worked with him in the yard the rest of the week, but he never found any of the bones. He did however seem to enjoy the treats.

CHAPTER 8

Big choices were not commonly offered around our house. Small choices came and went frequently enough though. Things like, I could grab another meatball if I was still hungry or sit in a variety of seats that were not predetermined to be defacto thrones. I was given the rare opportunity to decide in which car I wanted to ride on the way back up to the cabin. I was informed that this time, we would be staying much longer, probably till the week before school started again. I would need to pack more clothes and "anything else that would keep me occupied".

The second car wasn't a car at all, but instead an old, rusty truck with a loud engine. It had big tires and chunks of rust fell onto the ground whenever the door was slammed. The Father planned on driving back to the city from time to time for work, and this way the Mother and I would still have the truck for going into town. I liked the truck for the cool factor but chose to ride in the car because he wouldn't be driving it. Uncomfortable silence was going to happen either way but anxiety from unspoken thoughts is preferable to the stress of listening to his.

Ben kept licking my hand. I thought maybe he was tasting me. The monotonous, repeated clunking of tires over tar lines on the highway and bad 8-track tapes tempted me to offer myself to be eaten. Would he do it? I let him keep licking, even pushing my wrist into his mouth. Go ahead, I'm good. When my eyes weren't closed, I hated the back of the Mother's head.

I worked quickly and quietly to unload the vehicles as soon as I could without any controversy. I couldn't wait to get back to the find. Mikey was on me the entire time, even going into the bathroom with me.

"Get out!" I told Mikey. "I got this."

"Who?" the Mother asked. Apparently, she heard me through the door.

"Who what?" I said.

"Who should get out?" she asked.

"Stupid spiders," I answered. Of course it was a lie but I knew she wanted to believe it because she didn't answer. Damn her for eavesdropping. Stupid you. Just one more thing that she wanted to take from me, one more thing they wanted to control. Thanks to her not even letting me pee in peace, I wasn't just in a hurry, I was angry too. Should have just peed outside.

This time I had a small notebook and pencils, a pocket knife, a magnifying glass, most likely because of television, and the same ax. I also brought along food, for Ben too.

"Find the bone buddy, where's the bone?" I must have said it fifteen times. Ben was excited but he didn't seem to know what I was talking about. Stupid spider. I made myself laugh.

"Don't defend him, he sucks at this," I fired back at Mikey. Yeah right, he'll get better, right.

I was relieved to see the find unchanged. Mikey and I made our way inside. I wasn't letting Ben in anymore.

"Don't worry about him. He's not getting in here. I was hoping he could help us find, you know, the pieces. We did some training."

I told them about my time in the car, about how boring it was. There wasn't much to say. I let them know that parents had bought the place and that we'd be seeing more of each other. That was the biggest news. When I told them I expected something, something physical, any kind of reaction, something more. *I thought you'd be happy.*

I was feeling less-shy around her and at the same time I was getting used to his decayed ugliness. After the cold response when I told them I'd be spending the summer here, I wanted to lighten the mood. I snatched the hat off his detached head. Just sort of goofing around, I was going to try it on and ask them both how I looked in it. A patch of dried flesh that was stuck to the inside of the hat fell to the ground.

Looking more carefully at his head now, I decided I would have looked stupid in that hat.

The piece of him that fell away was undoubtedly loosened by a secret. I noted that the edges were slightly jagged around a hole roughly the size of a dime. I felt official, kneeling there holding his head in my hands, studying it. I flipped it over and found another hole. The backside hole was much less-clean around the edges and far more out of round. Pieces of his scalp still held jagged bone fragments in-place. That's what I was thinking. Mikey thought it was probably a bullet hole. It was me that figured-out someone must have shot him and put his hat back on his head.

Ben was sniffing around outside, scratching and digging at the entrance.

"Git!"

He jumped back as I flipped the flap open. He had the bone.

"Good boy, good boy."

I tried to keep him calm, but he most obviously wanted to play. He crouched down on his front haunches with his rear-end high in the air, wagging his tail like a surrender flag.

"Gimme the bone, give, give."

Much to my surprise he let me grab the end even though he made a half-hearted attempt to pull it away. The wet bone scraped across the tops of his teeth as I slid it out of his mouth.

"Good boy, good boy!" I showered him with praise for giving-up his prize. I examined the bone closely but was unable to determine which part of the body it came from.

It was a part of her, that's all I knew. I had a theory that wherever Ben stashed the bone is where I would find her skull. I didn't bother to dive into scientific details as to the why or the how. It was just an idea that I had that I never questioned to be anything other than the truth. I threw a convincing fake. While Ben was most certain that the bone flew deep into the forest, in reality and by means of impressive sleight of hand, I tucked the bone into the back of my pants. The search was on.

"You go left, I'll go right," I told Mikey.

Ben zigged and zagged through the underbrush, his nose combing the air for any trace of scent. This is the sort of ambition I pictured when I planted the bones in the yard at home. Neither Mikey nor I could keep-up with him for very long. After a few minutes of what felt like uncontrolled chaos, we were back to square one.

"Ben! Ben! Here boy!" we called over and over but heard nothing.

The usually-present wind that caused a soft hissing through the pines was absent, but I could still smell the sap. I could even feel it sticky on my hands even though there was none. Songbirds called sparsely, seeming to be so far away but really just very high in the old-growth canopy. Oddly enough, it was a sound that broke the tranquility that caused me to see it for what it was. Peaceful.

"Ben? Ben?"

It sounded like a yelp, the kind of noise a dog might make if it was hurt. I felt like it was too far away to be Ben, but it was hard to tell.

"Shh."

When I heard it again it didn't sound like a dog at all. It was clearer, less animalistic, yet still very soft and impossible to locate. Mikey was nowhere to be seen. I wasn't sure if he got scared and ran home or if he was still looking for Ben.

The third time I heard it, it soothed my fear. It swirled like a gentle breeze from behind every tree, pushing down from above while propping me up from below. It was soft, and inviting, and succinct. It came with the peace and tranquility of a new nurturing mother, but she couldn't be that, she couldn't be anything. She could only be the figure of a young girl standing at the edge of my peripheral, glowing like white fire.

CHAPTER 9

I didn't even hear Ben come back but there he was, sitting next to her, looking at her obediently. Whenever I tried to focus on her she would no longer be there, retreating instantly somehow to the edge of my vision. I couldn't hear her or make out any details of her face. She appeared to be wearing a shroud of blurry air and I might not have recognized her at all if not for her faintly visible pink shirt.

"It's you!"

Speaking to her, saying it out loud, helped me to believe it was true. And then she was gone, a reward for my validated faith.

I stood there silently for a few long moments. Ben took off again, back to wherever. After my racing heart returned to normal, I went to the place where I first saw her. I searched the ground thinking she must have been there to give me a sign. Where the hell are you Mikey?

There was nothing, not a trace. I sat there, defeated and overwhelmed.

The woods around me returned to being picturesque. I may not have noticed if not for a noisy red squirrel who wasn't happy with me being there. I absolutely did not know how to feel. I should have been scared because I didn't know exactly what I just saw. Really, I should have been scared because I did know exactly what I just saw. I doubted even seeing it while telling myself that I absolutely did. If you'd have been here at least I'd have a witness. He never believed me. He always had some explanation that he deemed logical. Not this time. Fear was logical, but for some reason the actual feeling of fear never came into my brain. Mikey settled my feeling for me without even knowing about it. I was angry that he wasn't there, I was angry that he was going to call me a liar or tell me I imagined everything. I was angry at him and therefore I couldn't help but be angry with her as well.

"Where are you? Where did you go?" I called out to her but received no sign or answer. Mikey heard me though.

"Where the hell were you? She was here! She showed-up right over there like a damn ghost! I'm telling you. I couldn't quite see her, but I could, you know what I mean?" Mikey vaguely noticed the area to which I referred but it was probably more to appease me than anything else. It was nothing like belief.

"I knew it. I knew you would pull this. If you were with me this wouldn't have happened. This is BS man, BS."

I walked-off in a huff. I headed back towards the find. I needed to talk to her. I barged-in toting all my anger like a slowly ripping grocery bag.

"What was that all about?" The groceries dropped onto the floor.

"I know that was you."

I picked-up the shirt and held it in my fist, up to the place where her face would have been.

"I saw the shirt. Your pink shirt so I know it was you."

I looked over at the man, his sideways head laying on the ground almost looked like it was smiling, taunting me like it was all some kind of a joke. I tossed the balled-up shirt at him.

"What are you laughing at?" I asked him.

For some reason I thought the words that just left my mouth were funny. I sat back and laughed with them. My anger disappeared as quickly as her form from the forest and my thoughts returned to the moment and place where I first saw her.

"Where's Ben? Have you seen Ben?" I asked Mikey as I stepped out.

"Ben! Ben!" I called-out for him as I walked slowly back to the spot where I saw her. I was just about half way there when I heard a yelp. This time it was clearly the dog. I knew I was half-way because of the bare branch of white birch that stuck out right at my eye's level. I saw it earlier on my way back to the find. I warned that if it poked me it would be my fault but I would still destroy it. The yelping turned into a sort of screaming, dog cry. I hurried through the woods to find him. My heart was beating so hard I stopped to feel my chest. The excitement, the thrill of not knowing what was happening to him, the pure physical rush was entirely exhilarating. While I stood there with my left hand on my heart, I couldn't help but smile. It was the most fun I had in as long of a time as I could remember.

It was easy to hear him before I could see him. He was scared. I stood a few feet away in the pines watching him. He would get a little head of steam attempting to break free of the snare which in turn would tighten and pull him back. Every time he'd yelp and cry. His mouth was opening and closing in an odd fashion, almost like he was both trying to lick peanut butter from the inside of his snout and sneeze at the same time. I stepped out of the brush as a hero, ready to save the day.

I went to work on the thin cable around his back leg. The white fur on his leg showed a ring of red as blood seeped-out of his skin. He growled and lunged at me.

"I'm trying to help you!" I screamed at him.

I gave up on his leg and started fishing for the other end of the cable. Whenever I got ahold of it, he'd take another run at an escape and escalate the situation. More yelping, more screaming. I found the place where the cable was secured but without any tools there was little I could do to free him. I ran back to the find stopping half-way when I noticed my old friend the bare-branched birch tree standing at the ready to make the situation worse.

"I see you. Thanks for making me slow down."

I didn't want to hurry too much. The tree reminded me of that, but I really couldn't help myself because the entire time Ben kept making those terrible noises. I split the difference, choosing a fast walk, making a game of it, patting myself on the back every time I athletically avoided a branch to the face.

"You're lucky I brought the ax," I told Ben.

I took a weak swing at the base of the small pine holding the snare. The lowest branches absorbed most of the blow and the tree did little more than shake. For Ben, this only made the situation worse. I swung harder and more frequently until I felt like I was actually getting somewhere. Even though the tree was now tipped over, the dull ax couldn't slice through the springy remainder of tree meat and bark. With every hit the tree bounced and Ben screamed. I dropped the ax and grabbed the cable again, hoping that fate would intervene and somehow, I could get it off. I worried for a second that if I was successful then I wasted my time getting the ax in the first place. I pulled the cable attached to Ben in an effort to recover a little slack. He clamped down hard on my left arm, at least two of his teeth punctured my skin.

"Ben!" I screamed at him as I crawled backwards and away. "You fucker!"

The rage I felt was new but somehow still familiar. It reminded me of accidentally hitting my head or badly stubbing a toe. There's that moment of sudden pain followed by anger, but you can't really blame anyone else, only yourself. In that moment of self-realization, you achieve a calm, sometimes even humor.

I thought about what the Mother would say had she heard me. I thought about how I was going to explain all this to them.

I thought about her. Maybe this was why she was there. They couldn't know anything about her, about the find.

If I could adequately cover the wounds, I would never have to tell them what really happened. I rolled-up my sweatshirt sleeve and took a better look at the wounds on my arm. The bite marks were close together and not very deep. Easily explainable if either of them even bothered to ask. A couple band aids was all I would need. Maybe that meant he didn't really mean to bite me, that it was an instinctual choice. Maybe he couldn't help himself. I knew the feeling, I did the same.

"We'll just tell them he ran away. Shut-up, I did the same thing he did."

I didn't want to look at him. The snare came off easily now, without all the pulling and screeching. I covered Ben's body with logs and big clumps of thick, lush moss. I noticed that the moss smelled a lot like the Mother's potting soil, the same soil I used for Ben's treats. The moss also worked well to wipe Ben's blood off the ax.

I just did the same thing he did.

Half-way back to the find, the little birch stuck its fingers out, pointing at me, judging me. Because it was already dead inside, it was easy to chop down.

CHAPTER 10

There was zero chance that I was going to tell the parents what happened to Ben. That afternoon, the afternoon he died, I wandered around quite a bit, looking for nothing, wanting to find nothing. My goal was to come back late. I started calling for Ben as soon as I was close to the cabin, just in case they would have cared enough to hear me. I asked the Mother if she had seen him while acting somewhat distraught and worried.

"Ask your father," she told me.

As much as my life was more pleasurable without speaking to him, I thought it best to keep up appearances.

"Have you seen Ben anywhere?" I asked the Father.

I could tell it was going to be a harrowing experience for him to have to put the paper all the way down in order to have this conversation with me. He glared at me for a good 8-10 seconds through his half-glasses. I wasn't sure why.

"What? What do you want now?" he asked.

"Ben, have you seen Ben around? I can't find him."

"What? I knew you couldn't take care of a dog. All the money I wasted on dog food, and the vet. Probably found some kid to take care of him." And with those sound words of wisdom he snapped his newspaper back into rigid submission and put me on figurative hold. At least the conversation was over. I had done my due diligence.

That was three days ago. I hadn't been back to the find. Ben was all but forgotten by the parents. Aside from the Mother saying something along the lines of her being sure he'd show-up in a crocodile-tear-jerking show of support, they both seemed in a hurry to sweep the whole issue into the dust pan.

The Father returned to the city for work the day after we spoke, leaving the Mother and I at the cabin alone. For how long I didn't know. That's the sort of information that would have to be deemed from a genuine conversation wherein I would have to act as if I cared. I planned to misrepresent my day by searching for Ben, but really, I just wanted to see her.

That morning, I could smell the dust of rain in the air. I ate cereal to a chorus of distant thunder. By the time I was ready to go, the winds picked up and the thunder grew closer. I stood outside hoping the storm would pass. I heard the rain falling before I saw it, coming down so hard it looked like strands of cable.

I stared out at the lake, at the heavy rain creating an entirely new kind of surface on the water. I couldn't see the trees on the other side but yet, I knew they were still there. I was hoping that something mystical would happen, that I would see her appear in the gray, watery light. Mikey laughed at the notion. His jealousy smelled like dead fish, like him.

I clicked on the television to frost my boredom. I could get three channels, not including the UHF public television channel that took way too much effort to tune-in when you knew there wasn't going to be anything worth watching anyway.

Mass for shut-ins. Church was on two of the available channels. Normally, I would have been forced to go to church with the Mother but on this Sunday, she didn't want to drive the truck into town. I listened for a few moments to the priest belting out every usually-spoken word in song, likely because he knew he was on TV. He begged the Lord for recognition and emancipation of the poor and downtrodden, hiding safely behind a carved podium, on a polished marble stage surrounded by golden statues. Sarcastically, I begged the Lord for something to watch.

Jesus died for our sins. In Catholic school, they told us this over and over. In the world, someone was always dying for us. There was of course Jesus, every soldier ever, even though shooting at, and getting shot at by people a million miles away who never intended on leaving their yards was somehow dying for me, and miscellaneous cliché movie heroes. The world pushed dying on us like it was the ultimate sacrifice, but everybody does it. Is it so ultimate if every single person that has ever lived or will ever be born will do the exact same thing? If everybody wins, winning isn't a big deal anymore. If Jesus died for my sins, why did the priest on TV just tell me I had to pay for them? Because of Jesus, sinning should be free.

Mikey and I headed-out to the find early that same afternoon. A light breeze broke water loose from the upper boughs of the hemlock trees almost as if it were still raining and we were as wet as if it were. As much as I hated being wet and cold, it seemed like proper-fitting discomfort for a grave visit.

"There she is! There she is!" I exclaimed in a loud whisper to Mikey.

She was over Ben's grave staring directly into my eyes. We were still a ten to fifteen second walk through the woods away from her. I couldn't tell whether she was floating or standing, the small trees and brush completely obscured her form below the waist. I could make out the pink shirt though and for that matter she seemed a hundred times clearer to me now. She no longer escaped to my peripheral and I could even make out features of her face. She was as I predicted, beautiful, young, with long blonde hair that kind of curled-inward towards her shoulders at the bottom. Her pink shirt looked exactly as it did in the tent, only brighter.

As I hurried towards her, she extended her right arm, signaling me to stop. Ignoring her request I moved even closer. So enamored was I, that it took at least four to five more steps forward before I realized she faded slightly with each one. I stopped, then backed away.

"See, just like I told you." Mikey was gone. I was nearly as stunned that he would leave as I was with her presence.

She pointed at me, to her eye, and then to the middle of her chest. She returned her arms to her side and after roughly two seconds she repeated the exact same motion, over and over again in a loop. For me, there was no sound. There was no more light breeze, no more dripping water. My ears faintly rang from the silence.

"You see me, you see me, you see me!" Once it sank-in I nearly screamed it.

She backed away from the grave and looked down towards it. She looked incredibly sad. Her left hand hovered over Ben's grave as if she was delivering a blessing. With her right, she repeated the previous motion.

Ben, you see me, Ben, you see me.

"Because Ben, I can see you?"

She didn't stop motioning but her face gained an impossible amount of pain.

"Because Ben died, I can see you?"

Still repeating the same motion, her eyes focused away from mine, towards the ax in my hand. I didn't think much about it. I had it with me since the very beginning. Now, at that moment I thought about it, and when I did the answer to her riddle occurred to me.

"Because I killed Ben? Is it because I killed Ben, I can see you?" She clasped her hands together in front of her chest while looking towards me longingly and then she was gone. There was no moment that I could recall when she disappeared. It was more like I just realized she was no longer there.

CHAPTER 11

"I can't believe you weren't there again man! Where did you go?" I confronted Mikey in front of the find. I wanted to talk with her, to them. I needed them. He was there waiting for me. I was mad at him for not experiencing her with me.

"Why you gotta be such a jerk? I know you saw her otherwise you wouldn't have left."

"Seriously? Then why is it every time she is here you are gone? I mean, you can't be scared, that doesn't make any sense."

"Whatever. That's bullshit. You've been a jerk about her the whole time. You're afraid she won't like you."

"No, I know it's bull because when you were laughing at me earlier, I could smell you. It's like, when you act foul, you smell foul."

Once I said the words aloud, I realized it to be more true than at any other time in my life. It's not that I never noticed them, his variety of odors, I just quietly accepted it as the way it was, hardly noteworthy. I could never recall him smelling like anything I loved. Everybody should smell like cookies.

"Right now you smell like dirty socks and lies. Why don't you go learn to swim somewhere? Jerk." That was purposely the meanest thing I could think to say.

The rest of the summer Mikey kept his distance and I was getting used to him not being with me all the time. Often, while walking to and from the find he would be walking with me, a few yards to one side or the other. He thought he was being clever, creeping around in the shadows, secretly watching me, but I knew he was there. Sometimes I would see him moving through the trees peripherally. If I was in a good mood, I would find it all very amusing but when I was not, he was my enemy, stalking me.

I sat with them in the tent. I felt like talking but I didn't really want to move my mouth. I was afraid I'd say something I didn't want to reveal like a silly fear, or a wild unsubstantiated theory. Besides, I felt like they could hear my thoughts easily enough if I opened that door to them.

"I don't know what to do now. I have no idea where your skull is, there's nowhere to go to look, no clue. I don't know." I sat silently for some time, nearly weeping, afraid to even think something that they might hear, ashamed.

The foot falls outside sounded all too familiar. They were coming fast and before I could get out there, were already trailing away.

"Ben? Ben?" I called. I was quiet then, listening intently, my heart racing. Moments passed but I heard and saw nothing.

Further out into the woods, about as far as a person can see into a thick forest, I finally saw something move. Sure, it could have been a dog jumping over a log, but it could have also been Mikey. Maybe it was just an unsuspecting forest animal, but I saw something.

"That you Mikey?" I yelled.

I worked my way over to the area where I saw it, hoping to find a clue, or maybe see it again. I caught another glimpse of it, way out this time. The forest changed there, it was a transition between upland and lowland. Ancient hemlock and cedar trees grew a thick canopy over a moss-choked and always damp forest floor, forever doomed to live in the shade. Even though it was darker, a person could see much further there.

I could see the color of something in the distance, standing-out against hues of black and dark green. Could be anything. Whatever it was stopped, allowing me to get a little closer.

There was a moment, maybe a half a second when I thought I saw Ben, looking back at me and wagging his tail. It was so fast that it was more of a thought, or maybe just a hope, rather than what was actually there. I crept closer, using the huge trees to mask my approach. I would have sworn it was her but it was moving, flashing in and out of view through the trees.

It wasn't a "her" at all, and "he" turned and looked in my direction but based on his lack of reaction, surely didn't see me. Slowly and purposely he moved, creeping ever forward, constantly scanning the forest around him. I had seen him before. He wore red plaid with a matching hat, his pants were dark. His gray and dirty beard didn't match the hair that jutted from under his hat. In his hand he carried something that I could not clearly see, but he carried it like a gun.

Because there was a her, there could also be a him, and this must have been him.

The entire pursuit was functionally silent on the soft forest floor. Higher ground offered him concealment in a brushy area ripe with birch and aspen. I was close enough now to be confused, to question everything I had seen earlier. The clothes were different, the hat, the shoes, pants, everything. I was close enough now to wonder if anything I ever saw again in my life I could trust as being real.

Warmler was his name. I didn't know his first, I just knew him as Mr. Warmler. The wolf in the snare had a nasally snarl, like it had too much spit in its mouth.

Mr. Warmler was the man that sold the cabin to the parents. I overheard that he owned most of the lots along the lake shore at one time, carving them off like pieces of cake in order to make a living. He lived alone in relative obscurity, reclusively tucked into a small cabin, far back in the woods away from the lake. Having no clue about his age, he looked like someone's grandparent, white haired and weathered.

Warmler hit the wolf on the head with a baseball bat hard enough that it didn't sound too dissimilar from a wooden bat actually connecting with a fastball. It took two more before the wolf was done. Warmler took a break, leaned back against a tree and lit a smoke. When he was done, presumably for good measure, he stood on the wolf. With one leg on its neck and the other on its ribcage, Warmler squeezed any possible life out of the wolf once and for all.

He wrapped the body in burlap and began to slowly drag it towards his cabin. I followed at a safe distance avoiding possible detection. In between where we both needed to go and us was the lake access road, and it meant we were both getting closer to home. I saw him cross the road but without the body of the wolf. I followed him almost all the way to his cabin before I doubled-back to check out the wolf.

It was easy to find if you knew where to look. Its eyes were blood-red, rolled partially back into its skull. It felt unfair, like it wanted revenge so badly for allowing itself to be trapped by a villain. I sat there with my hand on the neck of an endangered species, thankful to the old man for the opportunity, angry with him for every other reason.

I felt like they led me to him, to that very moment. I felt like there had to be a reason. Memory occurred to me as I stroked the fur on its body that it was trapped in a snare. Until that moment I had forgotten about the snare that trapped Ben, considering it an accidental left-over from some previous trapping season. Accidents happen, look at Mikey, look at Ben. Maybe that's what they were trying to tell me, accidents happen.

CHAPTER 12

I had trouble falling asleep that night. I laid awake in the dark wondering when Warmler would sneak over and recover the body. For all I knew, he already had the animal skinned and the fur stretched. Why else would he kill it? It explained why he didn't use a gun. He didn't want to put a hole in the pelt.

I was up extra early the next morning. It was light enough to see but the sun wasn't up yet. Occasionally, Ben would get me up to let him out about this time. It happened so often that I would have never been able to count how many times we watched old man Warmler's boat take-off fishing.

I made and ate toast, grabbed my fishing pole, my small plastic tackle box and headed down a path in the woods that would take me to Warmler's cabin. The still relatively dark woods unnerved me at first, until I realized the only thing left to hurt me was him, like he wanted to hunt me next. The path to his cabin carried past his door down to the lake. I could hear him coughing up his cigarette lungs inside while I crept silently by. I could see from the footprints in the dew he had already been outside that morning. I moved off into the brush and weeds, off the short grass, wary of my own tracks.

Warmler's boat was a long, old, aluminum rowboat fitted with a black outboard motor. It was big by rowboat standards with four wooden bench seats, five including the little one in the bow. A gray, sun-drenched plastic swivel chair was clamped off-center on the back bench for the driver to tiller the boat comfortably with his left arm. A half dozen or so fishing poles laid across the benches. Discarded fishing line, dead worms, and chunks of busted Styrofoam minnow bucket spotted the bottom. A metal, mushroom-shaped anchor with a nest of yellow rope sat on the bottom in the first section closest to the driver. The boat was pulled partially up on the sand and tied-off onto a tree. In the front section between the seats was a red gas tank attached to the motor with a long, black hose. Placing the tank in the front helps to balance the weight in the boat. Next to the gas tank was something wrapped in burlap, wired to two large rocks about the size of footballs.

I waited patiently for Warmler to amble his way down to the boat. He had his tackle box and a paper bag rolled down that probably was a lunch. I knew I should have had more than just toast. He untied the rope holding the boat onto the tree and was just starting to shove the boat off the sand when I stepped out of the trees.

"Mornin!" I said.

"Jesus Chri…What the?" He looked at me with his mouth wide open. Still frozen in the pushing position.

"The kid from down the lake. In the cabin, yeah." It seemed like he was talking to himself more than me.

"What the hell are you doin' here kid?" he yelled, making it painfully apparent he was speaking to me now.

"Well, you asked me to go fishin' with you that time and I was up and I kinda wanted to go fishin' so I remembered that, and I headed over but I was sort of afraid to knock on your door so I…"

I kept my head staring at the ground through the entire speech until he cut me off, reaching a point of frustration exactly as I intended.

"Yeah, yeah, enough already, I get it kid but you can't jus…well. What's your name again?" I told him as he climbed into the boat which had drifted parallel to the shoreline.

"Well, I guess you ain't a Pollock or an Irishman. I hate to see a kid want to go fishin', but you know…" He sat there, not saying anything for a minute. He lit a cigarette and looked out over the lake.

My heart was beating harder than any time I could remember. It was like I was in a dream. If he really asked me to go I couldn't. I couldn't allow him to make any decision on this planet that didn't make him appear to be the most evil person I had ever met. I couldn't ever go to sleep thinking there was ever any good in him and that he didn't deserve it.

I hopped off the rocky shoreline down about a foot or so to the sand at the water's edge.

"What are you doin' there boy?" he asked.

I don't even know what ever compelled me to answer him.

"This."

I bashed him in the lower forehead just above his right eyebrow with a rounded piece of granite slightly bigger than a softball. I expected the hit to sound more hollow, like the wolf hit, but instead it sounded more like stepping on a crayfish, or maybe a crab with a harder shell. I didn't think much about it besides initially choosing the stone. It was the right size, it was right there, I had to do it right then and there.

Warmler fell back into the thin area of the boat between the back bench and the outboard motor, managing to hold his face with the same cupped hands that filtered the terrifying noises he was making. Out of reach now, I had to jump into the boat in order to hit him again. I stood above him, straddling the seat while he blindly kicked at where he thought I was. With all his weight on the back corner, the motor, and now me, the boat dipped below the water line.

Warmler slid-out the back into the lake. The boat sprang back to buoyancy, tossing me backwards off my feet but still inside the boat. By the time I regained my footing, Warmler had crawled through the shallow water to a depth where only his head and shoulders were laid exposed on the saturated sand.

He grasped his face where I struck him. He growled and gasped, never uttering a recognizable word. Blood covered the back of his hands, draining away into the lake, diluting into artistic shapes in the shallow water. The boat was loose and starting to float away. I jumped out and pulled it by the bow with all of the strength and adrenaline of a madman.

The boat slid right up Warmler's back like a ramp. Already weak from my initial attack, he was nearly powerless to stop it from pinning his face down into the wet sand. I hopped back up into the bow of the boat, forcing maximum downward pressure on the hull. With his right hand he reached back awkwardly, trying to push the boat away. Considering the weight and his exhaustion, he stood little chance. He flailed and splashed about, trying as a last resort to do a push-up and force the boat off him. I could feel his lower back arching, striking the aluminum below my feet. At first, I knelt-up, staring over the bow at this villain thrashing for his life. Eventually though, for good measure, I sat down in the small front seat, leaned back against the bow and rested my eyes. It was one of those naps that felt like you only closed your eyes for second but remember at least ten minutes worth of dreams.

It took forever to get his old outboard motor started. My arms were trashed from repeatedly pulling on the starter rope. I set the boat on ghost ride and sent it out into the lake. The throttle wouldn't allow me to leave it set wide open otherwise it wouldn't go into gear, but after a little force and a terrible clunking noise the boat took off at about half speed. The unmanned motor wobbled for a little way before cranking itself all the way to one side. At that point the boat was just going to run around the lake in circles until it either ran out of gas or someone stopped it. With so many cabins on the lake, it probably wouldn't take long before someone would discover the boat. They might even get lucky and find the poor old man who somehow fell out of his boat and struck his head on the stones along the shoreline. Whether the incident was to be remembered as a tragic accident, or just desserts, depended on who found him. Justice doesn't care what people say. Even for poachers, accidents happen.

CHAPTER 13

After Warmler fell, I went back to the cabin to change out of my wet clothes. The parents were still asleep. The Mother couldn't be allowed to find them. Dirty clothes belonged in the laundry basket otherwise the world would have to endure yet another gross over-reaction. I hung them on the clothesline along with the rest of the garments. They were all victims of yesterday, tumbling down the list of importance when compared to an empty highball glass.

I still wanted to go fishing but thought it best to stay away from the lake, to let someone else discover the boat. If I were sitting on the dock, I would have seen the boat circling and anyone that would have seen me sitting there might have wondered why I didn't say anything.

Instead, I made scrambled eggs. I could see his face in my mind every time I cracked a shell on the side of the pan, an engrained snapshot. Maybe it was the sound. I tried to imagine pained faces on the shells but every one of them had a silly expression that made me smile. I was cooking all their brains in a melted pat of butter and tossing their skulls into the trash. There was not enough confusion, they knew their roles too well.

The driveway to the cabin was long and curved. You could hear a vehicle coming a few seconds before you could see it, unless it was dark. In the dark you could see the headlights through the trees. Hours passed before the tires crushing gravel that morning gave way to a Sherriff's squad like the slow unveiling of a prize. The Father stepped outside and approached the vehicle. The Sherriff was slow and old. It looked like hard work for him to even get out of his car. The two men shook hands and held a short conversation that I could not hear. The Sherriff motioned over his shoulder which begged the Father to point in the same direction for collaboration, towards Warmler's place, towards the lake where random visits by Sherriff deputies don't happen. My heart was a red rubber ball, frozen in mid-air post bounce. The Father turned, took a deep breath and walked back to the cabin.

He sat down at the table next to the Mother. "Some kids in a paddle boat caught a boat cruising the lake with nobody in it and brought it back to the resort this morning. They called the Warden and it came back to be Ernst Warmler's boat. They think he might have fell out of his boat, and they found someone. They want me to see if I can give them some help with identification," The Father's voice cracked.

I was looking-on and listening from the kitchen. I wanted to go in there and make a big deal, but I didn't know how to act. If I cared too much, then why would I care? If I don't care at all then why wouldn't I care? I backed away, I didn't want him to see me.

"My God! I mean…this is it then," The Mother said.

"Look, let me just go over there and…" The Father was too choked-up to continue.

"Don't you dare loos…" The Mother started to exclaim loudly before thinking of me, looking for me, listening for me, and not finding me.

She began again in a muted voice, "Just go over there and see."

He nodded submissively and headed out the door to the waiting squad car. The Sherriff let him ride in the front seat. I waited a few minutes until they were out of sight before me and my still-wet shoes headed into the woods and back to the find.

We sat together in silence. I couldn't help but feel like something was over, like I had done all I could have done, and it was time to say goodbye.

"Ben, the snare. Warmler, you showed me everything," I stared down at the dirt tent floor between us, taking a moment to gather my thoughts.

"You led me. You let me see, no more pain." Again, I paused to think about what I had just said, piecing together evidence to support my sudden claims.

"They're not going to bother me anymore," I laughed a little at the prospect of the parents no longer having the ability to make me feel small, unloved or hated. I paid for it.

It felt good to laugh, even if it was only to myself. I didn't feel like I needed a reward for my faith anymore. I no longer felt guilty for not being able to help them. I didn't feel the deep shame, or anger, or hate for them or anyone. I felt like every emotion I used to carry as baggage had been replaced in one swift moment with a sense of duty. A simple and verifiable duty to do what must be done, and for a specific moment in time to explain to me what that duty consisted of. No preconceived notions. My reward was freedom. Freedom from judgement as much as judging. Freedom from all man-made emotions. I cared not to care about anything besides what must be done.

This time when I left, I carried out the old, green, stinky tool bag along with everything that was inside, and of course the ax. I wasn't sure if I would ever return. A goodbye would be for me, so it could happen anywhere.

I could hear them arguing before I could see the cabin. It was like I was the tires crushing gravel and they couldn't see me yet. The loudest of words I could make out here and there, like "poacher" and "bullshit" told me all I needed to know about the content. It would figure the Father would be defensive, to stand there and defend a man of low character in front of the ever-judging wife. Maybe that's what he was supposed to go over there and see. The judge told him to get over there and make sure the old man was guilty so she could hate him in death as well as life.

I ducked into the trees and came around the back side of the garage where I put everything away. I didn't try to be overly quiet and once they knew I was within ear-shot they went silent.

The Father yelled out the door, "Come in here for a minute."

I walked in the door like I was taking the stand at my own trial. "They found Mr. Warmler this morning. He slipped and uh, fell out of his boat we're guessing and hit his head on the rocks. He um, died," the Father said.

He had a hard time telling me without choking back his emotions. I kept wondering why I should care and why he would care if I cared. I had never seen him act so temperate, so approachable. I looked him up and down, searching for more obvious signs of pain. I wanted to bathe in it. His hands were clenched, and he dripped with distraught. How enjoyable this melting candle of a man would have been yesterday, when I might have cared to feel the joy of watching him suffer. Today his pain was nothing more than a by-product. Still I managed a look of shock, trying my best not to make it appear too obvious that I was faking it.

"Wow. I um, I'm not sure what I should say." I looked over at the Mother, who was busy circling fancy candles she wanted in some sort of catalogue. She seemed to care even less than me.

CHAPTER 14

I wasn't allowed to go to the funeral. It was a curious decision that I did not argue. It wasn't like the parents to leave me alone, to trust me. For days, ever since the wake was scheduled I was looking forward to the solitude. It's not enough just to be in the room alone or to be awake while they are sleeping. True peace came from knowing they were gone. Anxiety is born in the gears of a clock.

Bouncing headlights on the wall were the harbinger of their late return. Every tick of the clock past zero hour was bonus time, and they made me waste it all, wondering when it would end.

They thought if they argued in the car I wouldn't notice. When he got out, he slammed the door with both hands, really getting his shoulders into it. As if daily interactions weren't uncomfortable enough, now I had to face him in an angry state of inebriation. I could see it on him before I could smell it, the booze, the drunkenness. Bottle in-hand, he was about to storm passed me. I needed to be ignored.

I was satisfied with his quick exit out the side door towards the lake. The Mother came in, less drunk but equally furious. She slammed everything she had in her arms on the table and went looking for him.

"Go to bed!" she barked at me as she also headed out the lake door.

The pictures on the table were what drew me in. Pictures of Warmler, and a few of Warmler with the Father from some years back. One even had Warmler with both the Father and the Mother. I never knew how long they knew each other. They never spoke of him, not that I would have been listening. The Father had changed quite a bit since those days, but I could still tell it was him.

The program, "In loving memory, Ernst Karl Warmler" with his black and white army picture on the front looked like it might be an interesting read. There were bible verses mixed with prayers and scheduled repetitive chants for the zealots printed in bold font. He was preceded in death by his wife, Anna Marie giving birth to twins, Walter and Ingrid. Walter was presumed expired after going missing years earlier. Ingrid landed firmly in the "survived by" column.

It was all passively interesting enough until for some reason I looked at the back of the picture. "Ernst and Walter at the lake" were the words written in ink. The Father's name was not Walter. There were two other photos that showed them both. In each one the Father was labeled Walter. I stood there, temporarily bewildered. She came in so quietly.

"Well, aren't you the little snoop." Angry and more than half drunk she stood behind me with arms crossed, presumably ready to engage in battle.

"Who's Walter?" I asked her, holding the pictures for evidence.

"None of your goddamn business!" she screamed. It was hard to tell whether she threw her empty glass at me, or if it flew out of her drunken hands. Either way, it shattered on the wall.

"I'm Walter." The Father was standing just inside the door.

"Yeah, but I thought your name was..."

"It's Walter. Mr. Warmler, my father, was your grandfather. It's time you knew."

"Shut up, just shut up Walter!" The Mother was irate.

"I am not your father, kid, never was."

"That's it you son-of-a-bitch." The Mother stormed out of the house.

I stood there in shock, trying to piece everything together.

"Well? You get it yet dumbass? Ingrid?" He asked before taking a long pull off the bottle.

"I'm not your father, I'm your uncle. Uncle Walter, nice to meet you!" He mockingly invited me into a handshake. Still in shock I took his hand in mine, he pulled me close.

"Get the hell out of here kid if you know what's good for ya." he said in a loud, drunken whisper. "Get the hell out of here and don't look back."

I pulled away with all my might and backed-up against the wall. "Then who's my Dad?"

He didn't answer me, he didn't even look at me. He was focused instead on her, on the Mother who had come back in with a spade shovel in her hands.

"Ask her boy," he said quietly.

She swung the shovel at him with all her might but missed, taking out a lamp and an empty candle holder with the overswing. Avoiding the hit caused him to stumble backwards and fall over a wooden kitchen chair. She clumsily swung at me next, barely grazing my face with the smooth backside of the spade, leaving whatever blackness it was digging in smeared across my now-bloody cheek.

"It was her, boy! She killed your dad, just like she killed your brother."

"Shut up! Shut up! Shut Up!" She screamed and swung wildly, bouncing the spade off walls, losing control every time, desperate to hit anyone.

He was laying on his back, too drunk to get away holding his arms up in the hopes of blocking the next blow. She stood over him, paused and focused.

"Fuck him! He deserved what he got!" The Mother broke down and started to sob.

"That sick son-of-a-bitch, whoring around with that little tramp that he just had to have, just had to rape. Sick son-of-a-bitch." Her emotions ran from hot to cold and back again. I felt like running but I was in a book I couldn't put down.

She glared at me, her eyes unrecognizable compared to the woman I had known. "That's right, he had a little spot in the woods where he'd take them. Well the last one was it for him. But you know all about that don't you. You know all about his little spot."

Instead of hitting Walter she took another swing at me, cracking the wall behind me with the miss. Not connecting only made her angrier, she swung and missed another handful of times before she was forced to take a breather.

"I followed you! I watched you! You're just like him! Just like your brother was! You're a plague!" She started to calm down. She acted like she realized something.

"And that means you gotta go too," she said quite calmly.

With all her attention focused on me she didn't see Walter behind her. Inept and drunk as he was, he managed to hit her with a sewing machine even though he was never soberly agile enough to get off his knees. She fell to the table and then the floor, unconscious.

"Look kid, I was hopeless, I had nothing." He slumped back against the wall holding his bottle between his knees. He took the occasional drink as he explained.

"Dad and I knew what she did, well, we expected with Mikey, but we knew when she killed your dad. And he did deserve it. She'd have gone away forever, and Dad wasn't going to let that happen. I didn't have shit anyways, so I just sort of moved into your Dad's spot into his life. Sorry man, life's a bitch."

I wasn't sure what to say. I heard every word he said but my visual attention was on the Mother.

"Hell man, she even cut that chick's head off. She was that pissed. She shot him, and I don't know if she was dead already or what, but she took an ax and cut the chick's head off. Dad was freaked out. He had it in a burlap bag, he got rid of it somehow, somewhere he said where it couldn't be found. She used that against him though, the bitch."

He paused for a moment and laughed to himself. "Made him stay quiet about everything. That was the blackmail, ya know? He hated her after all that, always said he should have let her go. The only reason we're here is because he wanted to fish with his grandson. Too bad you turned-out to be you instead."

"Fuck you," I said to him quietly.

"What? What did you say to me?" He threw his bottle at me. He tried to get up but was too drunk. He fell back into a sitting position, tipped his head back and closed his eyes.

CHAPTER 15

I would have liked to have gone fishing with my grandfather. She must have known, same with Mikey. Everyone knew but me. There really was no benefit to the secret, not for anyone, especially him.

When the season is right, usually the first cold days in the fall, a fire in the house smells sweet, especially pine or birch. The mantle over the fireplace in the cabin was made from birch. The white, paper-like bark was a dead give-a-way. A person might think that a building made mostly from pine would smell nice when it burned, but reality is quite the opposite.

The smoke pouring from the hole in the ceiling was blacker than the night sky it rose into. I thought I heard Walter scream at least once but the roar of the flames drowned out most anything that could be heard. Nothing inside could have survived the intense heat and smoke.

The trees were an entirely different sort of spectacle. The fire created its own wind. Long branches covered with leaves caught the unrelenting updrafts until they singed and shriveled away. Pines lit-up and fire jumped from one to the next like paper matches in a pack. The sound of snapping and crackling as they flared preceded awesome waves of hot air, so hot that I was forced to retreat to the dock.

Smoke soon burned my eyes and the air burned my skin. The small row boat that came with the cabin back when it was a rental was still tied to the end of the dock. I headed out onto the lake, illuminated by the flames that in minutes had spread in both directions along the shoreline.

My distorted reflection moved in the flamelight on the disturbed surface of the water. I was somehow the Mother, rowing for a young boy who accompanied her in the boat. She laid the oars inside and stared across the water for a few moments. She quickly and suddenly turned toward him, grabbed him by the shoulders and clumsily attempted to throw him over the side.

The boy struggled and fought back, screaming incessantly for his mother to stop. She bent him over the side far enough to dip his head underwater at which point the boy could no longer hold on. His last grasp, a piece of the Mother's life vest tore-away in his hands. He struggled to swim, thrashing wildly in the water as she rowed back into my reflection, and soon he, Mikey, was gone.

I rowed that boat around the lake a hundred times, kicking an old life vest out of my way every time, never noticing the missing piece matched the odd piece of cloth I found at the find. I could see it in his eyes at that very moment that Mikey knew. It had been too long since I had last seen him, and it was good to see him again. He watched me from the shore, I could smell his usual odor of sulfur through the smoke.

"You knew!" I yelled-out to him. Of course he knew.

To my surprise she appeared a few steps away, also with her back to the fire on the shoreline. She looked scared, and I felt like she was afraid for me. My father was there as well, his face tortured, melting with pain and anguish. I had never seen him before but knowing what I knew of him, I was satisfied with the introduction. They all moved towards each other, over-writing each other on Mikey, eventually becoming one. Together they created everyone a person knew and no one any one had ever known. They absorbed all color, black as coal, wearing a hooded cloak made of shadows. They showed themselves to be what they had always been as long as I had known them.

Multiple boats came to my rescue, one taking me in, treating the black wounds from the fire that bled on my face. I cried for my rescuers, providing them with details of the fight.

I heard them yelling at each other while I was in bed. Their screaming woke me up. It must have become physical, which was normal. I hadn't heard anything for a while and assumed it was over and fell back asleep. When I woke again something seemed wrong, I smelled smoke. I went down to see what was happening. By the time I got down there the room was in flames, thick, black smoke was everywhere. I couldn't see anything, and it was impossible to breathe. I tried to pull my mother to safety but was struck by falling debris. I tried again but it was too late, I had to get out. They fawned all over me, gleaning morbid satisfaction for their empathy towards a boy who had just lost his parents.

There wasn't enough left at the scene after the blaze for investigators to determine the exact cause. The small to medium-sized forest fire consumed a handful of cabins and nearly six hundred acres along the shore of the lake. The lake and water-rich topography of the area was really the only thing that slowed it down. Based on the information I gave them it was eventually determined that careless use of candles during a domestic disturbance was the most likely explanation. The Mother was fond of candles.

The Mother was identified through dental records, along with her brother, my uncle. My father, who was not found at the scene was wanted for questioning in their deaths as well as the probability of arson. I of course didn't see him.

CHAPTER 16

His eyes popped open as if he were frightened awake. Fear on his face was not obvious. In the darkness his bright blue eyes looked as black as the intent behind them. His arms lay across his chest as if he were lying in a coffin suggesting that he did not move while he slept. Comfort was a non-issue on a mattress that was solid wood with a few old army blankets strewn on top for padding. In moments he was out the door and into his vehicle, a twenty plus year old crudely camouflaged Jeep Cherokee with a short suspension lift and upsized tires.

It was early. Long before dawn. He pulled the Jeep down an old logging road that a person would never find in the dark unless they already knew it was there. The road was an undiscovered bone laying just below clutter of the forest floor. At the end there was enough room to turn a vehicle around, barely. He spun the Jeep around, the old suspension components creaking and groaning from the tightness of the turn. The yellowed plastic dome light offered dim help in recovering a handbag sized leather pouch behind the seat. With the dome's light fading away he made his way off into the woods quickly, carefully.

A human being's eyes are not suited for walking in the dark woods. Low clouds reflect sparse light from distant towns but on the ground where everything rots, there is no help. Still The Hunter glides freely through the blackness by means of a sense unavailable to modern men.

The gnashing and crunching of gravel under tires was more out of place in the darkness than the engines that drove them. The Hunter moved through the forest as the crow flew.

His straight path was enviable and he reached his destination relatively quickly. Two vehicles slowly approached The Hunter's squatted position in the dark. They pulled into a small clearing made for them and their like by the state. The men inside sought access by way of trail to overcrowded hunting grounds. By design the grounds were more managed than the sparse game the men intended to pursue. The car doors banged closed. Two bouncing balls of light in the darkness followed words to a song scribbled on a blackboard by a madman. The Hunter followed, safely tucked under the cover of their own boot falls. When the two men split off, The Hunter chose the man showing signs of fatigue. The tired bow hunter's light bounced more heavily than his partner's. His feet dragged and he occasionally tripped. The gear he carried clanged against his body and he grabbed for breaths that eluded him. He cared only to get where he was going, ignoring the journey. The man eventually found his marker and settled at the base of a large tree to assemble his climbing gear. His deer stand creaked and groaned as he made his way up off the forest floor.

As is often the case, burgeoning morning light plays tricks on a man's eyes. It is the prime time of the day for harvest. The bow hunter stood at the ready, strapped in, bow in hand and keenly alert. Every false shadow or sound was quickly investigated and just as quickly discounted. A barred owl invisible in a nearby tree startled him with its signature "Who cooks for you" spooky chant. The crack he heard next was promising. It took weight to make it happen. From his far left he became aware of two approaching silhouettes. The deer to which they belonged moved cautiously as deer generally do, but were not alerted. It was still too dark to shoot yet but patience dissolves faster than the darkness. He came to full draw and waited for an ideal shot. The deer froze, focused on something they sensed was not right but could not see or smell the danger. The whites of the man's eyes lit up his bow string as he strained to see behind himself. For he sensed it too. The odd whirling noise was not like wings. If he could only see it then the familiarity of it all might make sense. Amid enviable focus, it was all too suddenly too late.

He couldn't have seen it coming from the position he was in. As it was his eyes were just barely able to follow the counterweights of the three-ball bolo as they whizzed by his face. Then again and again as the cord tightened exponentially faster around his neck. His arrow flew high into the canopy out of sight as the man tossed his bow to grab at the thin rope around his neck. In his confusion and panic he may not have noticed that his safety harness suddenly fell limp to his feet. A second later the bottom half of his climbing stand dropped away to the ground. His fingertips dug into his neck tied tightly by the rope to which they barely grasped. His feet kicked wildly. Freeing his right hand he grasped at the scabbard on his belt. The upper section of the stand dropped away as well.

There would be two last things the bow hunter would see. Blue emotionless eyes inches from his face that belonged to a hunter of men who clung to the backside of the very tree he was about to die in and his knife, the one that was supposed to be on his belt, held at arm's length in front of him by the very same hunter, who never diverted his stare towards it. Instead, just holding it out there as a way to insult a dying man. The bow hunter managed a few symmetrical kicks like he was practicing swimming like a mermaid. The last noise he made sounded nothing like a human. He wiggled and twitched from head to toe for a few seconds before finally going limp. The

Hunter never took his blue eyes off of him. He watched intently as every last second of life drained away.

It began to lightly rain. The body hit the ground with a hollow thud. The Hunter collected the dead man's gear and stacked it neatly at the base of the tree. He flung the body over his shoulders using a typical fireman's carry and very simply and unceremoniously walked away.

CHAPTER 17

The spores were exceptionally small, so much so that they looked like dirty smoke. As a boy, he liked to watch them get carried off on a light breeze. He still steps on them occasionally, except now he no longer watches the smoke. Sometimes they simply just squish flat. Puffball mushrooms can be that way. Rich and edible one moment, hollow and dark the next. Somewhere in between this shift they caused him bitter disappointment and anger, simply because they were there.

The black, heavily gripped sole of his boot crushed yet another on its way through the forest, ever obeying its master's commands. The sun had yet to break the hill. The autumn had been unusually warm, and the fallen leaves crumbled absent the cool pre-dawn moisture that would normally soften the blow this time of year. The boots loved them. They hated wet, slippery leaves.

A barely lit forest offered little depth to a man's eyes, mostly sounds in the still air. Slow and steady rhythmic footfalls turned The Hunter's attention towards the top of the draw. Manifesting like an apparition in a dark hallway, a mature buck appeared, silent and without fanfare. He worked the underbrush, cautiously testing the wind as he made his way to the bottom of the draw. The Hunter drew his bow and held a stoic pose. The unexpected crack of a rifle fired in the near distance rocked the morning air. The buck froze in place, head to the ground, eyes up. It had to be now. The range was good but the underbrush too thick to push the arrow through. The moments ticked by without neither of the players moving their pieces on the board.

For a man in his mid-years he was well-defined and muscular. Dark, smoky gray hair and a short, sparse beard flecked with gray gave stark contrast to his bright, piercing blue eyes. Those same eyes that held the color of tropical oceans that now narrowed in response to the onset of fatigue as his arms began to shake. No longer able to hold it, he drew down his bow. Sensing movement, the buck lifted his head and stared with blind eyes into the trees. In barely more than another moment the buck bounded off quickly up the opposite side of the ridge and disappeared. The faint rustling of leaves from the now distant and fleeing deer was obscured once again by the rolling discharge of a high-powered rifle. The Hunter narrowed his eyes again as he turned his attention towards the disturbance.

The long valley, a half mile give or take, was more like the fat end of a paper clip than a horse shoe. One-hundred-foot bluffs cloaked in hardwoods protected the wild field that ran the middle of the long, narrow valley. Deep gouges and washouts occasionally cut through the steep sides like wrinkles on the faces of the old. The closed end matched the long sides as much as a man's fingerprints would match those of his brother's. The open end of the long field squeezed out onto a bald hilltop that dog-legged right, opening wide and spilling down into the dead furrows of a once-farmed field that wrapped around the edge of the bluff that formed the valley. It was on the exposed top of this hill, facing the valley, that an old thirty-foot pull-behind travel trailer clung to a two-track trail that eventually snaked its way to forgotten county road. Twenty-five yards behind the trailer on the edge of the hill, a small outhouse stood like a sentinel over the marsh below.

Mason Owens cheeked down on the stock of the rifle, resting it on the hood of his car using a sweatshirt as a cushion. His focus through the scope was clumsy. Even the way he squinted his left eye made the rifle seem like a distant cousin at best. As he squeezed the trigger the rifle bucked hard.

"Sonofa…shit!"

The scope tagged his right eyebrow. Cracking the skin slightly, just enough for want-to-be blue blood to form on the wound. He placed two fingers on his closed eyelid and set the rifle on the ground. He looked too well-groomed to be wearing so much camouflage. His dark hair stayed combed even under a ball cap, and he had the kind of beardless face you would associate with a used car salesman or banker. He looked like "Joe Fraternity" twenty plus years removed and reeked of expensive cologne and cheap anti-aging cream.

"What the fuck?" he said quietly to himself. "There's a black eye." He cupped his eye in pain as he hastily leaned the rifle against the vehicle. It slid down the fender, the front sight carving a light scratch in the paint on its way to the ground.

"What the fuck! C'mon! What are the odds?!" he yelled out loud to no one. Mason disappeared into the trailer, slamming the flimsy door hard behind him.

Impossibly hidden on the adjoining bluff, The Hunter watched Mason battle with his own clumsiness. In a previous life, even on a different day, he may have laughed. Today was not that day.

The trailer door flung open with a kick as Mason headed back to pick up his rifle, now sporting a shiny new bandage over his eye. He picked the rifle up and opened the action, ejecting the shell onto the ground. He checked the barrel for possible debris. Satisfied he released it, he chambered another round and settled in for another shot.

The Hunter turned his attention to the far end of the valley. A half sheet of plywood with a hastily spray-painted bullseye leaned up against the brush at the base of the bluff. Mason fired again, this time sparing his face. The bullet struck the dirt far ahead of the intended target, barely creasing the long field grass. It was too far for him to see, but not for The Hunter. Mason set the rifle down and picked up a pair of binoculars.

"C'mon, where are you?" Mason asked to himself. He worked the bolt and fired again. Playing a hunch that he had been hitting low, he increased his elevation. The bullet struck left of the target as a small branch creased and folded without breaking free of the trunk. It hung like a defeated flag.

"Huh, it's about fuckin'…" Mason's words trailed off as he talked to himself quietly. He messed around with small particulars, preparing to fire again.

CHAPTER 18

Through young trees, a small vertical log cabin sprouted with slow gradation mimicking the elder wood of the forest beyond. The door was solid planks on rusty hinges that matched the hue of the weathered logs. The door bar hewn from an oak branch lived on the outside, seemingly installed to lock a body in. Two small, four pane windows were built in on either side of the door with perfect equidistance that would have made any excessive compulsive maniac happy. The glass was far too filthy to be used for anything but dirty light, yet it was so clouded that the film seemed decidedly intentional. The rust on the galvanized steel roof gave tell to its age, and the chimney pipe that barely rose above the peak matched well enough that it could have been cut from the same cloth of iron. A hitching post unused for generations served as an aesthetic railing in front of the door.

Fifty man steps to the west, an 8-by-10-foot smokehouse was dug into the hillside. The walls were made from mortared field stone, and the same rusty corrugated steel capped the roof. The smell of the rich, thick smelling smoke trickling from under the peak was a lie compared to its light airy color. A two-track dirt path made claustrophobic by the surrounding brush cut harshly away from the cabin towards the main road. A mid-seventies Jeep truck with oversized tires and a crude camouflage paint job gathered dirt from the surrounding landscape.

The Hunter inside squatted in the hot face of a small woodstove. The dirty light filtering through the windows made the pile of kindling close by hard to see. The fire crackled, the dry wood burned hot and fast leaving little trace of its existence in the smoke. The back of the stove rang like a bell as he tossed ever-larger pieces inside. The pitcher pump below the window squeaked and groaned with the wisdom of aged steel as The Hunter filled a tin percolator and placed it on the stove. The smell of wood-fired coffee soon made the cabin authentic. The muffled shot from a rifle mixed with the crackling fire sounded like distant thunder from inside. He sipped his coffee with peaceful and stoic intent as he stared out through the impossibly filthy glass. He thought about his necessary return to the woods. He needed meat as much as he needed to address the artificial thunder.

A young turkey, commonly known as a Jake raised its head in stark attention, breaking from its feeding regimen, alerted by the sound of once again distant gunfire. A twang and a whiz mixed with the tail end of the rifle's echo. A black carbon arrow carrying a guillotine tip severed its neck. The arrow struck the base of a tree with the sound of a hatchet. The bird flailed and flopped while the flock around it scattered. Finally laying still, a few downy feathers hung precariously in the air above the dead bird. The movement of the bow was the only indication that The Hunter was nearby. The ghillie suit he wore hung and swayed like the skin of a monster that could disappear at will. Small branches and leaves of native flora intertwined with the suit seemed to grow right through him. The soulless figure approached and picked up the bird before blending away into the surrounding forest.

The bullet made a strong thump as it cut a perfect hole in the plywood ahead of its own report. It took Mason driving half the distance to the target to finally enjoy some accuracy. Nevertheless, he had finally breached the crude bullseye and his arrogance wreaked.

"Now that's a little more like it," Mason said to himself. He ejected the last shell from the rifle and carried it around to the back of the vehicle. Sliding it into its case with all the precision of a one-armed man, he winced and rubbed his right shoulder.

"I gotta get me a smaller gun," he said. The dull slamming of the hatch echoed through the hills, but the late model SUV's engine could barely be heard.

The Hunter took his time field dressing the turkey. Skinning the bird was never an option as it protected the meat during smoking. Plucking thick-shafted feathers feels and sounds somehow morbid and regrettable for most. The smaller down feathers become a nuisance as they float around and stick to everything. He stuck the large, barred wing feathers in the ground to save. A natural feather makes a superior fletching.

Mason stood in front of the smaller than normal camper stove, unceremoniously pushing a few fat sausages around in a frying pan. A small radio on a shelf nearby tuned to the only station he could get cranked country tunes through what sounded like a coffee can. Headlights bounced through the far end window of the trailer. The hollow sound of the closing door suggested an older truck, lacking the precision of modern vehicles. Paul Owens, Mason's younger brother stepped in.

Paul was younger than Mason by nearly ten years, the result of a parental oops. He was just a kid when their mother died. Mason was off at college and with Maria being older she sort of took over in her mother's role. She took him with her to an apartment in town after the house burned. When she passed for him it was like having two moms that died. It is possible that The Lord may have intentionally made Paul slightly simple in order to protect him from his life. Overall, he was physically smaller than his brother and kept a short beard that covered most of his similar face including his neck. The brothers may have shared the brown hair, but Paul kept his in a more relaxed style that fit comfortably into any factory or country-western bar.

"What's up big bro?" Paul asked.

"Oh, not too much. How was your drive up?" Mason said, paying more attention to his sausages than Paul.

"Not bad at all. It's kind of relaxing once you get off the interstate," Paul said. He stood in the doorway waiting, as if the conversation was going to get better or more intense. Getting nothing from Mason, he stepped back out, leaving the trailer door wide open as he grabbed gear from the back of his pickup.

"Shut the door, man! You're letting all the heat out!" Mason scolded his younger brother. Paul clumsily rumbled through the door again, a hard-sided bow case in one hand, a duffel in the other, and a case of beer tucked under his arm.

Mason glared at him, disgusted.

"You know, you could make another trip. It's not like it's a long walk or anything," Mason said.

"Or you could just shut the fuck up," Paul said. "I got it just fine by the way, thanks for all your help." He carefully set down the bow, tossed the duffel and carried the beer towards the fridge.

"So…you see anything today?" Paul asked, referring to deer activity. Mason reached out and shut the door and returned to cooking.

"Nope, nothing movin'. Too nice out maybe," Mason said.

"Well, they're out there. Remember last year?" Paul asked as he clanked open the latch on the fridge.

"Uh, yeah Paul, everybody remembers. It's not like you're going to ever let anyone forget," Mason said, annoyed. Paul tossed the case of beer onto the top of the empty wire rack in the fridge. He ripped open the box and popped the top on a can.

"Whatever. You're just jealous, that's all," Paul said before taking a long draw off the beer.

"You got lucky and you know it."

The first day of gun season the year prior brought less than ideal warm and windy conditions. Deer were spooky and holding tight to heavy cover. After hours of seeing nothing, Paul fell asleep in his stand. Mason gave up in disgust and headed back to the trailer. Approaching the wood's edge two deer jumped from the thick brush in front of him. Mason got off a panic shot, but they kept running and made it safely across the valley and up the bluff on the other side. The rifle shot woke Paul. A large-tined ten-pointer crashed through the woods in front of him like a freight train. The doe that had been with him split off and went directly over the top of the bluff. He fired quickly but missed. The buck kept trucking while Paul desperately tried to find him in the scope for another shot. On a dimple jutting from the hillside in the woods, a break in the overhead canopy allowed a small area of saplings to grow a few feet taller than the surrounding flora. That is where the buck slammed on his breaks, offering Paul a broadside shot at just under a hundred yards. The buck ran another twenty yards with his heart shattered from Paul's bullet before his adrenaline finally ran out.

Mason laughed out loud. "Damn lucky. If that sucker doesn't stop for you, you'd have never seen him again. And by the way, I've killed more big bucks than you could ever read about, if you could read." He rolled the sausages out of the pan onto a doubled up paper plate and slammed the pan back onto the stove top. He opened an upper cabinet and peered inside. "Didn't I have some bread in here?"

"Well, mine's on the wall at least," Paul said, as he swiped his sleeve across his chin, wiping off the dribbled beer. "And at least I still got a wall to hang it on," he said with all the tact and anger of a bullied little brother.

Mason slammed the door closed, picked the tongs up off the counter and pointed them indignantly at Paul. "Don't even fucking mess with me about that shit Paul…don't even!"

Paul knew he touched a nerve and instantly regretted what he said. He held up the hand not holding the beer in a defensive manner.

"OK, OK, you're right. I'm just sayin', that's all," Paul said. Mason turned and slammed the tongs into the spent frying pan.

"Just keep that shit to yourself man. I lost more in the last five years than you'll ever have!" Mason said, still reeling from the comment.

"I know, I know, I'm sorry, man. I guess I was out of line. Don't worry bro, you'll get it back," Paul said. Mason put his plate on the table and opened the fridge.

"Oh man, what happened to your eye?" he asked giggling slightly after finally noticing Mason's black eye. He moved in for a closer look but Mason bobbed and weaved his face to avoid him. "Looks like scope burn."

"Burn?"

Most people would picture some sort of flame or try to recall the physical nature of the injury at the mention of the word. Mason saw it more as a metaphor for his life. "Crash and burn?" he asked Paul. "I know a little bit about crash and burn."

"Here we go," Paul said sarcastically.

"Yeah, that's right. Here we fuckin' go again," Mason fired back through clinched teeth. "She put me here, man. When I was down she just kept kicking. She ruined me!"

"Oh, and you didn't do anything?" Paul said.

"I'm talking about business. She knew we were on rough times and she fucked it all up anyways. I mean, you know I could have come back but not after all that shit.

Custody bullshit, the fucking house. Houses! Bankruptcy! That's what really fuckin' hurts man, the bankruptcy. Is this all the beer you brought?" Mason pulled a can from the box inside the fridge.

"Yeah. You're still selling houses right? And what about the kids? You'd think that would be worse," Paul said.

"The kids? You mean her clones? Three more spoiled little girls there never were. Makes the little shit from Willy Wonka look like the ideal child. The minute they don't get new fuckin' ballet slippers, or computers, that's it. They stand there with their arms crossed tapping their feet by their mother all in row talking about their shitty lives. They fucking hate me, and to tell you the truth, I never saw them anyways. And on top of that, I'm still expected to pay for them. From what? A fucking commission on nothing? What's six percent of fucking zero? Now take like half of that and put it on my fucking bill! It's ridiculous."

"Well, you have to pay for your kids, man," Paul said.

"With what, Paul? With what? She spread her legs for a living the first time, let's see her do it again. Get the fuck off my payroll." Mason finally found time to take a long rant-cooling drink of beer.

"I don't really want to get into this with you again," Paul said.

CHAPTER 19

When things were good for Mason, they were real good. Golden good. For most of the recent past his life was on a roll. He met Mary at a real estate convention shortly after he started with the firm. She was a leggy blonde who screamed high maintenance. She brandished her blonde hair and polished looks like what the envious said was a weapon of sales destruction. Her numbers climbed, as did her reputation for climbing into other more personal places. She relied on those looks to compensate for her lack of intelligence, but was not smart enough to realize what she was doing. She was sharp enough however to latch her wagon to a race horse at a time when the track was in perfect condition to make a run at the trifecta. Mason was young, vain, and aggressive. He was smooth, much smoother than her, and he could sell anything. When he saw her he had every intention to lay her and was more shocked than anybody when afterwards he fell in love. From that point on, it was a typical life-of-excess, boring American story. For the first few years of their marriage, they were DINKs (Dual Income No Kids). They moved often into the next-best house they could make some money off of and move again a few months later. Vacations were tropical and often. Both Mason and Mary held their bronze complexions even in the dead of winter. Enter distrust.

Mary was pregnant. She used all her sales skills to convince Mason that she forgot to take the pill. A pill that she had taken for years and was as much part of her life as brushing her teeth or applying make-up, or as far as Mason was concerned any number of things that kept her in the bathroom for hours. He never bought it. That is not to say Mason was not happy when his daughter was born. He might have shown as much by being there for the birth, but as far as he was concerned, he did not remember anyone being there for his so what's the difference? Two years later there was number two and after that a third. Work was always a better place to be when babies were being born, even if that meant sitting in a bar with prospective buyers or coworkers toasting the child you viewed as a possession that got you free drinks and attention.

After the first one he did not care if there were a couple more. At three he began to notice the expense. He scheduled a vasectomy. When Mary found him at home with a bag of frozen peas in his lap, she thought he contracted a venereal disease and lit into him with all the expected scorn of a spurned woman. When she found out the truth, she could not figure out what was worse. Either way, in her mind there was distrust. As far as their relationship was concerned it was coming from both sides.

By the time his oldest daughter was six years old, Mason stumbled onto the opportunity of a lifetime. With some upfront capitol, he could get in on a project that entailed rehabbing an old warehouse district into high-end condos. He doubled his mortgage on his house and borrowed everything he could. To the tune of nearly one million dollars Mason had staked the future of his family and never mentioned a thing about it to his wife. Not even halfway through the project, the Fannie/Freddie bubble burst and America dove head first into the Great Recession. Partners that were heavily invested in broad real estate markets were the first to drop. Mason's capitol quickly ran out. The project screeched to a halt before the first unit was completed buried under a mountain of debt. Due to the size and scope of the development the story made the front page of the paper. "Third Ward Development First in Line for Bankruptcy," the headline read. Investors were named as it was a matter of public record. Mason lost everything and his wife found out about it in the paper.

Everything that was ever wrong with their marriage made an appearance in the ensuing argument. Mason was at least a little drunk.

"I got it figured out," he said. "Every day there's a little more crap. Every day it gets just a little deeper. Pretty soon your life consists of churning through crap. And you don't really give a fuck 'cause you're used to it! Well this is crap!"

Mary snatched a coffee cup off the table and threw it at Mason's head. He dodged to his left and bashed his head into the corner of the door jamb where he was standing. The skin was cracked open over the top of a quickly developing lump. Mason stumbled forward, bent over holding his head.

"Ahhhh! Fuck!"

He stood up overtaken with rage. His face contorted from the effort necessary to bring his arm back so far and so high and loaded with such force. Mary missed the couch by mere inches when she hit the floor. She was not conscious enough to have wished for carpet or even put her arms out to brace her fall. The huge red handprint across her face stood out like a port wine stain. Before she came to, her lip swelled and her eye began to blacken. All effects noted in the police report.

Most of Mason's time on work release was spent with lawyers. After his conviction for domestic violence, he was powerless in his divorce. Mary was awarded nearly everything including significant debt as it had occurred while they were married, but a civil suit brought later pinned the balance of the debts incurred from the condo deal back to Mason. Mason was also to provide support for Mary and the children, which he had no legal right to see in his house that he could no longer go home to.

Mason finally understood the meaning of hate. A person cannot really, truly hate something or someone unless they have loved that noun first.

Like he was shooting a real but tiny basketball, Mason put his empty can up on a graceful arch towards the recycle bin. "Nothing but net. So, is that all the beer you brought?"

"Nope, got more in the truck I'm saving for the game," Paul said. He motioned towards the old TV sitting on a table in the corner. "I hope that piece of shit TV works better than last year."

Mason pulled out another beer and shimmied into the restaurant style booth that was the kitchen table. Not bothering to cut it, he stabbed a sausage and tore off the end with his teeth. He pointed at the TV with a meat-filled fork and answered with his mouth half full of food: "It should, since Marty had to go digital it gets a pretty decent picture now."

Paul worked his way over and started messing with the TV as Mason paged through an outdoor gear catalog as he finished his dinner.

"So what's with the eye? You shootin'?" Paul asked.

"Yeah. Damn fox running through here this morning. Something's been scratching around the outhouse," Mason said never looking up.

"You get him? Or couldn't you see?" Paul asked, laughing.

"Fuck you."

CHAPTER 20

As the door slowly opened on the smokehouse, the little bit of evening light that remained illuminated the almost gone smoke rising from the stone hearth. The door was left open to take advantage of the failing light. The hunter dropped a few damp pieces of wood in the hearth then threaded the turkey onto a short pole suspended from the ceiling by a black chain. Another chain of the same length hung next to it, and he attached that to the other end of the pole, leaving the turkey hanging level and swinging slightly on the pole. On his way out he ripped a chunk from an undistinguishable black piece of meat hanging on a chain and hook closer to the door. Barring the door on the outside tightened the seal and the raw bird soon began to taste smoke.

Inside the cabin an old rocking chair that looked like it belonged there seemed inviting next to the fire. From the scabbard on his belt he pulled a stately knife and he settled in. With his right hand he slid the blade towards himself and sheared off a piece of the black meat. The leftovers sizzled faintly after being tossed on the stove top. As he gnawed meat off the blade, he reached towards a small table and picked up a kerosene type lantern. The poor light that it made smelled dank and horrible. He gave up kerosene some time ago, choosing to use rendered animal grease from the backs of pelts as fuel. Carefully he removed a book from a drawer in the end table. The gold lettering on the cover was nearly worn off, but still visible were the words "Holy Bible". The odd feathers of a turkey's beard serving as a book mark grew from the page tops. The rocker creaked as he leaned back to read, only his left side visible in the putrid light.

This time the headlights cutting through the field towards the trailer outshined the surrounding dark making the vehicle unrecognizable. This truck door closed with a tighter, more precise sound, clickier and not so hollow. Marty Fischer let out the groan of a tired man in his mid-fifties as he climbed the two metal stairs into his trailer. His gray hair and extra thirty-five pounds worth of years marked a man just prior to a long-term health downspin.

Marty and his late wife Maria, Mason and Paul's older sister, placed the trailer on the land close to twenty years prior. It was meant to be a temporary residence while they built their dream retirement home on the site of the collapsed farmstead. Maria was the older sister to Mason and Paul. The land had been in the Owens family for generations. The brothers paid little attention to it besides hunting season. There was little of the original house left besides some scattered field stone foundation and the base of a charred, crumbled chimney. The house had been burned by a lightning strike while Maria's father Jack was still alive. Jack Owens tipped his tractor over on the farm and severed his spinal cord. After losing his wife as well as the use of his legs he fell into deep depression. So dark and cold was his condition that he spent the last years of his abbreviated life nearly catatonic in a wheel chair staring out the window of his cube in a state run nursing home. Nobody ever told him he lost nearly everything he had. As he slipped away he gave a crying Maria at his bedside directions in the house to a box of mementos he kept of her mother that he wanted to be buried with.

Her mother passed as a relatively young woman from ovarian cancer, a fact for which her father never forgave God. The barn was technically still there but was more ancient ruin than any sort of functional building. The two former loft doors made it look more like a jack-o-lantern that someone had left on the porch too long. The meat slowly rotting until it finally caved in on itself. A person would find an occasional piece of rusted steel lying about that used to belong to some antique farm equipment that few could identify. Finally succumbing to the same cancer that took her mother it was also where Maria took her last breath.

The hospital was not where she wanted to die. Hospice was her only remaining option. As the end inevitably neared, Marty took Maria out to the land one hot summer morning before the nurse arrived. Hospice in their small apartment as far as she was concerned was not much better than a hospital room. The air was thick with humidity that morning and the bugs were nothing short of tragic. Even a healthy person had trouble breathing in the heavy, wet air. Almost two full days of forever included one more sunset as well as her last sunrise.

Now, so many years later the place itself was a memorial for Marty. 240 acres of peace where he and the brothers scattered her ashes. Ever since their grand plans the place was defacto his. Paul was a kid when it all happened and Mason led his own former life of excess, practically uninterested in most things rural. Marty still planned to retire there. There was life insurance but not enough to compensate a living for a man so young at the time. A double-wide a few hours away in small town America and an almost full-time gig at a home improvement store would keep him comfortable until the math worked out. That day got closer with each formerly brown hair that surrendered gray before giving it all up for the drain.

"Evening gents," Marty said to the brothers.

"Hey," Paul said giving an upwards head nod towards Marty.

"Hey Marty," Mason said.

Just as he was about to speak, the empty pan on the stove caught his attention. He shook his head with playful disbelief as he leaned over for a closer look. "I hate working Saturdays, what did I miss?"

"Not much, been warm, nothing movin," Mason said, looking up at Marty while tapping his empty can on the table.

"Well, we'll give her hell tomorrow anyways," Marty said.

Paul was still fumbling with the TV. "Hell yes. I hear you though, I hate working on Saturday. God knows I can use the money though."

"You and me both," Marty said as he opened the refrigerator door. Fumbling around in the box he slid out a beer. "Anybody?" he asked.

"Yeah."

"Yup, I'll take one."

The brothers answered in unison. Marty grabbed two more. With an underhand pitch he released one of the cans towards Paul who made a pretty decent one-handed grab. The other can he placed on the table in front of Mason.

"At least you only have a couple of years left," Paul said.

"Whoa, that's a little low man, I mean I know he's old and all but," Mason purposely laughed a fake tone at Marty's expense.

Marty grabbed a balled-up coat from a shelf and flung it towards Mason. It made a muffled thump as it bounced off Mason' face. The troubled smile it revealed when it fell onto his beer can revealed no animosity.

"You son of a…" Mason said playfully as he spit dirt from the coat off of his lips. The three men together laughed out loud.

"Say, anybody else coming up?" Paul asked.

"I talked to Barry the other day. He said him and Gordy are getting too old to bow hunt, so I should expect them in November some time to work on their stands," Marty said.

Brothers Barry and Gordy Ardent were the oldest members of the hunting party. Barry was the camp "old guy", usually the elder voice of reason. He was a retired local politician as well as a hobbyist chef, a skill that made him the defacto camp cook. He never was a serious type hunter but instead used gun season as a release, a way to dumb-down his false bravado community status and just be one of the guys. It was maybe the one time each year when he could park his arrogance and live in a mentally safe place where he had nothing to prove. His little brother Gordy was a dry-witted semi-pro gambler known to take or make a bet on nearly anything. "Little" of course being relative, as he breached the sixty-year hurdle with a few inches to spare. He was a pretty shrewd guy, definitely nobody's fool. A guy that did not say a whole lot, most likely the result of an older brother who so badly needed to be the constant center of attention that he dominated most conversations. Like his brother, gun season was more of a traditional commitment. As their lives had traveled such vastly different paths, Gordy saw it as a way to reconnect and remind himself why he needed to be away from his brother for the good of their relationship. The brothers grew up in the country, sons of a state government worker who did everything from road and sign work to tabulating election results. Barry used to help Mason's father with farm work when he was home from college and was hunting the land when Mason was born.

"Tom said he might show, but I doubt it. He's probably already shit-faced," Mason said, referring to his longtime friend from college.

"It's possible," Paul said.

Taking a final long gulp from his beer, Mason slammed the can down hard on the table and hunched slightly, cupping his hand to his stomach. "Whoa, I gotta hit the head," he said. He got up from the table quickly and scurried around in the overhead cabinets searching for and finding a flashlight. In a hurry, he rushed past Marty and flung open the door. The light bounced randomly in the dark, a result of his awkward fast duck-walk that allowed him to pinch his ass cheeks together as he went. If he ran, or even jogged he knew the impact would cause him to fill his pants. It was a situation in which every person is familiar. One of those "had to go right now" moments. In the grass, the light reflected off something bright that caught his attention. A few of the brass casings from his earlier target practice disappeared in the dark as he hurried by.

As his mind was focused on the task at hand, it took a moment for Mason to fully process what he had just seen. Due to the urgency of the situation, he did not have time to stop and pick them up.

Paul, beer in hand, pulled the curtain aside and watched him from window. "Run Forest run!"

"It's not funny! I think the guy might have an ulcer or something," Marty said, taking a look through the window.

"Could be, after, well, you know, Mary and the kids leaving and everything," Paul said.

A trip to the outhouse was never pleasant. Besides being relegated to a candle for light, all different types of vermin found it to be a convenient place to live. Mason was doubled over on the seat grimacing, the candle flickered at his side. A loud thud, like someone smashed a fist against the outside, disturbed his quiet discomfort.

"Hey! Stop fucking around!" Immediately another loud bang rocked the side of the outhouse. "Cut it out, Paul. I know that's you out there," Mason said. The next thump was more disturbing. It was quieter than the others but clearly contained more mass, like a bag of powdered cement. Then the unmistakable sound of claws dragging on wood and high-speed sniffing right away lent a different sense of urgency to the situation.

"Uh oh," Mason said quietly to himself. He started to bang on the walls and yell. "Git! Get outta here! Ya, ya! Git!"

Everything went quiet besides the perceived extra-loud pounding of his heart. *What the fuck is that?* For a moment he thought he heard the dry weeds outside crunch under footfalls.

"Hey! Hey!" He pounded on the wall again, not knowing if it was man or animal. He felt powerless and uniquely alone, like a child lost for the first time in a department store a few racks away from his mother. If it was beast it would run, if it was man; he'd feel like an idiot. Enough quiet time of intent listening had passed without further event. Mason decided that whatever it was went on its way, but it was not long before he heard scratching again. This time it was different. It was faint, the claws seemingly much smaller. He clicked on his flashlight and focused on the corner on the floor in front of him. It was rhythmic and steady but barely audible. *That's gotta be a fuckin' mouse.* He leaned in closer in an attempt to pinpoint the exact location. He heard a faint hiss.

He looked away from the light, brow slightly furled racking his brain trying to figure out what could be making that noise. It was only seconds later when the bone-splitting crack of an M-80 type firecracker sent Mason reeling backward into the wall behind the seat, blasting the candle off the bench and smashing his flashlight into the wall. Outside in the darkness a man laughed hysterically.

Paul and Marty in that order came barreling out of the trailer, obviously also in the dark as to what caused the explosion.

"Assholes!" Mason yelled out while he fumbled for matches in the dark.

Marty shined his light in the face of the laughing man who was standing next to the outhouse. "Yup!" he said.

The man, who was grabbing his belly in laughter, was "good old" Tom Lasour. The sort of guy that a person might consider "good old Tom", but he was not really that old. In fact he was about the same age as Mason. Taller and thinner, his face showed the age of an older man who spent most of those years enjoying too much tobacco and booze. He tried to keep his thinning hair relevant with gels and creams that gave him a distinctive odor. There was, however, no product that was able to adequately mask the boozy after-smell of a functioning liquor alcoholic.

Either the best or the worst job in the world for a drinker is being a bar owner. "Tommy's" was a corner bar in an old neighborhood south of Milwaukee that originally catered to third shifters from the nearly defunct heavy equipment manufacturer next door. He learned years ago that tending that bar would lead to his personal demise, so he made a point to never drink there. That made it all that much more important for him to not be there, so he could drink.

"Tom? Is that you? You're such an asshole!" Mason yelled. He was obviously angry, but something in his voice said he was happy Tom was there. There were times in Mason's life when he felt like Tom was the only friend he had.

Mason came charging out of the outhouse mumbling profanities. The flashlight in his hand made it difficult for him to close his zipper in the melee. He finally saw Tom.

"It is you, you fuck. I should have known. What the fuck did you do? Walk up here?" Mason asked.

Tom was getting straight now and had finally calmed down after he had a good laugh.

"I parked down by the main road and snuck up here so I could fuck with you guys. So did I scare the shit out of you or what?" Tom asked with a half-baked smile.

Paul was still having a good laugh at Mason's expense. Marty was laughing too, but he at least had the good taste to turn and walk away in an effort to spare Mason's feelings.

"Ha ha, real fuckin' funny," Mason said as he finally finished securing the button on his jeans. "There's always gotta be a funny guy in the group. A real funny guy. Now where the hell are you going?"

"I'm going to get my car," Tom said.

"Well, nothing left to see here," Paul said gleefully. "I need a beer."

Marty just sort of laughed to himself while shaking his head in what could have been either disbelief or disapproval. He followed after Paul. Both men passed by an angry Mason, who quietly stared each one of them down. When they were both inside Mason grumbled and turned to follow when a thought stopped him. The brass. Mason thought. He clicked on his light and began to scan the grass. He walked a zig-zag pattern back and forth over the area but could find nothing. After a few minutes he was forced to stop and think about it.

They were right there, Mason said to himself. He shined his light down the path that Tom had taken to his car. Mason held the light still, beaming in that direction like he was threatening the dark with a light saber. Did Tommy grab them?

The loud crack of the firework still echoed in the hunter's cabin as he turned down the key on the lamp.

CHAPTER 21

A bell-topped alarm clock broke the silence of the pre-dawn darkness. The usual and expected moans and groans from the men nearly drowned out the bell. Somebody flailed hopelessly at the clock as it danced across the table, intent on completing its job. From the back room of the trailer Marty stepped out and clicked on the lights.

"Let's go gentlemen, rise and shine," Marty said exuberantly.

"Shine this!" said one of the men from inside a sleeping bag. Another miscellaneous voice answered, "Yeah, maybe when he's done you'll have a nice shiny button."

"Fuck you," said Tom as he flung the bag off his head, revealing that he was of course the first voice of dissent. Paul then flipped his bag down to get more air with which to laugh.

"Now, now boys," Marty said, scolding them like children, "the deer are waiting."

Tom let loose with an overly loud yelling yawn and stretch too obnoxious to quantify. Mason and Paul also contributed assorted noises from differing areas of their bodies as men are apt to do. Mason sat upright, aggressively rubbed the sleep from his eyes, and eventually came to focus on Tom.

"Jesus Tom, you look like shit," Mason said.

"Fuck you too!" Tom said, running his fingers through his disheveled hair.

Without much fanfare, the men all began to mill around getting dressed, assembling gear and such. For a decent amount of time nobody spoke a word until Paul finally broke the silence.

"I for one can't wait to get out there. There's a big buck with my name on it," Paul said.

Mason froze and glared at Paul before turning to Tom.

"Hey Tom, you ever see a deer with "Fag" written on the side?" Mason asked. Both Mason and Tom erupted with laughter. Paul was decidedly confused with the insult while Marty walked outside shaking his head in disgust, which in turn made the men laugh harder.

"Fuck you!" Paul said, finally getting the joke.

After a short time the wood-on-wood bang of the spring-loaded door on the outhouse echoed in the darkness. Marty walked back inside the trailer and dropped a newspaper on the table where the others were tiredly sipping coffee. Paul picked up the folded paper and perused.

"Everything come out OK?" Tom asked.

"Fine, fine. You should know I was thinking of you the whole time," Marty said.

"I'm flattered."

"You're something anyways," Marty groaned while sliding into his coveralls. He picked up his bow and headed to the door.

"Well, I'm heading out," Marty said.

"Wait, I'm heading out too. Let me out, I gotta go," Paul said, as Tom had him blocked-in in the tiny booth. He started to hip check him, spilling a little of Tom's coffee.

"Where's the fire, man? Let a fuckin' guy wake up first!" Tom said, irritated. He slid out and let Paul free. Once out and geared up, Paul shoved his brother Mason on the front of the shoulder.

"C'mon man, let's go," Paul said.

Mason stretched his arms out high and wide and let out a bear-like groan. "I think I'm going to take my sweet time and get out there when I'm god damn good and ready. I'll let you guys chase em' all back to me."

"Now that sounds like a plan," said Tom.

"Well whatever, I'm out of here," Marty said as he walked out the door. Paul made a sound as if air was escaping and brushed Mason off with a forward wave of his hand before joining Marty outside.

Speaking in hushed voices the two men walked carefully into the dark valley.

"Where you going?" Paul asked Marty.

"Far end of the valley where I usually go. You?"

"The west ridge in that old gray permanent someone built," Paul said.

"Alright. You shoot anything come get me."

"Will do."

Marty continued to walk straight down the center of the valley in the tall grass while Paul branched off towards the bluff and thicker woods. He dug around in his fanny pack and found a flashlight. The beam was yellow and old, the sort of light that comes free with a couple batteries. Climbing the steep hill Paul switched the cheap light into search pattern mode as he tried to find the tree stand in the dark. The trek was taking far too long. What should have been a ten minute plus walk was now pushing twenty as Paul reached the clearing on top of the bluff, well beyond the location of the stand.

"Shit," Paul said out loud.

He was already exhausted. The sweat trickled from below his camo ball cap and he was grabbing pretty hard for air. His thighs felt like cables, that they should be tight and strong enough to bound up the hill effortlessly, but his muscles were spent. Leaning heavy against a tree he dropped his gear and took a break to re-assess the situation. The benefit of stealth that accompanied a dark walk to the stand was gone.

In the cool, still air the dim light whisked erratically through the trees. To the Hunter, he could almost hear the beam shake the leaves like a passing light breeze. He looked on silently from his tree stand on an adjoining bluff to the west. Just knowing there was a man that close burned him inside.

Wheezing heavily, Paul finally found the steps of the old stand. Gray and none-to-safe looking, the two-by-four ladder was never-the-less a welcome sight. A simple plywood triangle wedged and framed into the triple tree trunk waited on top, grossly out of level. The complaints over Paul's weight registered as creaks and groans that carried down the hillside. Finally topside, he flopped over to grab some well-deserved air. The common but completely unreasonable reaction for a smoker is to light up. The warm smoke triggered an instant cough.

The now still light shone through the trees like a laser. The cough became a signal to the woods that a man was present, and reinforced the Hunter's distain.

Back in the trailer Mason and Tom finally motivated themselves from the table and were finally getting ready to head out.

"So what's up with you and the old lady?" Tom asked.

"I don't even want to talk about that bitch," Mason said.

"She going to take you to the cleaners or what?"

"Cleaners! That bitch gets everything!"

"Well at least you'll get half, right?" Tom asked half-heartedly.

"Half? Half of half is more like it. And I'm fucking broke as it is!" Mason said. "Really, I don't get a God-damned thing."

"Didn't you get anything from your sister?"

Mason answered like a spoiled young boy, "Fuck no, Marty got everything. Life insurance, all that shit my Mom left her; china, jewelry, everything."

"Well you didn't want any of that shit anyways. I mean, it's not like the guy was going to give you any insurance money. You still have the land though right?" Tom said.

"Yeah, that's still out there but what good does that do me besides a place to stay? I mean really? Marty pretty much laid claim to it with Maria and all. It's not like I can sell it. He'd never go for it, and I doubt Paul would either. Figure in the taxes and it's just one more thing I have to pay for," Mason said.

"The way things have been you probably couldn't get shit for it anyways. You're better off."

"Tell that to my accountant I can't afford to pay anymore," Mason said as he walked to the door.

"You got problems man," Tom said as he picked up his gear to go.

Mason stood with his right hand on the knob, pleading with the air above and between them. "All I need is one big deal ya know? Something to get me back in the game."

"Wish I could help ya man, but you know I ain't got shit," Tom said.

Mason looked at him and grinned slightly. "Yeah I know…but you're used to it."

"Whatever, fucker," Tom said as he pushed Mason out the door.

CHAPTER 22

The darkness slowly gave way to dim light. The sun is up somewhere but shadows from bluffs can make a morning seem longer. Dew is now visible on the tall grass and weeds in the valley. Marty's path cuts through it with remarkable accuracy. A doe with a yearling appeared at the valley's edge, having melted out of the hillside. All the guys were in their prospective deer stands. Immediate anticipation gives way to longing for light, and action.

An unlucky gray squirrel was an early riser in front of Mason's ground blind which was tucked into the steep hillside. The noise was distracting to Mason. When the squirrel finally foraged close enough he drew back and held on it, debating. Mason's waning strength ended the debate earlier than anticipated. The arrow carried high, barely grazing the squirrel's back. It escaped immediately into the trees, disappearing safely in the limbs that it called home. *Little bastard.* The squirrel had every right in the world to be there; Mason had little. It is curious how a man's feeling of superiority gives him the right to kill out of annoyance. The squirrel needed no coat to stay warm, no fire to cook, no gun to kill. That little squirrel was in every way far better suited to survive than any man yet is deemed inferior due to wit and sentience.

At the same time Paul sat dozing. His head bobbed forward, slowly at first, then full speed like a person committing suicide off of any high place. Seconds would pass before body and mind agreed and he would start to tip over, catching himself before falling out onto the ground. The temporary increase in heart rate triggered by surprise and fear would buy him another few minutes of attention.

Tom took an altogether different attitude towards the hunt. He loved being in the outdoors and figured the best way to celebrate that fact was with a drink. He also had an old permanent stand in an old oak at the edge of a field but was often found relaxing on an adjoining stump. He slid a half pint of liquor from inside his coat and took a hard pull reminiscent of a seasoned drunk.

Marty on the other hand was flat-cold serious. He stood in his climber completely at the ready, his back rigid and straight against the tree. Eyes and ears constantly scanning for any irregularity. He held his bow low, arrow knocked with the release clipped to the string.

Mason was fidgety. His mind was so far off of deer that he scanned tree limbs hoping the squirrel would come back, something to stave off boredom. He got out and side-stepped down the steep bluff looking for his arrow. If not for the bright yellow fletching he would have never seen it buried in the leaves. He checked for hair then slid it back in the quiver that dangled from his belt. Even though it was early, he could not bring himself to return to the blind. His thoughts were poor company and his mind was best distracted.

He hiked back up to the top creeping slowly along the bluff's length. From such a vantage he could see down either side, possibly placing himself in a point of ambush.

Eventually, without thinking, even more without remembering, he approached an area of the bluff top that wreaked of familiarity. Sandy sedimentary rock that broke through the forest hill was layered like fine pastry. It told the tale of an ocean that rose above it so many eons ago. It was a unique landmark. Unique enough that Mason suddenly remembered exactly where he was. Towards the west, down in the adjoining valley Marty waited, ever stoic.

Mason hunched down and laid his bow on the ground. The bluff did not instantly fall off from the edge of the rock. Instead, a small plateau of brushy undergrowth about the size of a city lot buffered the drop to the west. Towards that edge a short natural berm of eroded rock and then a harsh thirty-degree slide to the valley below. He pulled a tiny pair of binoculars from a cargo pocket in his pants and crept to the edge of the berm. He had a good view of Marty below. Backing off he turned onto his back, patting down his body, searching all remaining pockets. His hands clung tight to his body. He squeezed his pockets and stared upwards at the sky, as if somewhere up there was the answer. The missing item's importance slipped away with the passing seconds and soon he was back to the edge, eyes planted in the lenses of the binoculars, spying on Marty even though there was nothing to learn.

The two deer that foraged at the valley's edge earlier had made their way to the end. They grazed slowly back into the wood-line, just yards away from Marty. Marty's body language changed, he raised his bow slightly but still short of shooting position. He was no longer searching, his glare now fixed. Mason quietly watched the scene unfold. He could barely see the deer approaching Marty. Small sections of their bodies shape shifted through trees an impossible distance away.

"Why does that shit never happen to me?" Mason whispered to himself.

A glimmer of light, or some sort of reflective flash like a distant camera diverted Mason's attention away from Marty.

It came from somewhere on a distant bluff. Through the tree tops it was impossible to locate the source. *What the?* Mason never heard the footsteps coming until they were right on top of him. Very slowly he turned his head around, careful not to move any other part of his body. Their eyes met. A young buck, six points, hooved the ground and bobbed its head, a show of aggression. Mason's heart pounded hard on his chest as if it were in his breast pocket. He knew the buck would not stay there long. He contemplated a slow grab for his bow hoping the deer would not notice but without picking up Mason's scent it was movement that the buck was waiting for. Mason decided on the quick grab method and lurched hard and fast for his weapon. The buck wheezed loudly, his shoulders went low as he planted his front hooves into the ground and sprang ninety degrees north in less than the merest instant. He flew through the woods with reckless abandon, snorting and wheezing as he ran. The same animal that had so gracefully and silently slid up the ridge moments before.

The alert from the buck did not go unnoticed. The adult doe in front of Marty snapped to attention. Her tail stood tall like a cartoon skunk. Nervously she began to trot, eventually breaking into an elegant bound, her white tail waving like a flag surrendering into the trees. Unaware of why, the yearling followed, knowing only that it must. Marty too had heard the distant commotion on the bluff and searched in vain for an answer.

Paul was fast asleep curled up in the fetal position on his deer stand. The sound of crashing hooves startled him awake. He was dazed from deep sleep and it took him a second to re-realize his surroundings. Twenty yards in front of him stood a wheezing, tired six pointer, the same buck that Mason encountered moments earlier. Not really even believing what he was seeing he reacted relatively quickly for a man that was sleeping only seconds ago. He picked up his bow, the arrow knocked and ready. He swung the bow around and came to full draw in one poetic motion. His aim was handled in a fast two-count before he released. The arrow skipped off the ground underneath the buck's belly. The buck jumped straight up like a bucking bronco at the rodeo. When its feet hit the ground the acceleration was impressive and he was long gone.

"Son of a bitch!" Paul said, quite loudly. Immediately he knocked another arrow and took aim at a nearby stump. He could not come to grips with the fact that he could have missed that badly. After careful aim the arrow once again strikes the ground low. Now cradling the bow he looked it over carefully.

"Shit!"

Without a functioning bow Paul gathered up his gear and climbed down from his stand.

Marty could see a long ways across the valley through the tree tops from his stand. He saw Paul in the distance exiting the woods into the weedy valley below.

"Huh, it's pretty early there bud, did you get one?" Marty asked as he tried to get a better look at Paul through his binoculars.

Paul knew he could be seen by Marty but it was not an emergency so he did not bother to flag him down. The lack of a signal gnawed on Marty for a few hard moments before his curiousness forced him down.

Mason was still watching from the top of the bluff. The noise Marty made during his descent would mask his own exit. It was the perfect time to leave. He ducked back from the berm and rose to his feet. In a slouching run with quick steps being careful not to let his profile breach the bluff he made way back to his stand.

Paul was walking slowly along the wooded edge. A loud whistle, the sort that can be made by some by putting two fingers in their mouths and blowing hard, stopped him in his tracks. It was Marty signaling that he was coming out. Paul lit up a smoke and waited.

Tom was off wandering in the woods, something he is prone to do. As he had in the past he would eventually make it around to stumbling across the other hunters, an unofficial sign that the morning hunt is over. He also heard the whistle though only faintly. Unsure of the direction, and unsure of his location, he made for where he thought Marty's stand would be.

"What's going on? You get one or what?" Marty asked Paul, slightly winded.

"I took a shot at one but I missed low," Paul said.

Marty was still trying to catch his breath. He leaned over with his hands on his knees. It seemed as if lately he did that after every short walk. Movement caught his left eye. It was Mason coming out on the other side of the valley following the usual path that led down from his stand.

"Yeah, I think something's wrong with my bow," Paul said.

Mason was not quite there yet, but without any real wind to consider, sound travelled well in the valley.

"Did I hear that right? You missed low?" Mason carried out the "low" like a game show host.

"Yeah, but I'm telling you I think my knock may have slipped because everything is low."

"Whatever little brother, it's not the arrow, it's the Indian," Mason said.

"Fuck you I'm serious!" The tone of Paul's voice made it clear he was upset.

"Any size?" Mason asked as he too leaned onto his knees searching for more air.

"A decent six, respectable." Paul looked down at Mason. "You're outta shape man, that's not that long of a walk."

"Fuck you, live once," Mason said as he straightened up.

"Let me see it once," Marty said. He set his bow on the ground and reached for Paul's. He knocked one of his own arrows and placed it on the arrow rest. Marty held the bow out at arm's length trying to keep the bow string perfectly vertical. The arrow should be ever so slightly pointed up, or at the very least level with the horizon. Paul's arrow pointed slightly to the ground. "Yup, she slipped all right."

Mason nodded his head at Marty, "How about you? See anything?"

"A couple of baldies, something spooked 'em though but I never did see what it was," Marty said.

Tom was right on track to the backside of Marty's stand. Even drunk, he has made the walk dozens of times. When he finally reached the tree he leaned back with his head against the trunk, exhausted. He dug around in his coat pocket for a flask. Before he could unscrew the top he felt a wet spot on the back of his head. A thin streak of water dripped off the bark. He collected the liquid on his finger and raised it to his nose but all he could determine was the stink of his own booze. His eyes followed the stream up the trunk to its source, a larger wet spot on the trunk just below the height to which Marty had climbed.

"Jesus Marty!" Tom said, chewing Marty out even though he was not there.

Most bow hunters are consumed with covering their scent. A white tail deer has tremendous sense of smell and many hunters carry bottles of their own urine away from their stands. Marty was not one of these hunters.

Marty, Paul and Mason started back for the trailer.

"I wonder if Tommy's done," Paul said.

"Oh. I'm sure he'll be down shortly, if he's not back already. Besides, he's probably dry by now," Mason said, referring sarcastically to Tom's obvious drinking problem. The three men laughed out loud. In the past not one of them missed an opportunity to honestly voice their concerns with Tom regarding his drinking. As a functional alcoholic, Tom's dark contention was that it couldn't be that bad if he were still alive, and he had no intention of changing. Tom felt that if it was that big of a concern that his friends needed to constantly lecture him then he would solve the problem by just not coming around anymore. The guys chose familiarity over contempt and no one mentioned it to Tom again.

"Damn it!" Paul nearly shouted.

"What now?" Mason asked.

"I'm pissed off that there's something wrong with my bow. The whole weekend is shot now."

"Excuses, excuses," Mason said.

"Fuck you! Try it! I'm telling you!"

"Me? Hell no, I'm not taking a chance fucking around with your shitty equipment. Probably stick my arm or something," Mason said.

Paul fired back, clearly annoyed, "Well excuse me Mr. big time real estate guy. We can't all afford the latest and greatest shit."

"Fuck you Paul. I'm sick of your shit. You're a fucking failure and it's nobody's fault but your own. You're too fucking stupid to get a job that pays you anything and it's everybody else's fault all the time."

"You guys cool it!" Marty yelled at them both. "Let's go get a bite. I think I might know a guy to see about that bow of yours."

"Who?" Paul asked.

"The neighbor. For the life of me I can't remember his name though. He was over here once. I was unloading my truck and all of sudden he was just standing there. If I remember right, he's some sort of archery rep, or repair guy or something like that. I don't even know if he lives there anymore but we can run over there after a while and check," Marty said.

"The neighbor where?" Paul asked.

Marty stopped and pointed up over the bluffs to the west, "Over that way behind your stand. He's got the adjoining eighty, or hundred I think. I'm not sure."

"Sounds good to me. It's worth a try anyways," Paul said, some sense of hope returning to his tone.

"How come we've never heard of this guy before?" Mason asked.

"I don't know, likes his privacy I guess," Marty said. The three men walked on together, slowing their pace as each was breathing slightly heavier as they pushed through the long grass. Conversation dried up as it simply required too much breath.

Tommy was finally getting to the end of his rounds. "Fuck, you too?" he said as he crested the hill behind Mason's stand. "Doesn't anybody hunt anymore?"

He headed for it anyways, it was a solid place for a rest on the climber's comfortable cushion. One more time he fished the flask from his pocket. Mason's guess about Tom running out of booze turned out to be frighteningly accurate. Tommy tipped the flask straight up in the air, taking the last few drops of booze on his tongue. He tipped so far back on the seat he nearly came off, needing to put his hand on the ground to keep from falling. As he stood to leave he noticed something on the ground under the climber. He picked Mason's laser range finder from the leaves which was about half the size of a standard pair of binoculars, slid it into his pocket and headed in.

"You want to head over there now? Or get a bite to eat first?" Marty asked Paul back at the trailer.

"Well?" Paul looked to the sky for an answer. "I guess I was hoping to get out again this afternoon so…yeah, let's go over there. You coming?" he asked Mason as Paul laid his bow in the back of Marty's pick-up.

"Me? No. I'm going to hang around and wait for Tommy to get back."

"Alright, suit yourself," Paul said.

As the truck was leaving, Paul leaned forward to watch Mason from the passenger mirror, who was consequently jogging to the outhouse. "There he goes again, the poor bastard. Maybe he can shit some of the asshole out of himself."

The jab caught Marty funny and he laughed out loud. "Brothers."

Mason's pants hit the ground with a quickness, even before the door was latched. He was not settled in for more than a moment when once again a large startling thud contacted the outside of the little building.

"What again? It's getting a little fucking childish don't you think?" Mason yelled out, angrily.

"Motherfucker," Mason whispered. He heard footsteps approaching from outside and it enraged him further. "Just leave me the fuck alone man!" he yelled.

"Whoa, whoa, calm down man!" Tommy said. "I was just seeing if you were in there."

"Whatever fucker, I'm getting tired of this shit," Mason said through the door.

"Whatever yourself fucker, hope you get stuck in that motherfucker!" Tommy screamed back. He kicked a clump of grass and dirt at the door and huffed back to the trailer, slamming the door hard as he went inside.

Mason was pleased, "Good, drunken idiot."

CHAPTER 23

Marty's mid-nineties Ford pickup crawled slowly up the twin dirt path driveway. With all the humps and puddles he shifted the manual truck no further than second gear, and the engine whined. Brush and small trees closed the road in like a tunnel, the edges so thick that they would be impassable to a man. Nearly an eighth mile in, the road turned sharply left. The wood of the cabin was blackened by the years and almost seemed wet with mold.

"Seriously? A guy lives here?" Paul asked.

"Supposedly," Marty pushed the squeaky clutch pedal to the floor and rolled to a stop. He leaned forward on the steering wheel, spying out of the windshield. The extra inches closer to whatever he was looking for may not have been as beneficial as the security of being behind the glass, like everything outside was in a zoo, or a museum.

"See anyone?" Paul asked.

"No, but there's a truck here. He's gotta be around here somewhere."

As if suddenly emboldened by his own statement Marty moved quickly to get out of the truck. His over exuberance became punishing. The truck lurched forward still running and in gear. Without the correct transfer of gas to clutch, the engine hovered near death, sounding like big ping pong balls and exhaust. Marty, who was not quite clear of the truck, was knocked to the ground. Paul screamed as the moving vehicle ran down a handful of potted spruce trees before abruptly slamming into a well-established white pine. Paul never did put a seat belt on for the short ride and paid the price as momentum carried his head into an unforgiving windshield. His loose bow caught air in the bed of the truck and hit the back of the cab with a cracking authority. The engine quit on impact.

Marty was shaken but sans any serious injury. His age and the shock of the moment showed in the climb to his feet. He limped with all the quickness he could muster. Paul was sitting upright in the cab lightly checking for the growing lump on the top of his forehead.

"Holy shit! You Ok?" Marty asked, panicky, shaky.

Paul's voice was muffled, speaking down into his chest. "Yeah I'll be ok. Thanks though, helps to put the fucking thing in park!"

"Yeah! Sorry! I can't believe I did that!"

Paul angrily kicked his door open and immediately went for his bow in the back of the truck. He looked it over closely. "Well, your guy ain't fixin' this."

"What?"

"Well the sights are busted off," Paul reached into the bed with his other hand and picked up bits of broken plastic that used to be on his bow. "And who knows what else now?" Paul was disgusted and angry. He threw the bits back into the bed, or more like threw them at the bed. Then he haphazardly tossed his bow in after them.

Marty heard him but at the moment was more concerned for his truck. He hunched over the front bumper that was squarely lodged against the trunk of the tree.

"I guess it looks alright."

He brushed a few fallen needles off the hood and looked over at the fuming Paul. "Hey, I gotta tell you I'm really sorry about that. I don't know what I was thinking, I, I…" Marty's voice trailed off, unable to explain his actions.

"Whatever!" Paul shouted. As if to just end it all now he waved his hands off mimicking the sign an umpire makes when the runner is safe. "Let's just get the hell out of here!"

Marty looked around and under the front end of the truck. The mowed over pines, squeezed from the five gallon pail pots that were crushed under the axle.

"Yeah, well, I think we'd better let the guy know about this," Marty said. He turned towards the cabin and cupped his hands around in his mouth to form a makeshift megaphone. "Hello! Hello! Anybody here?" he shouted.

"C'mon man, he's not here. Nice trip though," Paul said sarcastically.

Marty repeated his call and waited. "Hold on, let me leave a note."

He fumbled around inside the glove box for a pen and any piece of paper. Half of an envelope and a golf pencil would serve. He scribbled a quick note and headed for the cabin.

"Hurry up!" Paul barked as he climbed back into the truck.

Marty walked cautiously, like a child forced to admit his latest fault, to the cabin door. He knocked lightly, not really wanting anyone to answer. Leaving a note was far easier than actually having to face anyone. A spade shovel and a rusty spud bar leaned against the cabin wall and the door frame. Marty used the shovel handle to hold the note against the door and ambled back to his truck. It cranked over and over but refused to start.

"C'mon you piece of shit!" Paul slapped the dust off the dash. The engine barely caught, it ran a little rough to get going but came around quickly and returned to its signature whine.

"Good girl," Marty said.

"Good, now let's get the hell out of here!"

The Ford backed easily off the tree. The buckets of trees popped and clucked clear of the bumper as Marty turned around and crawled back down the dirt road.

Mason walked into the trailer. All was quiet besides Tom's light snoring. The smell of dirty socks and booze breath made him grimace. He was just about to read the riot act to Tom and ruin his nap when his attention was diverted to Marty's truck rolling back up the field. Marty went in first, immediately going into the back room.

"That was quick," Mason said. Marty offered no response but the weak slamming of the thin interior door. Paul walked in slowly after, rubbing his head. "Nice lump. What the hell happened?"

Paul was still angry. He answered Mason but held a cold stare on the door that Marty had disappeared behind. "Some nitwit hit a tree."

"What? Where? What happened?" Mason asked.

"Dr. Alzheimer back there got out of the damn truck and left in gear, or needed to shut it off or something.

Whatever he did not do sent the damn thing into the trees with me sitting there."

Mason let out a faint snort, the kind a person makes when they are trying in vain not to burst out laughing.

"Fuck you man! It's not funny! My head hurts!" Paul snapped. Mason lost the battle of the laugh as Paul shoved his way past him, right hand still cupping the goose egg above his forehead. Marty came out with the cheap sounding click of the door latch.

"Yeah, I'm sorry. What an idiot. I still can't believe I did that," Marty said apologetically.

Mason came around to the conversation quickly. "Well, at least you had some excitement, nothing happened around here except numb nuts over there getting drunk and messing with me on the crapper again."

Tom was laid out on his back, a camouflaged ball cap pulled down over his eyes. His arm was slung out into the aisle like a dead man which Paul took no care in avoiding as he plowed his way through to the television.

"Should be close to game time anyways," Paul said. The older buttons on the television clicked loudly without report. In his already agitated state, Paul smacked the set hard on the top. "C'mon you piece of shit! Everything is a piece of shit!"

"Hey! Don't take it out on the TV!" Marty scolded him.

"The damn thing worked fine last night!" Paul retorted.

Mason was seemingly ignoring them both as he leaned on the door of a mostly empty refrigerator. His voice sounded robotic as it initially echoed through the box. "What the hell do you want? We're in the middle of nowhere." He slammed the fridge door closed and addressed the men in a suddenly serious tone. "Looks like we'd better take this thing to the top!" The reply from the men was silent. Tom rose up slowly, bending at the waist like a vampire rising from a coffin.

"I heard that," Tom said.

"Figured you would," Mason said.

"Fuck yeah, I'm in," Paul chimed in.

"I guess the least I could do is buy you a beer," Marty said to Paul still apologetic.

Tom sprang to his feet. "Hell yeah! Heard that too! Marty's buyin'!"

While Marty held his index finger up to signal a halt to that particular line of thinking Tom rushed past him and out the door.

"Shotgun," Tom yelled from outside as he hopped into the front seat of Mason's SUV.

"Looks like I'm driving," Mason said as he also quickly headed out the door. Marty still stood silent, his lips frozen in mid word. Paul gave him a little shoulder bump as he followed the lead of the others. Marty's muffled protests could be heard outside after he slammed the camper door shut. Eventually his voice would disappear with the sound of the fourth closing car door.

Inside the trailer the air became still. The interior door with the tiny window looked inward. It was an emotionless eye that saw everything but remembered nothing. It never judged and never cared but yet the new silence made it seem lonely and sad.

"I thought you had shotgun," Mason said to Tom by way of the rear view mirror.

"I did, but Marty said he was too old to sit in the back or some shit like that."

"No. I said I wasn't buying a damn thing if I had to be all cramped up back there," Marty said.

Paul and Tom shoved at each other in the back seat like children.

"Move over man, you're crowding me," Tom said.

"Fuck you, I'm right up against the door," Paul gave Tom a harsh push as the two nearly came to blows. "Ow! What the fuck you got in your…"

He smacked Tom's coat pocket to try and determine what jabbed him.

"Oh, hold on." Tom reached into his pocket and removed the range finder he found earlier that day. "Here, I found this this morning." He handed it over to Paul.

"Where?" Paul asked him.

"Well, I was looking for you guys and stopped to take a break by Mason's stand and I found it laying in the leaves."

Marty turned in his seat and took it from Paul. "Here, let me see that." As he played with the buttons Mason snatched it from his hands and spiked it deep into the center compartment. He slammed the door hard and kept his arm over it to make sure it stayed closed.

"What the hell is that all about?" Marty asked.

"Nothing! I don't know, just, never mind," Mason stumbled on his non-answer.

"He's getting old, that's what's the matter," Paul chimed in from the back seat.

Mason took his hand off the council door and adjusted the mirror so he could focus his look of disapproval directly at his brother.

"It was an impulse buy, that's all. I was just curious," Mason explained. "It's embarrassing."

"Well does it work?" Marty asked.

"I don't know. I lost the damn thing somewhere before I got the chance to use it."

"And then he forgot about it, because he's old," Paul chuckled.

Mason once again focused cruel intentions through the mirror at his brother, "Yeah? Well who missed today young guy?"

"Ha!" Tom chimed in.

Marty just shook his head and gave his attention to scenery outside his window.

"Fuck you," Paul said defeated.

After a moment of brief uncomfortable silence Mason leaned into the brakes hard as he pulled the vehicle onto the shoulder. "Ahh shit!"

"Now what?" Paul asked.

"I'm pretty sure I left my bow sitting outside. I don't want it sitting out in the rain." Mason cranked the wheel hard to the left and checked his mirror.

"Wait, what are you doing?" Paul asked. "We're not going back, the game's about to start. Your precious bow can get wet you know."

"It's not like you ever shoot anything with it anyways," Tom said.

"Fuck you!" Mason said, annoyed with the banter.

"You don't lock the door anyways so what the difference?" Tom laughed.

Marty craned out the window trying to study clouds he could barely see from the tree lined road. "I think you'll be OK, a little water won't hurt it anyways."

"Yeah, c'mon man, I'm thirsty!"

"Don't be such a bitch!" said someone from the backseat. Miscellaneous complaints were hurling forward from both men now non-stop.

"Alright! Fine! Fuck it! I'll just have a fucked up bow that's all!" Mason revved the engine and slammed the vehicle in gear, spinning out of the gravel shoulder and squealing his tires on the rough old blacktop highway. The uncomfortable silence returned temporarily until Mason slammed his fist hard onto the dashboard.

"Don't worry. Calm down, it'll be fine," Marty said in a soothing, singing tone as if he were talking to a child.

"No, it's not that, something's rattling in here and it's driving me crazy."

Marty turned his head from side to side, changing his ear position to try and pick up on the noise. "I don't hear anything."

"Whatever, ya' fuckin' nut job, we're here anyways," Tom said as he snapped his pointer finger forward into the shape of a gun.

CHAPTER 24

If not for the mid-seventies dimly-lit beer sign precariously hanging from a rusty post at the road's edge it would have looked like just another metal pole barn. The faded letters on the bottom of the sign were reminiscent of a once clever play on words. "The Table Top" which a body would guess referred to both the geographical location of the bar as well as a most obvious fixture inside. The metal siding was gray and chalky faded. The also metal roof just a darker version of the sides. A small window in the numerously dented steel door looked like bulletproof glass. The open sign on the inside of the glass was probably taped up there back when tape was invented. One dirty window not far from the door framed a dying neon sign advertising a beer nobody in those parts drank.

Mason pulled into the gravel parking lot fast enough that his front wheels locked up for a second when he stopped. Parking in the lines was of no concern. The few other vehicles that were there ignored any compulsive tendencies that would reflect any sort of organized row.

Paul barged in first. The interior was what would be expected. Knotty pine walls; varnished particle board for a ceiling. A few dollar bills stuck to it with cute little sayings and pictures. Some tourists who stopped there did it once and then it became a thing. Almost everyone who does it will never be back, so their bill becomes a symbol of their immortality. The owner harvests a few times a year when his wallet is thin, always leaving a few for sucker seed. A few old tube TV's sit high on shelves above the back bar, their roundness looked ancient in the modern flat world. A bar box Valley pool table covered in so many chalk spots that the color of the felt was in question was the fixed centerpiece. A surprisingly modern juke box played barely audible country and western tunes as if what already existed was not atmosphere enough.

Paul took a seat at center bar. Tom stepped next to him but pulled the stool away preferring to stand. Marty and Mason took seats to his left. A weathered blonde barkeep dealt a hand of coasters as if were the toughest thing she'd done in forever.

"What'll it be boys?" she asked the men.

"I'll take a High Life," Paul said reaching for his wallet.

"Make that two. On me," Marty said.

"Better make it three," Tom added.

"What the hell, me too," Mason said like he did not really want it but could not decide.

"Ten bucks," said Ginger. The barkeep's voice labored through tens of thousands of packs of cigarettes.

Marty looked shocked. "Ten bucks? For a round? I like it." He swung his wallet out for once with pleasure.

Paul held up his bottle for a toast. "To bad driving!" A collective "here-here" from the crew with the only ringing bottle connection coming from Marty.

One of the locals at the end of the bar was looking them over and made an attempt at a friendly ice breaker. "You boys out huntin'?" he asked, referring to all the camouflage clothing.

"Nope! Just like to blend-in," Tom said loudly, in a jerk-like fashion not even turning towards the man he was treating like shit.

"Smart ass," Mason scolded him quietly. The local man did not bother with any more small talk.

"Shut up you guys I can barely hear the game," Paul scolded them both.

"Who cares, it's just pre-season anyways," Tom said. He turned away from the television and surveyed the bar. His gaze came to rest on the pool table. "C'mon, let's get a game."

"No, I just wanna watch the game. Play somebody else," Paul said.

"Any takers?" Tom asked out loud to the bar.

The local man that Tom had treated poorly chuckled and mocked him.

"What? You? You got some game man? Got any money? Lessons ain't free!" Tom set his bottle down hard and motioned towards the table like he was inviting a celebrity to walk the red carpet before him.

The man never budged. He still held his beer bottle with both hands as well as his chiding smile.

"It ain't me you gotta beat, it's him." He motioned towards the bathroom with his head just as the flimsy door squeaked open.

The man that walked out was familiar to any man that ever looked into a mirror and framed his own insecurities. He was what most would hope to be at any age, and what even more never were. He was the hunter they did not know. Some of the locals knew of him but did not really know him. Only one person in the bar knew his name.

"Another one, Blue Eyes?" Ginger asked. His eyes were so bright and so piercing that the first time Ginger saw him in the bar some years earlier she thought it would be a solid tip-generating, fun and flirty nickname. Being noticed for his eyes was nothing new for him. Women were drawn into them for most of his life. The irony was they were a focal point for his outward appearance. As eyes are supposed to be the windows to the soul, for him they were the total depth of how others saw him and a trait people couldn't get past. For this reason alone he never bothered to offer his Christian name. Any other reason he had he figured men hadn't earned the right to know. Other people in the bar rarely addressed him partly due to his stand-off-ish nature, but mostly because he did not seem like the type of guy another guy would call Blue Eyes and still be able to claim heterosexuality.

"Yes please." He was imminently polite. Ginger poured him a short high ball of absinthe straight-up, no ice. A nearly unpalatable green spirit said to have psychedelic properties.

"Blue Eyes?" Tom exclaimed. "I have to play a guy named Blue Eyes?"

Marty couldn't take his eyes off the man but was not glaring at him in a rude way. More like he was trying to place him, like he had seen him before. Then it clicked. He got up and gave him a one shot atta boy pat on the back of his left shoulder.

"Hey there fella. If I'm not mistaken we met once a few years back. My name's Marty. I believe you're my neighbor." He extended his hand for the traditional shake.

Blue Eyes set his drink on the bar. He never really fully turned but took hold of Marty's hand anyways. Instead he addressed Marty through the imposed advertising on the mirror behind the bar.

"I believe I am," Blue Eyes said to the mirror.

Marty was slow to respond and it took him a few moments to understand where the man was looking. After he topped that hurdle it took a few more seconds to absorb the situation and continue the conversation.

"Funny meeting you here 'cause as it turns out we stopped over there to see you today. Say, I hate to say this but I might as well admit that I don't quite remember your name."

"What did you need?" Blue Eyes asked him.

Marty took a good long drink and focused into the mirror. "Well Paul over there was pretty sure his knock slipped, and I thought you were a bow guy so we were going to see if you could fix it. Turns out we had a little mishap with our truck in your driveway and the bow got a little beat up anyways. I don't know if you saw my note yet or anything but…"

Blue Eyes turned abruptly to face Marty and cut him off mid-sentence. "There are no mishaps."

Marty rocked back slightly uncomfortable with the sudden closeness. "Well I…"

Once again Blue Eyes cut him off. "The problem was you failed to plan. Something unforeseen happened and you were not prepared. You say mishap, I say you failed to think and react adequately."

Marty was taken aback and the few seconds of face-to-face time seemed like minutes while he formulated a response. "Look, I don't know where you're going with this but…"

Again, cut off. "I know, you've made that obvious."

Marty now took a full step back away from Blue Eyes and stood stunned silent with his mouth slightly agape. In the middle of the tension Tom slammed his empty bottle down on the bar and interrupted the moment. "Whadya say there partner? Blue Eyes? Play for a drink?"

The Hunter kept his glare affixed to Marty. "Do you really want to see where I'm going with this?" He turned and walked towards the cue rack pausing just long enough to make eye contact with Tom and give an approving nod to his challenge. Of course Mason couldn't help but notice the action and spun his stool towards the pool table. Paul may have been the only oblivious patron in the bar instead choosing to focus on a meaningless football game.

Tom joined the Hunter at the cue rack. "What's the game? Eight ball? Bar pool? I suppose you local guys know the good cues right away."

The Hunter laid his choice on the felt and gave it a push. The stick's warp signature made it look like a candy cane rolling across the table. "It'll play. I'll rack."

"Wait a second, we can flip for the break," Tom said struggling to get a coin from his front pocket.

The Hunter ignored him as he slid quarters into the slot and engaged the table.

"Alright, whatever man," Tom shook his head a bit disgusted with his opponent's rudeness.

It seemed as if the Hunter was taking an inordinate amount of time to rack the balls tightly. There was enough time for Marty to move closer and take a seat at a pub table near the pool table. Finally, he pulled the rack away and backed up to the wall. Tom revved up and struck the head ball hard. Had the spread of the balls corresponded with the sound of the break it would have been far more impressive. No matter how he begged, no balls fell and Tom slid back to his stool. "Wide open."

The Hunter approached and carefully studied the table. The blue chalk slowly ground on the tip accompanied by a shrill wooden squeak. He fell into his shooting stance quickly, almost cartoon-like. He aimed for nearly a second and fired, banking the eight ball cross side through a crowded center table. Game over. Tom, as well as everyone else in the place watched quietly stunned. The Hunter walked back to the cue rack and snapped it into the plastic wall clips.

"Nice shot. Color blind? I'll take a High Life bottle," Tom taunted him.

The Hunter motioned to Ginger to set Tom up with the drink then turned his attention back to Marty. As all eyes were still on The Hunter Marty twisted in his chair with anticipation as he slowly walked that glare back to the uncomfortable closeness of Marty's face.

"I don't know what that shit's about but I'll drink on your dime all night," Tom said in a taunting laugh.

Marty slipped off his stool barely reaching a standing position before the Hunter got to him. "Just what was I supposed to learn from that little show?"

The Hunter did not answer for a few seconds then leaned carefully towards Marty's ear and gently whispered, "Control."

"What?" Marty backed away quickly having had enough of the proximity.

The Hunter, still bent forward, whispered, "Simplicity whistles to a complicated tune." With that he turned to leave, dropping a bill on the bar on his way out. "Thank you," he nodded to Ginger and stepped out the door.

Mason got up and walked over to Marty. "What the hell was that all about?"

"I don't know. I think maybe he's been out in the woods too long."

"Well, that was fun. Anyone else in here wanna buy me a drink?" Tom said.

The local man slid his stool back and crossed slowly in front of the men as he ambled his way to the door. He laughed quietly to himself and walked out saying goodbye to no one.

"I'm in I guess," Paul chimed in.

"Yeah now that I took the table," Tom said.

"No let's just get the hell out of here," Marty spoke loud enough that everyone could hear.

"What? The game's not even over yet. It's only halftime," Paul complained.

"Yeah. I'm pretty tired, I could go," Mason said.

Paul was irritated. "What? Where the hell you gotta be anyways?"

"It just so happens little brother that I have a meeting in the morning."

"Yeah right. With who?"

"None of your fucking business!"

Tom intercedes. "Boys, boys, let's just grab some wood, calm down, have a beer or two and then we'll all leave happy."

Marty agreed. "All right one more."

"Rack 'em Jack," Tom called out to Paul.

Marty walked to the dingy window and became lost in the lingering dust kicked up by the last vehicle to leave the gravel lot. "Yeah, one more isn't going to hurt anything." Nobody else could have heard him.

After a time the men finally poured out the front door although some begrudgingly. Their girlish chatter suggested that they had achieved the edge of drunkenness, but not so far gone that mean words could not be deciphered. Mason waited impatiently next to the driver's door for the men to clear out of his way. He diverted his eyes from the bumbling men in disgust. A slight chill trickled down his spine, under his shirt right next to the skin. A rifle casing was slid over the top of the vehicle's antenna. One empty piece of brass from a deer rifle. *So that's what was rattling.* It did not have to be his. After all this was deer country. But he knew it was. It was shiny; still new. He would at least have to check the caliber but it looked about right. He did not dare go for it. So badly he wanted to ask who put it there. So badly he wanted to know. It was most likely the same person that picked up his brass outside the trailer. *Of course it was.* Who would have to be lied to if they hadn't been already? Why everybody, of course. *Can't trust any of these fuckers.*

CHAPTER 25

The short days of fall can drone on under overcast skies. Days like that happen to everyone, even animals. The sun lights the landscape like any other day except on gray days it has to work a little harder. Shadows don't really exist. The joy of summer is gone, wicked away from all things. Even rocks and mud puddles lose their ambition to show color and the whole world seems bathed in black and white.

A coyote's life is built around spookiness. For a coyote, it is a perfect day. His color blends well with the drab. His habits of thievery and small murders bode grim for depressed prey that seeks the warmth of the sun. This day he would thrive. His keen nose caught the scent of death. No wind made a stealthy approach a challenge. Instinct forced him to hunt from down-wind. He was not graced with reason or understanding as to why a dead possum laid half-buried in leaves, he only knew that it was there. He stopped short of the body and stretched his neck, ever cautious intending to steal. A bevy of hardy green flies took flight as he closed. One more step before the snap. If there was any breeze at all, a human's ears would have been incapable of detecting the faint yelp that was hopelessly buried within a million trees. Fear and anxiety compelled him to chew at his leg above the steel jaws of the trap that held him. The animal heard him first, then he smelled him for wind was barely needed in order to detect the invasive stench of a human. The pity lies in the fact that coyotes cannot see color and therefore he could not truly appreciate the blue eyes of The Hunter. His stance was as tense as the trap spring that kept him prisoner. His snarl and low growl were universally understood.

The Hunter approached very slowly. As he neared the animal he crouched with his head down, attempting to show subservience. He stayed that way for some time until the growling stopped. He picked his head up slowly. When their eyes met the coyote was momentarily stunned, as if he were a sinner looking into the eyes of Jesus. Then he sprung. The chain of the trap was pulled wire-tight from the stake, stretching towards freedom but The Hunter's lunge was too fast. All he could do was wail in horror as The Hunter pinned him sideways to the ground. The Hunter laid prone on the animal with all his weight. He held its head tight to the ground and kept his left hand wrapped around its snout.

Eventually the animal's will waivered, and his struggle lessoned. Hard breaths took over for a faint whine. The Hunter's blank, emotionless stare made him seem as if he was lost in deep thought on the edge of a trance. He pulled the snout slightly closer and plunged his face into the heavily furred neck of the coyote. He bit down hard, the anger on his face and in his eyes were a mirage merely a direct result of the circumference of his bite. The coyote made one last admirable attempt at escape but without immediate access to air and his lungs compressed by The Hunter's body, he had no choice but to die.

There is nothing like a human scream to break the silence of the forest. It is almost never one born of joy and is usually as lost as its own sound. He hated the coyote for forcing him to take it, but he could hate it, because he loved it first. Spittle from the back of his throat caught the guard hairs that were stuck in his teeth and sent them fluttering down onto the face of the limp animal. Looming behind him he felt a dark, familiar presence. Like that of a man, but also like a wolf or even a forest god. It was close. It watched him with unknown intent. If it were a hungry animal, it would want the kill. If it were a hungry god, it would kill. In one fluid motion The Hunter unleashed the hatchet from his belt, turned and sent it whirling towards the perceived presence. With a dull thud the hatchet buried itself deep into the bark of a tree. Whatever was or was not there was decidedly gone. That was the exact moment that Mason heard the scream.

It was an untimely distraction as Mason was bearing down on his rifle stock in the process of touching off a round. From The Hunter's ear it was as if the echo of the scream melded into the two-tiered report from the rifle, the latter becoming responsible for the first respectively. The scream was now in need of justice or possibly retribution.

The invasive report from the rifle stole the Hunter's moment. He left the body temporarily. He had to take the moment back.

Mason was getting low on rounds. He needed to make sure his last few shots counted towards his goal. *No more screwing around.* He took a few minutes and sucked the plastic close on a bottle of water. *C'mon man, just do it.* After his short breather he bared down on the stock once again, totally focused. An eternity passed. *Shoot! Shoot already!* The trigger had already been partly depressed when his eye caught what appeared to be a person in the peripheral view of his scope. Too late. He flinched hard trying to look over the weapon for a better view. The distance made it impossible. Quickly regaining his target in his optics, he searched the field of vision for anything. A shaking branch was the only evidence that suggested nothing in particular. He waited. He watched and listened. Nothing, not a sound. Still, he had to check it out.

Mason walked towards the end of the valley a little quicker than normal. The sight of a person had him unnerved. When he reached his target he smiled. "A hit." He stuck his finger in the bullet hole on the board and ran it through a few times like he was a fly tasting it. He went tromping around in the field edged brush and then up into the woods. Nothing. "Well, I guess I'm losing my damn mind."

The hunter's face took on enough emotion as to possibly suggest pleasure, maybe even a faint smile. He laid down in the leaves, skewed among the deadfalls near the top of the ridge, watching, enjoying the moment.

CHAPTER 26

Another weekend of crappy fall weather had Paul disgruntled. He walked through the field towards the trailer in a huff having left his stand early. The light mist was a slow soaker and it made hunting miserable on a cold windy morning. He walked in the trailer to find Mason at the table sipping a cup of coffee paging through an old hunting magazine someone had left behind. The news on the TV in the background provided adequate company.

"Nice morning," Mason said, never looking away from his magazine.

"This is bullshit. I can't believe I got up early for this," Paul drove up that same morning.

"I didn't even hear you come in this morning. I think it's supposed to clear up later though. I guess Barry and Gordy are coming up later to work on their stands."

Paul was peeling the wet clothes off his body. "Uh oh, sound like a card game later. You going out?"

Mason leaned towards the window and squinted his eyes skyward. "I don't know. I'll see what the weather does."

"Must be nice to just be able to go out whenever you want," Paul said.

"You think so?" Mason slammed his empty mug on the table. "You think I'm happy living here in this little shitbox while that bitch is enjoying what little I had left?"

"All right, all right, calm down man. You know that's not what I meant," Paul held his hands out as if to signal to Mason to slow down.

Mason got up from the table and threw his cup into the sink, breaking the handle off "I'd go out right now if it wasn't so damn shitty. If anything just to get away from you."

Paul was hunched over messing with the TV. "Go ahead, nothing is moving in this rain anyways. Hell, might as well go to the bar." The two men traded an unexpected but knowing glance and within minutes were headed out the door.

Even a light rain in the forest is noisy. The branches and leaves add a constant non-rhythmic drip to the steady hiss of the rain. An occasional wind gust skews the symphony until it approaches a white, pelting noise.

Blue Eyes' stance over the hole was rock solid, like a tripod over an open mineshaft. He thrust the hand held posthole digger deep into the sandy mud. He was already nearly thigh-deep in a roughly four foot wide starter hole. It had to be wider on top so that he could dig deep enough. He slid the body down head first. Seeing the bottom of the bow hunter's boots made it final to him. He offered no ceremony. There was as much joy in him as sorrow, because after all, he never loved the man. He backfilled the hole then carefully spread forest duff over the freshly dug ground. Directly over the body he planted a Colorado blue spruce nearly four feet tall. Next to it he planted an absolutely dead spruce about half the size. He spread a handful of needles in the dirt below it and once again covered the area with leaves and branches. He shouldered his tools and casually walked away.

Ginger hip-checked the swinging western style doors to the kitchen, both hands occupied by plates of food. She slid them in front of Mason and Paul who were sitting at the bar sipping a few beers watching the TV while country music played off the juke box quietly in the background.

"Those guys going to meet us up here right? Or are they going to the trailer?" Paul asked Mason.

"I'm pretty sure they'll come here first. I don't think it'll rain all day so I expect they'll be here soon."

The squeal of the front door drew everyone's attention. A dripping wet Game Warden approached the bar.

"What can I get for ya?" Ginger asked.

"Just a quick burger today, to go," he said.

"Be up in a minute." She scribbled the order on her little pad and headed back into the kitchen.

The Warden took off his hat and shook off the rain. "You boys been out hunting at all?" he asked Mason and Paul.

"Made it out a few hours this morning but it was miserable. Nothing moving in this rain," Paul said.

"Really? Where abouts?" the Warden asked.

"We've got an old family farmstead off of C, just down the road." County C was on the far edge of the property barely touching a few feet of frontage. The driveway was actually on Andersen Road, well off the beaten path. It was probably named after the farmer that back in the day owned most of the section. No hunter wants a Game Warden hanging around, until they need one.

The radio attached to the Warden's collar by a coiled up stretchy wire started chattering. He turned his face towards the mic like he was about to speak but stopped and turned the volume down.

"Nice. There's some great hunting around here. What's the family name?" the Warden asked Mason.

"Owens. I'm Mason and this is my brother Paul." Mason reached over and the three men exchanged turns shaking hands.

"I have to ask you guys. As you've been out, have you possibly ran into anyone who may have been lost, or maybe saw someone walking down the road, or even a guy in a field in the distance that seemed out of place?"

Mason turned his glance slightly downward and reflected. "No, can't say that I have." He swung around on his stool and looked to his brother. "You?"

"No, I haven't seen or noticed anyone. I didn't even see a squirrel this morning."

The Warden put his wet hat on. He was the kind of person that liked to talk with his hands. "Well guys, I need you to keep your eyes open. We're out looking for a hunter that may be missing from the state forest. We think he might be wandering, possibly injured and definitely lost."

"May be missing?" Mason said.

The Warden reached into his inside pocket and removed three business cards, one for each man and one to leave on the bar. "His name is Steven Resant, white, 37 years old dressed in camo. His buddy was out there with him but hadn't seen him since they let out in the morning. When he didn't come back at the designated time his buddy went over to where he knew he would be hunting and found his gear but couldn't find Mr. Resant."

"Maybe he's tracking a deer or something," Paul said.

The Warden leaned forward on the bar arching and stretching his back. "It's possible. His buddy seems to think otherwise though."

"In that case I'm surprised you guys are out looking for him so soon," Mason said.

"Steven Resant is the son of Representative Alexander Resant. Congressman Resant also believes otherwise and has insisted that a search be started immediately."

Ginger hip-checked her way through the swinging doors again sending the light pine crashing into the back bar even though one hand was free. Upon their return the hinges seemed to cry from the unnecessary force. It was more of a habit than a necessity, a passive aggressive way to establish bar dominance. She carried a brown bag with the top stapled closed. The grease spots that soaked through the bag looked like a model of a solar system.

"My cell number is on the card. I'd appreciate a call if you see anything." The Warden thumbed through his wallet. "What are the damages?"

Ginger waived him off. "Never mind that. Just stay warm and find that poor man."

"I'd argue with you if I had more time," the Warden said as he grabbed the bag off the counter. "Well gentlemen, duty calls. Good luck out there."

"Good luck to you too," Mason said as the Warden nodded, tossed a bill on the bar and walked out the door.

Through the dingy window Mason watched the Warden and two men outside pantomime what he believed must have been a similar conversation although markedly shorter. The two men rounded out the hunting party. Barry and Gordy. The Ardent brothers. Their self-proclamation that they are both too old to bow hunt put them at the trailer twice per year. Once in the fall to prepare their deer stands, and once for the nine-day gun season. Combined, the brothers will only spend a fraction of that time actually hunting.

Barry was the oldest, nearly seventy and comfortably retired. He and his brother inherited a family investment business started by their father years ago that came with little responsibility and a lot of money. A few terms as a supervisor on the county board left him beaming with self-importance sprinkled with a touch of arrogance. Although he remained politically active a crushing defeat some years earlier left him far too embittered to subject his ego to another dent. Although clearly the voice of reason, he seemed at times to only exist in order to sap the fun out of every waking moment in camp. The guys still looked forward to him coming though. As a hobbyist he was a damn fine cook and proud of it. With Barry as the defacto camp chef everyone ate well all week, extremely well. A full stomach made the political rhetoric easier to swallow. He was noticeably a great connoisseur of his own creations, carrying more weight than a man facing such a height challenge should probably carry. His thick, lush head of blue-gray hair seemed to almost repel the fine droplets of rain, like there must have been some hairspray involved. Rumors abounded that he had some work done on his face, but of course he denied the allegations. Either way, it is hard to hide seventy.

Barry swung the front door open and held it for his brother, Gordy, a man that was clearly cut from a different cloth. He never really had a serious job to speak of, but always managed to get by, sometimes quite well. He was only three or four years younger than Barry but looked easily ten years older. His lifestyle of pseudo professional gambling had taken its toll. It takes a special sort of individual to achieve longevity in such a profession. Somewhere between the money, booze, women and the sleepless nights most players usually get lost. Addiction and early death are rampant. Gordy was smart. His wit was dry. Depending on his mood he could either be entertaining for some smart-ass comments or he could be totally withdrawn seemingly being forced to exist in an uncomfortable world. It was his eyes that made him a gambler. His stare was intense. The natural furl in his brow made it difficult to determine his mood. People always thought he was grumpy. If he liked you, you were golden. He came along to hunt for the ride, because it was something he always did with his brother. Since they were kids regardless of their individual life circumstances, they would meet up for the annual gun deer season. It was not only the tradition. Even if just for a short time, it was something Gordy really enjoyed. Being in the woods was a welcome break from the dingy bars and casinos where he made his living.

"What'll you gents have?" Ginger stood behind the bar repeatedly slapping a filthy rag into her hand like a baseball player seasoning a glove.

Barry leaned up close and looked up and down the bar for inspiration. "I think I'll have a Manhattan," he said.

"Bud Light," Gordy said from behind him.

"Bottle or can?" Ginger asked.

"Bottle."

"Gentlemen!" Barry announced. "And I do use that term loosely. Good to see you guys. How's the hunting been? Seeing any deer?"

"Can't say I've seen much. The kid missed one last week but other than that the weather has been pretty shitty," Mason said.

"Fuck you. My bow fucked up," Paul said.

Barry let out a laugh loud enough to take over the conversation. "I don't suppose you went back and checked on my stand."

"Hell no, I wasn't going to go way the hell back there. There's no deer back there anyways," Mason said.

Gordy remained silent, simply spending the time taking consistently long pulls from his bottle. Barry swirled the ice in his glass. "The further away we can get from you guys the better."

"Aren't you guys kind of old for this sort of thing?" Mason asked with rank comeback intent.

"That's what we bring you young guys along for," Gordy finally spoke as he was just finishing his beer as Mason finished his demeaning question.

"Yeah, but what's in it for us?" Paul asked, being of course the youngest in the conversation and desperately trying to stay relevant.

"Life lessons kid," Gordy said. "So you don't end up to be the guy they're looking for."

"Some politician's kid anyways," Paul said.

"Actually, I heard about that. Alex and I know each other quite well and I've met Steven on occasion," Barry said. "I should really let his dad know I'm out this way and helping."

"You're not really helping at all man," Gordy said.

"I'm here, and my eyes and ears are open, the way I see it that's more than most," Barry retorted.

"I guess," Gordy said with some amount of disgust.

Mason stood up first, followed closely by Paul. "Well, let's get this show on the road," Mason said. "You putting your stand in the same place you did last year?" he asked Barry.

"No, I think I'm going to get along that ridge a little closer to where Gordy is. There were a lot of deer moving thorough there last year," Barry said.

Barry and Gordy were not tree stand guys. They liked to sit on the ground preferably near the tops of a bluffs with easy access, usually surrounded by ground blinds constructed of any brush and limbs that may have fallen nearby. The "stand" was actually a misnomer and more of a generic term relative to "Kleenex" being the bastardized term for any disposable tissue.

The men tossed appropriate bills with rounded up tips included onto the bar and walked towards the front door. The grand enthusiasm of youth washed away by the associated impending doom of physical exertion.

CHAPTER 27

Paul brought a small handsaw and Gordy had an ax. Barry shouldered his shotgun and Mason carried nothing. As if it were a necessary trip, a walk they have all made hundreds of times before, they headed into the woods like a small guerilla army doomed against overwhelming odds, little chance of success. Finally, through the tall grass, Mason, free from burden, parted the brush at the valley's edge. A grouse busted cover at his feet tearing through the brush with all the grace of a crashing airplane. Barry shouldered his shotgun a squeezed off a failed attempt to take the bird.

"Nice shot," Gordy said.

"Thanks. If I could hit one we'd have some pretty good eating tonight," Barry said taking no offense.

"Then you'd better hit more than one then," Paul said.

"I don't think he brought enough shells," Gordy dug him again.

"Yeah, yeah, I just gotta get warmed up that's all. Anyways, I really only have to get one. For me," Barry said jokingly. Wild game was one of his culinary specialties. Actually harvesting enough fresh meat to feed four or five guys falls solidly into the easier said than done category. Sometimes its grouse, but turkey has happened, of course fresh venison tenderloin and even a squirrel / rabbit small game buffet. More often than not though, dinner comes from the grocery store so when fortune strikes, everyone in camp looks forward to the feed.

"Over the river and through the woods…" Barry sang the tune quietly to himself to take his mind off the hike up the relatively steep bluff. Nearing the top, the men approach a clearly unnatural pile of logs cabined around the base of a large oak.

"It actually looks pretty good. We'll have her fixed up in no time," Gordy said as he stepped inside and began shoveling out leaves and forest debris. Mason and Paul brushed in the outside with branches that had fallen nearby all in attempt to make the blind disappear against the hillside.

"Well, you guys got this. I'm going to head over and try to find a spot on the other side. Paul, let me have that little saw would ya?"

"Yeah, Yeah," Paul said as he handed it to Barry. "Don't lose it."

"Why would I lose it?" Barry asked. "When have I lost anything?"

"Not too close," Gordy said. "Don't want you molesting my hunt."

Barry did not bother to answer and with an annoyed wave of his hand angled off over the bluff top where the undergrowth catches decidedly more sun. It thickens to the point where the walk likens itself to a jungle adventure. He ventured slowly. Scanning ahead for decent shooting lanes was hopeless but light near ground level did soon become apparent. Sandstone laid down by an ancient sea exposed by glaciers 10,000 years ago formed the edge before a steep drop. Behind him the thick sub growth would obscure his form from below and a nice flat, natural seat is always appreciated.

Many cold hours in the blind demand a comfortable seat. Barry stood and started kicking away the loose dirt and rock in front of the natural seat where he laid his shotgun. A handful of fallen branches in the area adjacent and below him would be sufficient to build the blind up in front. The perfect starter was mere feet away. As he retrieved the branch a grouse flushed from the thick cover behind him. The sudden flush startled him, his heart beat as if he'd just run a mile.

When it comes to the Ruffed Grouse, often times there are more than one. Just when you let your guard down a second will re-startle you, moments later an unexpected third and maybe if you're lucky you're ready for a fourth that may never come.

Barry, however, was ready. He crept ever slowly and quietly back to his shotgun. Standing at the ready his still pounding heart was now fueled by anticipation. He took a step towards the flush. One then two, even though he was ready they were too quick. Grouse are short distance flyers but will often instinctively notice a brilliant escape route. As it would happen the third bird offered a line, although sometimes in the thick brush a bird's line has to be judged rather than always seen.

Time seems to ever slightly slow down when you just know it is the perfect shot. Tiny breast feathers hover in midair at the point of impact, while the bird arcs to the ground. What never happens, however, is when the bird screams.

"AHHHHHHHH"

As blood curdling of a noise as anyone might be able to imagine came from the brush beyond. Knowing what it had to be, in a panic Barry charged forward through the thick brush and the continuous screams using his shotgun as a shield against the many whips. He did not have to go far. Less than twenty yards into the brush Mason knelt on the ground with his head pushed into the ground, screaming. The hand holding the right side of his head provided the proper age lines to sponsor a stream of blood.

"Oh my God!" Barry tossed his shotgun to the side and nearly dove to the ground to render aid to Mason. "Oh my God, oh my God." His voice was shaky. His trembling hands patted Mason all around in a useless attempt to provide comfort. "Are you OK?"

"Fuck no I'm not OK! You fuckin' shot me!" Mason screamed about as loud as a person can through teeth clenched in pain.

"Oh my God, I'm so sorry. I never saw you. I shot at a grouse and…"

Near hyperventilating, Barry takes a moment to catch his breath. "And then the screams! I never saw you." Nearly in tears, he was far too shocked to offer adequate help. He tried to pull Mason's hand away from the wound for a better look but Mason fought the advance.

"What the fuck you doing! Get away from me!"

"No, no, I've got to help you. We have to see it. C'mon, let me help you down." Barry was finally starting to get his head on straight. Mason rolled down on his side and allowed Barry to slowly remove the shaking bloody hand from his head. Blood was still erupting from two BB sized holes in Mason's ear.

"Well it looks like I may have pierced your ear. I guess twice," Barry said feeling a bit relieved having expected much worse. "I could have been way worse."

"What? Did it hit my head?"

"No, no, like I said it pierced your ear. One through the lobe, one a little higher and maybe one that skipped off at an angle, left a trench. That's it though, lucky," Barry said. Now having talked himself out of his panicked state. "It's just bleeding a lot."

Finding it easy enough to hone in on the commotion, Paul came in following Mason's trail. "What the hell happened?"

Barry reached into a breast pocket and removed a white handkerchief folded in four and applied it directly to Mason's ear.

"He fuckin' shot me. That's what happened."

"What? How bad is it?" Paul had a sudden rush of panic as he to rushes for the ground next to Mason.

"Calm down. Calm down, it's not bad. Just put a few holes though the earlobe that's all. You know, pierced his ear."

"Fuck you!" Mason screamed just as Gordy finally found his way into the melee.

"What's going on?" Gordy asked the crowd.

"Barry shot Mason," Paul said, almost as if it were meant to be joke on a sitcom.

Gordy was absolutely calm. He only shook his head in disgust as he calmly set his tools on the ground. "Why am I not surprised?"

"It's not that bad." Barry was now defending himself. "It could have been a lot worse. Just a couple of little puncture holes." The politician in him was already lobbying for a pardon based on circumstances. "I never saw him. It was complete accident. It could have been any one of us."

"Let's have a look." Gordy leans in and assesses the wound. "Yeah, I guess it's not too bad. Let's get him up and get him back and cleaned up."

Barry grabs him under his arm and to help him up on his knees. Mason pulls away and stands up on his own.

"Not you, motherfucker! Not you! I don't even want to look at you right now man. Just stay the fuck away from me!" Mason snapped hard on him.

"Look, I know you're upset right now, but let me help," Barry pleads.

"No, no!" Mason pushed Barry away and stood under his own power. The blood on his angry face painted an unforgettable stare for Barry's memoir. "Upset? Upset? Fuckin-A I'm upset! Why? So you can feel better? Fuck you! Gun Safety 101 Barry! 101! Be sure of your target and beyond!" Mason's teeth were still slightly clenched in pain.

Paul stepped in and placed his hand on Barry's shoulder. "Look, everybody calm down. It's not bad. It's not that big of a deal."

Mason turned his screaming fury towards Paul. "Oh no! No big fuckin' deal! Motherfucker just fuckin' shot me! That's all!"

"Look! That's not what I meant! Your ear! It's not all that bad. It's not like we have to take a trip to the emergency room or anything."

"Alright, alright. Let's just get him back and get it cleaned up and then we can see what we've got. Barry, you just sort of hang back. You know, come in a little bit," Gordy said.

"I really think I should be there, especially if he has to go to the hospital," Barry said. "I mean, if there is a shooting, accidental or not the police have to be notified."

"I doubt we have to go, but if we do you'll probably either be back by then, or Paul will come out and get you. Ok?"

"I'm certainly not okay with it. I'm not comfortable at all. Look Mason, I know you're upset but…"

"Save it!" Mason yelled cutting him off. "Just save it! Now let's fuckin' go!" He immediately walked away. Gordy pointed towards Mason and started after him. He turned to Barry and gave him the universal slow down sign with his hands and theatrically mouthed "Hang back".

"This is ridiculous. It was clearly an accident. I know he's pissed but this isn't right. What am banished? Am I voted off the island? If he goes in without me I could be facing charges for God's sake! Above that I'd like to make sure he is OK. I mean, it's a tragic event for both of us."

"Where were you even?" Paul asked.

"I found a new stand sight just through the thick brush over there. There's a nice natural outcropping that gives me a pretty good look down the valley. There were grouse flushing behind us and I shot the last one that jumped. That's when I heard the screaming. I had no idea he was coming through there."

"Did you go flushing birds?" Paul asked.

"No! I was building the blind and they started flushing, I grabbed my shotgun quick and shot one."

"Hmm. Maybe Mason flushed the birds," Paul said with head down and eyes up. The sort of position a person is in when delivering as a matter of fact bad news.

Standing with his hands on his hips, looking completely worn out, Barry focused on where he had come from before noticing where he was at. "Maybe."

"Maybe?" Paul was now annoyed. Whether Barry couldn't admit fault or the shock of the situation caused temporary ignorance, either way he had had enough. "Let me have that saw."

"Oh. I think I left it back over there," Barry said pointing back over his shoulder.

"And you never lose anything huh? Well there you go. You shot a bird right? Bring that thing back and get my saw. By then it'll be long enough. Maybe you can get another one," Paul said.

"I suppose I have to do that anyways," Barry said looking off into the woods.

"There you go. I'll see you back there in a few minutes." With that Paul followed the beaten path of the other men back towards the trailer.

Barry picked up his shotgun and took a moment to gain his bearings. He was only mere steps away, his back still visible in the impossibly thick undergrowth to The Hunter, who was kneeling next to a tiny pool of Mason's blood.

One leaf, pooled with blood The Hunter lifted and poured down the side of his head letting it drip down over his ear. He reverently twisted his neck towards the sun. A second leaf with blood he carefully cradled. He stared at it angrily. He inhaled the blood like cocaine. His head flew back, his eyes stung closed from the burning in his nasal cavity. When blood drips down the throat there is no better way to get the taste.

Barry finally stood at the spot where he thought he downed the bird. Puzzled he began to walk concentric circles thinking he must have been close. After just a few minutes, he came upon the bird. Once found, the camouflage that kept it hidden seemed suddenly and strangely ineffective. He looked it over closely, lightly juggling it in his hand, spinning it around, and shaking his head in disgust before sliding it into the game pouch on his vest. After a few turns he eventually meandered his way back towards the blind. As he approached, through the brush he could see a figure of a man, sitting in his half built blind.

"I thought you headed back!" Barry yelled to him but there was no response. "Are they taking him to the hospit…?" Barry froze in mid-word as it was clear that the man sitting in the blind was unknown to him.

"Excuse me? Hello?" Barry leaned close to the side of The Hunter's face and asked again. "Hey bud! In case you didn't know this is private land. You're not supposed to be here." Again, there was no response, not even a look in his direction. "Excuse me are you ignoring me?" Carrying his shotgun in his right arm he lightly swung it forward gently poking The Hunter on shoulder. "Hey!"

With impressive speed The Hunter grabbed the barrel with his left and pushed it towards Barry's feet while pivoting the butt towards him, which he grabbed with his right, effectively twisting the gun from Barry's hands.

Blue Eyes stood and glared down the barrel directly at Barry's head. "Sit down."

"Look, I don't know what this is all about but…"

At that point The Hunter kicked out Barry's right leg sending him straight to the ground.

"Jesus! Ok, Ok! Calm down." Barry crab-crawled into the seat where he expected to hunt later in the fall. He kept his gaze down not wanting to see the gun, avoiding the Hunter's eyes, desperate and afraid. "What do you want? I'll go! It's all yours! I'm outta here!"

The Hunter spun the shotgun in his hands and pressed the butt against Barry's chest. He placed the barrel tightly under his own chin and held it closely in place with both hands. "Please, don't shoot me," he asked in a whisper, almost mockingly. For Barry it was one of those moments in life where a second seemed like five or ten or maybe thirty. Barry very slowly placed a shaky hand on the stock behind the trigger. His index finger hovered precariously close to the guard.

"I'll do it," Barry said.

"Please…don't," the Hunter said once again in a fake monotone response.

Barry's lower lip clinched in anger at the reply. His shaking hand made the entire gun tremor.

"I'll do it." The words became much harder for him to say, as if they were being pushed up through wet concrete.

"I wouldn't. Why would you kill me?" The Hunter asked.

Time stopped before the dumbfounded Barry let The Hunter rip the shotgun from his hands.

"What about you?" The Hunter asked. "Would you kill you?"

He shoved the barrel under Barry's chin, planted the butt down into his crotch and braced it with his knee. "Do it!" he said.

Fight or flight being what it is, it seemed as if was Barry's time to have his moment. "Fuck you!" he screamed at Blue Eyes. "Fuck you! I'm not doing shit! You think I'm afraid?" He tried to pull the shotgun from his neck but The Hunter was too strong, "Fuck you! Fuck you," he screamed and began to cry as he struggled. Barry's right hand covered the trigger guard with the grip of a desperate man, the other on the barrel fighting up against the leverage of the other man to no avail. The Hunter moved his face in closely, nearly nose to nose, Mason's blood stained on his face.

"Why would you do this to me?" The Hunter said in a long, drawn-out whisper. At that he took a pencil thin stick and rammed it into Barry's nostril. The ensuing scream was cut short by the blast of the shotgun as the hand that guards the trigger is the first to reach for the pain. Blue Eyes pushed the thin stick into the ground and broke the bloody end off well beneath the leaves, turned, and walked away.

CHAPTER 28

As they left the church Mason, Marty and Paul stood in a circle at the bottom of the sprawling concrete stairs. Tom stood atop in the doorway shaking Gordon's hand.

"How's he doing?" Marty asked Tom as he came down.

"He's pissed!"

"Yeah, that's what I got too." Marty said. "You'll never be able to convince him that Barry committed suicide. Never." He pulled his long black overcoat tighter by the pockets.

After most of the last of the attendees filtered out, Gordon slowly walked down the steps to join the men. "Guys, I really want to thank you all for coming. It would have meant a lot to him knowing you all came." He sprawled his arms around the shoulders of both Marty and Mason.

"Of course man, of course, why wouldn't we?" Paul said.

"Maybe if I'd have reported the shot?" Mason said. "You know if the cops had come it never would have happened."

"Maybe that's what he was afraid of," Paul said.

"No! No way!" Gordy snapped back at Paul, his eyes fixed with subdued rage. He changed his tone to a forceful whisper. "No way! There's no way my brother killed himself over this. You guys were there. Paul, you seen him last. Was he suicidal?"

"Well, no," Paul said in the same whisper tone. "I mean, he was upset and everything but I didn't think he was suicidal."

"Exactly! No way my brother offed himself. I'd bet everything I own! Something ain't right!"

"What did the cops say? I mean, is there going to be an investigation? Do *they* think it's a suicide?" Mason asked.

"Those fuckers. Well you were there; Sheriffs and the Warden and those guys were there after we found him. They did not look around really at all. It was dark, said they'd seen this sort of thing before and considering the accident just wrote it off right away as a suicide. That's bullshit!"

"The Warden was talking about me failing to report a crime, I thought he was going to take me in but I guess considering everything…who knows, they could still charge me, and you guys for that matter," Mason said.

"It's not over as far as I'm concerned," Gordon said. "We gotta get out there and look around. I'm heading out there in the morning. Who's with me?"

Paul looked to Mason knowing he was able. "I gotta work," he said.

"I'm there anyways. What time?" Mason asked.

"I might be able to make it up there in the afternoon but Friday would be better," Marty said.

"No, I'm going in the morning before anything changes. I'll be there early," Gordon said. "Tom, you in?"

Tom kept his chin tucked down into his overcoat pulled tightly, rocking gently to stay warm "Yeah, I guess I don't have anything going on. But just what are we supposed to be looking for?"

"I'm not sure, I'm not sure. I'm hoping between us we'll know it when we find it," Gordon said. A few moments passed as they let it all sink in. "Alright boys? I gotta get back in there. I'll see you guys in the morning. Thanks again, thanks again," he said as he shook all of their hands and climbed the stairs back into the church.

"Wow," Tom said. "Mason, you staying around here tonight or are you heading back?"

"No, I'm going to head back now I think."

"You sure? Want to grab a bite or something? C'mon you can crash at my place."

Mason knew lunch would eventually digress into some heavily mournful drinking. "No, I just want to get home. Thanks though, and I guess I'll see you in the morning from the way it sounds."

"Yeah, I guess. I don't know what in the hell we're looking for," Tom said.

"Closure," Marty said. "Closure."

There were still a few hours of daylight left when Mason got back to the trailer. He changed clothes quickly. The spent shells still bothered him. He scoured the ground for more but found nothing. *Is there anything I really have to do?* he thought to himself. *I'm the victim here after all.* He rubbed his thumb and forefinger gently over the scabs on his ear, his eyes fixed distantly, thinking, *They'd know.* He thought while considering picking up the makeshift plywood target that was coincidentally not far from the scene, *I'll burn it. But they'd know. But if I lead the way…No, there's a trail but not to there. It's tipped over.*

He rewarded his next idea with a subdued fist pump, *I'll come down from the woods.*

Carefully Mason followed the trail put forth by others. He wanted no hint that he or anyone else had been off the beaten path. He wanted this over with as soon as possible. Two tragedies on the same parcel will be suspicious. *It can only be one shot,* he thought. He giggled at the unintended pun that came to mind. *I only have one shot at this.* A man at the end of his rope it could be argued holds on just a little tighter. *No way I don't get caught,* he thought, gently shaking his head in self-doubt. *Fuckin' Barry.*

CHAPTER 29

The distant star-like glare of the small fire behind the trailer could have lived inside the light in Blue Eyes' stove. Purposefully different yet so much the same. He carved a piece of meat off the bulk he held in his hand, dropping it on the wood stove by way of knife and thumb. The meat sizzled. Movement caught his eye indirectly. A field mouse on the wood pile was taking great interest in the goings on. Blue Eyes cut a tiny piece for it, but the mouse's fear overwhelmed his hunger and he scurried away from the offering. Blue Eyes just left it.

"You'll be back."

And so he was. He moved quickly and with purpose, stopping unexpectedly and starting again at nearly full speed seemingly without reason. He was on that chunk of meat in no time and just as quickly he was full speed and gone like a liar that had gotten away with something. The Hunter set out more.

He tapped his chest pocket with the back of his knife as if just realizing something was there. He dropped the knife blade down next to his chair where it stuck deep enough to stand. He removed a small handful of spent rifle casings and bounced them in his hand. The clinking noise they made gave him satisfaction. He placed them end-up on the hot stove, admiring them. As they heated the smell of spent powder mixed with the odor of burning meat. Sometimes he liked it well-done. He flipped the meat and picked up a log to feed the stove. Again, his mouse friend scurried off to points unknown.

"Back again?"

Finally done to his satisfaction he took the meat off the stove and tore off a piece for the mouse while he chewed the rest. His offering went unnoticed. The sound of the scurrying rodent at his side angered him.

"Sneaky."

Its tiny nose sniffed overtime at the blade of the knife.

"Not what's given but what you can take," he said to the mouse quietly. "We need more wood." He pulled the knife from the floor and replaced it in the scabbard on his belt. The chair rocked itself still as he walked outside; the mouse watched from the safety of the nearly exhausted pile.

Another empty beer can hit the coals with a sizzle. Mason stood over what was left and unzipped his fly dousing the fire with his own pee. The ensuing steam hissed a foul odor like dragon's breath.

"Damn that stinks," Mason said aloud, staggering slightly as he zipped back up. He stopped for a moment at the door pondering the uncertainty ahead. An obnoxiously loud beer belch complete with liquid spatterings echoed off the trailer. "That's what I was waiting for," he said as he swung open the door and retired inside.

Sounds carry great distances on clear, cold nights especially when the lion's share of the leaves had already fallen. Blue Eyes recognized the sound as having come from the halls of lonely depression, a place he used to visit often. The amount of wood he held in one arm in order to open the door with other was impressive but heavy non-the-less. He guided the drop all at once attempting to place the perfect pile. The shriek from the wood offered him more concern than had anything in his life in a very long time. The look on his face was pained. The mouse jutted from the pile and hit the side of the stove with a soft pong like the ringing of a far distant bell. It lay motionless next to the stove.

"No!" he yelled. He kicked the chair back and fell to his knees. He reached for the rodent extremely slowly. He was almost afraid to touch it, not because he was afraid of mice, but because of what he might find. He picked up the lifeless body and held it closely, cupping it in both hands. His chin pinned tight to his chest and his body shook with nearly uncontrollable weeping.

"The fuckers!" he screamed as he quickly rose to his feet, rage replacing grief at an alarming rate. "Those fucks!"

He threw the spent mouse hard against the back wall. He turned and smacked the empty shells from the stove top scattering them throughout the cabin. It was not enough. He stormed outside, the anger on his face overwhelming. His fists were tightly clenched, ready to fight.

"Show yourself!" he yelled out into the darkness. The Hunter heaved-in the air. *It is you.*

It was hard-faced with sunken, dark, indistinguishable eyes that lived in the shadow of a protruding brow. It had always looked that way, as far back as he could remember. It has haunted him just as long. A shadow, a thought, always just out of sight living on the edge of his peripheral. In his mind it was judging him and his own rage gave it life. "You knew. You let them." His voice slowly built to a crescendo. "Leave me alone!" The gravel in his voice sounded animalistic. He alone would hear the echo and enjoy the rage.

CHAPTER 30

It was Gordy slamming things around in the kitchen of the trailer that rudely awoke Mason that morning. He tossed a disheveled death stare in Gordy's direction on his way outside to pee. Tom's approaching headlights illuminated Mason's failing arc of urine.

"Why so fucking early?" Mason yelled.

"Nice prostate," Tom said getting out of his vehicle.

"Fuck you. What the hell are you doing here so early?"

"Gordy said first thing so here I am," Tom said.

"Yeah,but you though? It's not like you to be up before the sun."

"Fuck that, I'm always up for hunting."

"We're not hunting today though," Mason said as he zipped up his fly.

"No? Do you think he killed himself?" Tom asked.

"I don't fuckin' know anymore. Who knows?" Mason said.

"It just doesn't seem like something he'd do. I mean, we weren't going to the cops, he was long out of office, and he just wasn't the guilty feeling type. You know what I mean?" Tom said.

Gordy watched the two talking from the low window of the trailer.

"Yeah but it looks like he did it though," Mason said.

"Why though? I don't think he could do it," Tom said.

"Well nobody else pulled the damn trigger. It's not like anyone else was out there," Mason said.

"Paul was," Gordy said now standing on the metal stairs of the trailer.

"What?" Tom asked.

"Yeah, tell us more," Mason said with about as much sarcasm as a person could muster.

Gordy walked slowly towards them. "He held back remember? He was last one to be with him. And if I remember correctly, you told him to hang back."

"Well excuse me I was a little pissed off at the time. So what are you saying, Paul and I conspired to kill your brother? You fucking think we'd do that? Seriously?" Mason said irritated.

Tom stepped in between the two with his arms spread to keep them apart. "Whoa, whoa, everybody just calm down." Although Mason took a half of a step forward, Gordy turned to the side in a failed effort to hide his tears.

Gordy's voice was muffled as he used his gloved thumb and forefinger to wipe his eyes. "Look, I don't know what I'm saying. I just can't make a whole lot of sense of it. Barry wouldn't have done this." He sucked it up hard and turned towards his friends again. "I need your help. I'm sorry, I just don't get it."

"Look, I get it. But Barry was like family. Sure I was livid, he just shot me. What the fuck do you expect? Hell, you were right there. You seen him. You saw how he was acting. To think Paul or I had anything to do with it pisses me the fuck off to tell you the truth! And you're not even saying you don't think that!" Mason yelled.

"Look, look, Gordy, you don't seriously think these guys had anything to do with it did you?" Tom asked.

"No. I don't know. Tom, you weren't there either? Alright!" Gordy put his hands up in a defensive posture, his demeanor now was one of focused anger. "Ok, ok, I might be a little fucked up and off the wall. Maybe I'm not thinking straight. Something happened though. No way it went down like they say. And I'm going to get to the bottom of it with or without you."

"Well I guess it's without me then," Mason said. Tom looked over at him slightly shocked. "You think I had something to do with it? Or Paul? Fuck you! Just fuckin' have at it man. Just fuckin' go and see for yourself." He started for the trailer in huff. Tom grabbed him by the shoulder.

"Hey! Let's do this together. He's not saying it was you. He's just saying shit out loud because he's fucked up right now. It was his brother man," Tom said.

Mason stood there and took a deep breath focusing angrily on the ground at Gordy's feet. "Alright. Let's get this over with," he said as he lifted his head and looked deeply into Gordy's eyes. They stared at each other for a moment. Both men's eyes were glossed over with potential tears. "Let me get dressed."

The air outside the trailer was consumed by uncomfortable silence. Tom and Gordy took turns pacing waiting for Mason to get dressed. It was light although the sun had yet to break the trees. The long grasses and dead for the year weeds shined white with fresh frost.

After a few minutes had passed without the two speaking a word Mason came out of the trailer reeking with a lack of enthusiasm.

"Well, where to first? What are we looking for?"

Both Tom and Mason looked to Gordy as this was now decidedly his show.

"Let's just go back there and see what we can find," Gordy said. The three walked single file, their back trail highlighted by the lack of frost, like an etch-a-sketch. They went first to the last place they saw Barry alive, where Mason was shot. Gordy began to scour the leaf litter on the ground with his foot like it was a metal detector. Mason and Tom just sort of stood around pretending to look for what they knew was not there.

"Is this where it happened?" Tom asked.

"Well, this is where he shot me. That happened," Mason said, the tone in his voice showed he clearly was not over it yet.

"Yeah, but is this where he…you know, did it?" Tom said trying not to say the words.

"No. It was over the ridge, by a new spot he found." It did not take long for Gordy to give up looking "I guess there probably wouldn't be anything over here. Let's go over there."

After so many had been through the area including police and emergency personnel, the path was well worn. The spot was eerily still. The tree Barry leaned against before the gun went off was painstakingly obvious. Gordy stood there next to it, staring at it, the dried blood turned brown against the gray bark.

"You see now Tom?" Gordy said.

"Yeah, I got it," Tom said.

"No note, no sign, nothing. My brother loved to talk. Hell, he made a living at it. No way," Gordy said. He took a deep breath. "Well, let's have a look around."

Once again, he combed the leaves looking for any clue. A few trees away from ground zero his foot dislodged something that was not stick nor stone. He reached down and picked up Paul's small hand saw. He juggled it in his hand deep in thought. Mason and Tom both looked at other then back at Gordy with the universal "oh shit" look on their faces.

"So what. Paul borrowed it to him before he took off," Mason said.

Gordy held tightly to the saw. "I guess. And I suppose he's going to want it back then."

"You still think he had something to do with this don't you?" Mason asked.

This time Gordy held his opinion close to his chest. "I don't think anything," he said, never looking them in the eyes. "You guys think you could give me a second?"

Tom gently pulled a once again swollen Mason by the coat sleeve. "C'mon, let's head back, c'mon. This isn't going to do anybody any good."

Mason shrugged him off and walked away still angrily staring at Gordy.

Gordy watched them until they were out of sight.

"Keep your friends close boys, keep your friends close," he said softly to himself.

CHAPTER 31

The days leading up to gun season had a typical holiday feel to them. Stores buzzed with last minute shoppers stocking up on whatever they were told would give them an edge to bag the big one. Visions of sugar plums dancing in the heads of children were replaced by bucks frolicking in the minds of grown men. Kids will miss school and adults will skip work. Wives will soon become temporary widows and men that don't hunt will have their virility questioned. Small towns braced for the invasion of an orange-clad army that filled restaurants, hotels, and town coffers. A heavily armed force numbering more than half a million statewide all hoping for a kill.

There were of course the overly serious types. The kind of guy that sucks the joy out of the activity with the attitude that all those around him are inferior hunters, simply obstacles that may accidentally luck into one of his deer. Then there are the party types. The focus of this particular hunter is usually to just get drunk. Often, they never make it out into the woods instead choosing to sleep off their hangovers and sometimes occasionally make it out to hunt in the late afternoon. There's the toy guys, they buy every new-fangled gadget on the market that promises success. And the nonchalant guys who haven't fired a shot in years. They just like to be part of the scene. Their collective purpose is not as singular as their orange coats would dictate. Instead, the gun hunt is more like an overall theme where each individual is allowed to insert their own special tradition.

The bluff country was especially attractive for its propensity to produce big bucks, and lots of them. Small towns could prosper on the reputation of the surrounding countryside. It was the time of the year the Hunter despised the most. Each man in the woods was one too many. The natural balance of predator and prey was about to be degraded for the entirety of the cold season. Their presence in the woods to him was akin to roaches in the kitchen. Simple vermin.

Mason walked down the valley with a fist full of helium balloons. He tied them from top to bottom on Marty's deer stand even going as far as drawing an unhappy face on the balloon he intended to tie to the top, a macabre gesture that made him laugh to himself. This was it, the dry run. It was the Thursday before opener. His last chance to practice the shot. There was no shooting allowed on the Friday before opener outside of approved ranges. He needed no extra attention. The first shot failed to connect on anything noticeable. The second tagged a blue balloon near the middle. Three and four sailed most likely high while five struck home. Number five would have been a body hit. A mid-section connection by a 300 Winchester magnum round powerful enough to rip a dirty hole through Marty as well as take a fist sized chunk of meat with it on its way out. Mason noted the limb where he aimed nearly four feet above the intended target. Butterflies came to life inside him with the thought and excitement of what he was about to do. He aimed slightly higher for the last shot. The red balloon on top suddenly had a reason to be unhappy. The heavy bullet that pierced it was its last nightmare. Mason had his marks. The deer he'd say was a lot closer than that, he must have panicked, it was a big buck, a wall hanger. The kind of deer that makes a grown man shake. Obviously and most regrettably he must have flinched. The rubber from the spent balloons caught fire and turned to burning liquid goo in the tiny pit behind the trailer. The pit that had become a graveyard of sorts for circumstantial evidence.

Late Friday afternoon they started to filter in. First Paul, full of enthusiasm, the thought of Barry pushed to the back of his consciousness. Next was Marty who usually was first but had to pull an extra four-hour shift at the home improvement store to fill in for a call-in. Tom rolled up champing at the bit to partake in his traditional Friday before the opener feast, once again to be meticulously drained from a bottle. Usually, the crew headed for the Table Top to drink, bullshit and squeeze every attainable moment of the jovial atmosphere that is opening season. Barry and Gordy generally met them at the bar, but this year was of course going to be different. Nobody was even sure if Gordy was even coming, especially considering the event a few weeks prior.

"Well? Table time?" Paul asked, referring to the battered pool tables at the bar.

"I'm game," Tom said.

"There's a surprise," Mason said.

"I don't know. Just doesn't seem right this year somehow," Marty said.

"Is Gordy even coming?" Paul asked.

"I really don't care if I ever see the guy again to tell you the truth," Mason said. He grabbed a beer from the fridge.

"I'll take one of those. Why, what's up with you and Gordy?" Marty asked. Tom, who was ready to leave a moment ago opened his eyes wide, flapped his lips with an extra-large exhale and looked for a chair.

Mason went on a rant. "You're not going to fucking believe this. He's sure that somebody killed Barry. On top of that he thinks it was one of us. More specifically he thinks it was either Paul or me that had something to do with it."

Paul nearly did a spit-take. "What?"

"Yeah! He thinks because you were out there with him last that you must have talked him into it or something. Or forced him to do it somehow. And he thinks because I wanted him to hold back that you and I were in on it together! Hell, he even thought Tommy because he wasn't here, like he snuck in or something."

"He said all this?" Marty asked.

"In so many words, yeah," Mason said.

"He did say he was confused and sorry though," Tom added.

"Still pretty screwed up though," Paul said.

"What did you say?" Marty asked Mason.

"I told him to fuck off!" Mason said.

"Yup, pretty much," Tom said.

"First of all, that's crazy," Marty said. "I can't believe where he went with that. From what I hear it was pretty cut and dry. I mean, you think you know a guy, but do you really?" There was an unintentional moment of silence. "So is that it now? Is Gordy even coming up anymore?"

"I'm not sure," Mason said before sucking down the last few drops of beer from the can. "I guess we'll find out."

"Wow! I can't believe he thinks I would do something like that. He's known me my whole life," Paul said.

"Yeah well like Marty said, you think you know a guy. That goes for guys that are still alive too," Mason said.

"Let's head up there and get a bite and I guess we'll see if he shows up?" Marty said.

"I don't know, I've got beers here," Mason said as he crushed his can and threw it at the sink.

"C'mon man, its tradition," Paul said.

Tom placed his hand on Mason's shoulder as he passed. "C'mon bud, it'll be fun."

"Alright, alright. What the hell. If he shows he shows," Mason grumbled.

"I figured that was it," Marty said. "Let's go I'm hungry."

CHAPTER 32

The car ride to the bar was unusually quiet. Everybody had their own reasons, even if it was just the discomfort of the quiet. That was Tom's boat. Paul fumed and pouted about what he had heard Gordy said about him. Marty never was much of a conversation starter, more of a responder. No sense in adding to the tension in the air. Mason, of course, was planning to kill someone.

That might be the sort of thing that takes over a person's mind if they planned it. It may also be proof of being sane, if killing a family member can be the act of a sane person. The problem for Mason was that he did not hate him enough. That was part of the reason he was so quiet, he was trying. Surely guilt had to play a role.

"Gordy's car," Paul said as they passed it in the extra busy parking lot.

"You sure?" Marty said.

"Yeah, that was it for sure."

"Huh," Mason said as he pulled his SUV into an available space. "Let's go see if he's still fucking crazy."

Once inside the crowded bar they found Gordy shooting eight ball, a game he was occasionally pretty good at. "Gentlemen!" he said, "Looks like we were first this year."

"We?" Tom asked.

"Yeah, me and Barry," Gordy said as he pulled a necklace free from his shirt and dangled what appeared to be rifle round on a thin leather bootlace. "Loaded with Barry." It took a moment, but everybody seemed to get it at once. "Look, I know what you guys are probably thinking. You gotta know

I was in a pretty dark place. Denial was heavy. I still don't get it, probably never will but I at least wanted to let you know that I'm sorry for some of that shit I said." He reached out to shake Mason's hand. Mason resisted at first. The hopeful to bury the hatchet glares from the others peer-pressured him into it. Handshakes are rarely so cold.

"Well alright! Let's get after it!" Tom exclaimed as he clapped his hands and wedged his way through the crowd to the bar.

"What'll it be?" Ginger said as she happened to be at that spot behind the bar already mixing drinks. "Oh it's you guys. Never mind, I know what it be then," she said and went about her business mixing drinks, eventually lining up a round for the five men.

"To Barry," Marty said as he held his glass high.

"To Barry," they toasted. For a few it was even genuine.

CHAPTER 33

The repeating chimes of Paul's cell phone alarm caused a mighty collective groan. On such mornings words are rarely exchanged. Contempt is easily achieved when so many are in such a small space. It used to be part of the fun but now with the dark cloud of Barry's death looming it was nothing less than uncomfortable. The seed of mistrust that Gordy planted had already sprouted roots. The chiming repeated.

"Paul!" Mason yelled as he came out of the back room. What used to be a small bedroom with a queen-sized bed was now a small bedroom with two bunks. Marty was on top.

"What?"

"Your damn phone that's what." Mason hit the button on the coffee maker and headed for the outhouse.

"Rise and shine gentlemen," Marty said following him out of the back room.

Even before everybody else had a chance to step out for a morning piss Gordy was nearly ready to go.

"What's the hurry man?" Tom asked.

"What? I can't be ready? I should mutter around here and listen to this shit? Don't worry I wouldn't dare break tradition and actually get out in the woods on time," Gordy snapped at him, poured himself a cup of coffee and went outside.

Not that the rant went unnoticed, but besides a few chin stretches it was not all that unexpected considering the circumstances. Normally the smell of a fat man's breakfast would literally overtake the trailer opening morning which is why guys put their blaze orange cover-alls on outside. This year however guys were on their own for food. Barry was the cook of the group after all, and nobody wanted to step into those still-warm shoes. The men gerbiled around slowly getting ready until Paul checked the clock. "It's about that time."

Gordy stood facing the depth of the dark valley with his rifle hanging from his shoulder on a sling, waiting. The rest of the guys finished up putting on their gear and started out. Tom and Paul headed to the long, western, heavily tree-lined bluff that makes up almost one whole side of the property. Mason, Gordy, and Marty head down the valley's center, branching off respectively to the east as they progressed to the end of the valley.

The thick, heavy brush line where field met trees at the very end of the valley was the worst part of Marty's walk. His stand was only a few yards beyond the field edge which in general are thick with sun-loving brush and trees. They can be highways for deer that wish to remain concealed. With no easy way through Marty put his head down and plowed through. Just as the brush thinned and only feet from his ladder stand his light caught a bright reflection of something in the leaves in front of him. He knew what it was before he picked it up.

So sure was he that he even had time to wonder what a picture of his wife was even doing there. He bent to pick it up and almost had it.

The blow to Marty's face sounded like a heavy mallet smashed into a raw turkey piñata. He did not even have a chance to scream. The Hunter was standing behind a large oak just beyond where he laid the picture frame. The heavy rock tomahawk he held over his head was four plus pounds of river-rounded granite affixed to an oak branch handle. He followed through hard with the pendulum type uppercut.

Marty's eyes nearly looked at each other over the massive indentation in the center of his face. They blinked with all the emotion of a plastic doll. Shock spared him for the moment until blood clouded the last of his sight. His lower jaw flailed while desperately trying to speak but there was no upper pallet to contact. He lay paralyzed, shaking violently, churgling on the blood in his throat. The Hunter quickly rolled him over and removed his coat and bibs before they could be covered with blood. Finally, he snatched the hat from Marty's head. Marty was nothing more than limp, quivering meat now, his choking last gasps barely audible. The Hunter kicked him back over and watched him die as he slipped into Marty's orange clothes. He took the butt of Marty's rifle and pushed it into the cavity in his face. The many tiny pieces of broken bone still held together by skin and cartilage crackled and conformed to the base of the stock. He laid the bloody rifle carefully on Marty's chest. He slid the tomahawk handle down his belt inside of the orange suit and disappeared into the forest.

Paul's heart raced at the sound of approaching footsteps. He quickly checked his rifle even though it was still too dark to shoot. As the sound drew closer he noticed an odd cadence to the steps. His still pounding heart sank when he caught a glimpse of blazed orange.

"Hey! Who is that?" Paul yelled in a whisper tone. There was no answer.

"Hey! Who is that?" he asked again. The approaching man coughed and wheezed. He fell to his hands and knees. He waived up at Paul for help and put his face down as if to vomit.

"Holy crap Marty? Is that you? You OK man?"

The man on the ground nodded his head yes and continued to wave for help.

"Hold on man I'll be right down," Paul said as he quickly climbed down from the creaky stand. He rushed to the man's side and placed his hand on his back. The coughing abruptly stopped. With a quick strike The Hunter reached up and grasped Paul's throat with such force as to take him backwards onto the ground. With a sort of Roman Greco style pin Paul was trapped, unable to move or scream. After a few moments without air, he blacked out and lost consciousness.

The first noticeable breeze of the morning finally woke Paul from his blackout. Rope tied his forehead, shoulders, waist and neck to the tree. His hands were bound behind his back and legs were tied to the ladder stand in which he was placed. A gag was so deep in his throat it was even difficult for him to breathe through his nose. His mouth was taped closed. He could do little more than wiggle and could see only as far as his peripheral vision would allow. Within it he could see Marty's body, motionless, spattered with coughed-up blood. He tried to scream but that only made it even harder to breathe. His panic and fear was palpable. His frightened eyes searched for answers through his tears. He sobbed so hard he choked on the gag nearly blacking out again.

He could also see an orange hunting suit, neatly folded and placed by the tree next to Marty. On top was a hat. Leaning against the trunk a rifle. It all was familiar, but shock had all but destroyed his common reasoning. He soon realized the suit was in fact his. As was the hat and the gun. He became aware of the fake orange fur on his collar that tickled the sides of his face, an option his suit did not have. He furled his brow upwards towards a thin brim of the hat he wore. His hat had no brim. As he wiggled his shoulders he felt the sleeves. His right hung straight down while his left was pinched into the action of the rifle that laid across his lap. Marty's rifle.

CHAPTER 34

It was light although the sun had not yet rose high enough to break the tree line. Mason never even sat in his stand. He had in fact only gone far enough so as to not be seen. He worked his way down the tree line adjacent to the fielded center of the valley obliviously hidden. He crouched low and slow against the bare hillside outside the trailer until he was behind his vehicle. It was of course parked with the explicit intent of using it as a bench rest for his rifle. All part of his plan. His heart raced from a combination of haste and anxiety. He checked his rifle for a chambered round, removed his hat and placed it on the hood where he laid the rifle.

"Has it really come this far?" he thought. "Fuck him. Fuck Marty."

He removed his gloves, his hands wet with sweat. As he got down on the rifle a light breeze from his right made him bend his stare towards the encroaching sun. As if premonition had graced him, at that same moment the sound of cracking branches only barely proceeded three deer bounding out of the thick brush. As soon as they cleared the field edge they stopped. Their ears swept to and fro and their tails twitched like surrender flags. They pranced on the edge, afraid to cross open ground at the same time looking back at what had spooked them from safety in the first place. Mason watched enamored. His muscles wanted to swing the rifle in their direction. The Hunter took one large two-legged jump forward and that was enough, the deer flattened their backs and bolted across the valley floor.

In a matter of seconds, they would be gone. Opportunity as they say was knocking. Mason focused hard and fast through his scope, raising his braced shoulder in anticipation of the shot. He did not connect. The deer continued their run towards the safety of the tree line. He fired again although he never swung the rifle. Once again he missed. The third round felt magical. The ejected shell seemed to nearly stop in midair. He could hear every click and slap of the action. This time he could see the hit through the scope. The bullet cut Paul's suit over his ribs, entering on the left side of his body just behind his pectoral muscle. The velocity of the high-powered round turned his heart to cheese before leaving him forever though a half dollar sized hole in his right shoulder. The shock of the impact gave Paul his last greatest burst of strength but if even for a fraction of a second. The rope around his forehead slid up taking the cap off his head. The rope around his neck stretched causing a deep gash that sans a heart could barely bleed. The rifle was jarred from his lap, discharging as it hit the ground. Paul hung in the stand, his chin nearly touching his chest. For the first minute or so he twitched every few seconds as tenseness left his muscles.

Mason stood up, pushing the rifle scope closer to his eye, trying to get a better look.

"Why didn't he fall? A safety harness? I didn't know he wore one. This will work. I didn't even notice."

He quickly slung the rifle over his shoulder and walked towards the trailer. *Wait,* he thought, *I've gotta go look for the deer. Yeah. I gotta go down there.*

He put the rifle down and hurriedly picked it up again, trying carefully to think out his next steps. "Yeah, yeah."

He headed out down the valley trail carrying his rifle at the ready as if a deer were going to pop out at any second. Only his focus was not on the trees, but on the man in the stand. The man that he was sure was Marty, a man he had known for most of his life. A man he had just killed. Never had his heart beat so hard. No thrill ride in the world, no parachute jump, not shooting a trophy buck, nothing could bring this much exhilaration. So much was his lack of regret that his face carried the look of anticipation associated with more of a grand opening surprise than a cold-blooded murder. He hurried his pace.

Four shots in the valley got everyone's attention. Tom was just dozing off before their harsh resonance startled him awake. The three deer pounded up the bluffside, not out of sight but definitely out of his range. His half-asleep mind boggled momentarily with confusion. Who was over there? Who took the first couple of shots? The report was from two different rifles no doubt. Initially they came from Paul's direction but not quite. Or was the echoing sound simply playing tricks on him? He pulled out his cell and shot Paul a text. Was that you?

No answer could mean a myriad of different things. He was walking or maybe tracking. Maybe he was gutting a deer. He knew Marty had an old flip phone, but he had never even sent Marty a text. Ever. He could do little more than hunt. After a few minutes curiosity got the best of him. He climbed down from his stand and headed down the bluff towards the direction of the shots.

Gordy too was alerted by the shooting. Sitting on the back side of the bluff distorted the sound. Pinpointing the shot location was difficult, although he could at least tell they were close. In his mind the last shot had to belong to Marty. Maybe the one person in the group he could trust. They were close to the same age, much older than the rest. Being as how he was well aware of the physical limitations of advancing age, he would go lend a hand, maybe gain an ally and at the very least relieve his mind of the quiet conspiracy that grew from his dead, preoccupied forest stare. Besides, he was close.

Considering the topography of the land he was not going to be able to see Marty until he was relatively close. But he was still far enough that he laughed to himself slightly when at a glance he assumed he was walking up on Marty sleeping in his stand. With his rifle slung over his shoulder he cupped his hands around his mouth and yelled, "Good thing you're wearing a harness."

He expected to startle Marty and was now only steps behind him. That's when he saw the ropes. Two hurried and nervous steps later he saw Marty.

"Jesus!" he yelled.

He rushed to Marty's side but once he was on him, he knew right away that Marty was dead. He backed away slowly. His mind trying desperately to comprehend the scene unfolding around him. For a moment he even forgot about whoever was in the deer stand. He swung around and looked up carefully.

"Paul. Oh my God." He set his rifle down and climbed up to Paul as fast as he could manage but once again, his efforts were fruitless. "Oh my God! Oh my God!" he said over and over as he climbed down.

He paced the ground for a moment in front of the stand for a moment talking out loud. "Okay, okay, get ahold of yourself."

He froze. It finally dawned on him that this was of course no accident. He saw the folded clothes, the bloody rifle laying on the ground, everything. His eyes opened wide on the edge of panic. Brush breaking. Someone was coming. His eyes searched wildly for his rifle. By the time he saw it he was too scared to move.

CHAPTER 35

"What are you doing over here?" Mason asked Gordy as he parted the thick brush. Of course he was shocked to see Marty on the ground. He was already mentally prepared for that. So much so that he even ignored him. A second later, looking up in horror, Mason found his brother.

"Paul! Paul!"

He threw his gun on the ground and nearly flew up the ladder. He knew when he looked into his brother's eyes, when he saw his body tied to a tree that it was his shot that killed him.

"Oh my God! What are you doing here?" Mason yelled in a screaming cry. "Oh my God! Paul! My brother man! My brother!" followed by a sob that can only be made when you lose a loved one.

"Who did this? Who did this?" Mason cried quietly and desperately with his face buried in Paul's chest, pounding his fist on the tree. He dropped to the ground. "Who did this? Who put him up there? It was you?" He screamed at Gordy with all his might. "What? Revenge?" As he drew closer he noticed Gordy was holding a rifle on him, balanced on his hip. It was Mason's rifle.

"What are you kidding me? You fuckin' shot him. It had to be you." He glanced over at Marty. "And you didn't even…"

Gordy stopped in mid-sentence and looked back at Mason. "Ahhh, I get it. You thought it was Marty up there! What were you doing, trying to cover this up? Don't move Mason. I'm warning you," Gordy said. "I'll kill you if I have to. I knew it. I knew this shit, I knew something wasn't right.

Barry, man, Barry. I knew he couldn't have done it. It was you, you fuck. It was you. I knew it. I knew it. I should fucking shoot you, you fucker. You fuckin' murderer!" He ended shouting. He appeared to gain temporary composure as Mason raised his hands in surrender.

"Fuck you man! You better fucking kill me or so help me God you're a fucking dead man," Mason said. With that kind of motivation Gordy slowly raised the rifle and took aim through the scope. Mason was too close so he re-focused on the iron barrel sights underneath the scope.

"What the fuck is going on?" Tom asked as he barreled down the hill onto the scene. His mouth hung wide open, kept that way by disbelief and horror. There was no chance he could comprehend everything he was seeing. It was very simply horror. Seeing Gordy about to shoot Mason, Marty on the ground, and Paul in the stand he really just raised his rifle instinctively and pointed in the obvious place. Square at Gordy. "Put the fuckin' gun on the ground man!"

"Shoot him! Shoot him," Mason yelled.

"Fuck you, fuck you!" Gordy yelled at Mason, hard enough to spray angry spittle. "He fuckin' killed these guys! He killed Barry too!"

"Fuck that Barry's the one that shot me! I just got here and found him!" Mason yelled back. "Shoot him Tommy!"

Gordy swung his rifle and pointed it at Tom. "Drop it Tom. I swear."

"See? See? He's going to shoot you Tommy! For God's sake do it!" Mason knew he could not have a witness.

"Put it down Tom. I'm dead serious here. This has to be done," Gordy said.

"Fuck him Tommy! He killed Pauly! He killed my brother man!" Mason pleaded.

From the corner of his eye, he saw Gordy's gun lying on the ground. It was a lever action rifle that most seasoned hunters are familiar with. It was one long lunge away. While Gordy held his weapon on Tom, Mason took the chance and dove for it. He fully intended on pumping as many rounds as possible into Gordy who by chance swung earlier than expected. A split second later and Mason probably would have been dead. That's why Tommy did it. He really had no choice.

That close to the source, the bullet passed easily through Gordy's chest. It was so fast he barely flinched. The wave of instant pain was a different story. He let go of the forearm of the rifle and cupped his hand over the wound as he fell to his knees screaming. He got off a one-armed shot with Mason's Win Mag carving Tommy's breast bone in two. Tommy's eyes rolled back, and he fell to his knees. He was dead before he went all the way to the ground.

Gordy fell over gun side down and tried to train the rifle on Mason as he crawled for cover. Mason had made it to Gordy's weapon and slipped behind a tree, messing with the action making sure it was loaded. He hit the tree Gordy hid behind, but was actually trying to hit the exposed orange he could see.

"Fuck you! Fuck you!" Gordy yelled at Mason but gasping for air and bleeding profusely, it ended up being more of a loud, gravely whisper. "You won't get away with this!"

"You shot Tommy you son of a bitch. Tommy! Tommy!" Mason yelled but of course there was no response. "You fuckin' shot him!"

"Game Wardens! Game Wardens!" A stern voice yelled from just beyond the brush. Mason could barely make out the orange vests. "Place your weapons on the ground!"

"Officers! Officers!" Mason yelled. "He's got my rifle. He shot my brother! He shot my brother!" Gordy no longer had enough to yell back as his breaths became harder to come by.

"Put you weapon on the ground!" The Wardens approached slowly with their semi auto handguns trained on Mason. He tossed the rifle on the ground and placed his hands alligator high above his head.

"Stay down! He's right over there," Mason said. "He killed everybody! He killed them all!" Mason began to cry.

One of the Wardens kept his pistol trained in Gordy's direction while the other pulled Mason back and processed him. Sherriff's deputies with guns drawn were also closing in from multiple angles.

By the time officers got eyes on Gordy it was too late. The deputies carefully approached and removed the rifle from within his reach. His eyes were closed. No doubt the result of grimacing in pain before upon death his face muscles retracted back to death neutral.

Mason was escorted to an ambulance where the EMTs immediately treated him for shock. He knew deputies were close and wanted immediate answers. He grappled with his story, not yet able to decide the proper time to break out of his false fugue state. Opportunity appeared in his favor yet again but these men were no fools. He needed to solidify details that were confused by his brother's death. He couldn't grasp the "how" yet but what especially tore him up was the "why". He knew it was his fault no doubt, but should he even tell them that he took the shot? Ignorance could be his friend.

Large childlike puzzle pieces fell into place. Mason after all did not even have his own gun. Tom's bad luck of getting shot by Mason's rifle worked huge in his favor. For that matter Paul was also killed by the same gun, the same one deputies removed from his possession moments earlier. Mason began to sob as he recounted, effectively breaking him out of his self-induced coma.

"Pauly," Mason cried aloud. "Tommy boy! My God, my God! Why?" The deputy and the detective with him that were waiting there hoping for answers looked at each other and shook their heads with mutual pity. At that point they would have bought any car on the lot. Grim reality sold his cries at a steep discount.

"I'm sorry sir. I know this is an impossible time, but we could really use some details while they're fresh in your mind. If you could just take your time and try to describe for us exactly what happened," said the detective. "Take your time. Mason is it?"

Mason turned towards the wall of the ambulance, still whimpering trying to gain composure. "Yah," he said quietly.

"Last name? Mason do you know what happened here today? Can you give us anything that might be able to help us out right now?"

"Owens. Mason Owens."

"And what happened here Mason?" The detective asked again. "Did you know these men? Are you familiar with the deceased?" At that point a deputy outside the ambulance tapped the detective on the shoulder and handed him the driver's licenses of the deceased. He looked them over patiently waiting for Mason to answer.

Mason looked directly at him now. His eyes shocked wide open by fear, not of being shot, but being caught. This was the game winning shot every want-to-be hero goes over and over in their mind. If he missed it was game over. Worse yet, even he did not know all the details.

"Mr. Owens?"

"My brother. My little brother." He began to cry again. "He killed him."

"Who killed him Mr. Owens? Who killed your brother?"

Mason answered as if it only just came to him. "Gordy," he said quietly. "Fuckin' Gordy!" he screamed. "I got up late. It's my fault I got up late. I could have stopped him."

"Stopped who Mason? Stopped who? Try to calm down and start from the beginning. Can you do that? Can you try to focus for us?"

"Sure, sure." Mason choked back his tears and tried to sit up. The paramedic adjusted the angle so he could sit upright. He was as ready as was ever going to be. "I got up late. The guys were yelling at me to get up as they headed out. That's what woke me up. When I finally got up and was getting my stuff I couldn't find my rifle." Mason wanted to be dead sure they knew he did not have his gun. "We keep a spare 30/30 in the closet for a back-up so I just grabbed that one but I couldn't find shells. I needed something. I saw Gordy's spare on his bunk so I just grabbed his."

"And you had cartridges for that rifle?" the detective asked.

"Yeah sure, it's a Win Mag like mine. I figured he must have grabbed it by mistake. So I had bullets in my coat."

"So you knew at that point that Mr. Ardent had your rifle?" Mason gave the detective a startled look when he mentioned Gordy by name but then he remembered the licenses.

"Yeah, yeah," Mason said.

"Then I would guess you went out hunting as well Mr. Owens?"

"Yeah. I went out. By myself cause everybody else was gone already."

"Approximately what time would you say you left?"

"I'm not sure, maybe 6:30 or 7:00. It was just getting light."

The detective took careful notes, then turned the notebook over to Mason and presented him with a pen. "Mr. Owens do you think it would be possible for you to draw me a map of where you were in relation to where we found you? If you could also approximate the locations of the others that would be a huge help here."

Mason took the pen in his shaking hand and began to map out the property. He tore out his first attempt and crushed it into a ball with one hand. "Wait, wait that's no good."

The detective picked up the discarded map and unfolded it while Mason worked on a new one. He folded it once and tucked into his inside coat pocket. "I was here." Mason pointed out a spot on his map and made a small "x". "Paul's stand is over here, Tommy hunts over on this ridge and Gordy is back over this way," Mason said pointing out areas on his map.

"Then this is would be Mr. Fischer's deer stand?" The detective asked. Once again Mason was given pause by the use of a last name.

"Yeah, that's where it all happened," Mason said.

"Where all what happened Mr. Owens? What exactly happened out there today? Wait, excuse me." The detective stepped out and summoned over the local Warden as well as two deputies. He handed them Mason's map. He also pulled the crumpled first attempt from his pocket and handed that one over as well. Mason couldn't hear them but he could see the detective giving direction with his hands. His heart sank. He hadn't really thought it through. If they went and checked it out it would be obvious he was not there. He hadn't been over there since before Barry. "Sorry about that Mr. Owens. Please continue."

Mason worked hard at choking back a few tears and seeming distant. "You, you think you could give me a minute?"

"Absolutely, absolutely. Tell you what, it doesn't appear you're suffering from any injuries so when you're ready we'll be right here OK?" the detective told him as he placed his hand on Mason's leg. "If we're going to sort this out though we are going to need a little more help from you."

"I understand," Mason said as he bit his lower lip and looked away.

CHAPTER 36

The detective knocked on the metal ambulance door more for warning than permission before he stepped in. "Feeling any better Mr. Owens? Again, I know it's difficult but we could really use your help."

"Sure, sure," Mason said.

The Warden who had gone to look at the stand locations knocked on the open door. "Pretty close on this," he said as handed the maps back to the detective. "There's not really anything out there. No equipment, no blood. No sign of struggle…All the leaves were cleared off of them, dew knocked off the steps, that sort of thing. In other words, I could see they were used this morning but not much beyond that."

"Ok, thanks Tony," the detective said. "So you were saying Mr. Owens. You went out to your stand." Mason could not answer. "Mr. Owens, you're in your deer stand, then what?"

"Uh, uh, yeah. I'm sitting there and I hear shots," Mason said, still reeling from what the Warden said.

"How many shots? Were you able to determine the direction of the shots at that time?"

"Um yes. Or…no, no, I wasn't sure. That's the thing, they were coming from my left. I didn't know who'd be up there. That's actually why after a while I got down. To go check it out," Mason said.

"How many shots were there?"

"I guess two or three, I'm not a hundred percent sure." The detective nodded and continued to write in his notebook.

"So how long after the shots were fired did you get down form your stand?"

"I don't know, ten minutes maybe? Something like that," Mason said.

"If it seemed odd to you that someone would be firing from that location why didn't you investigate immediately?" the detective asked.

"I don't know, guys move around, you know? But the more I thought about it the more I thought maybe someone got a deer," Mason said.

"So is it your habit to go see if someone in your party got a deer after you hear shots? I mean, why not just send him a text?"

There was a pause. "Because I didn't know who to ask. Like I said they came from an odd place and I didn't know who was shooting. Normally I would. And yes, when someone shoots one I usually like to help with gutting and dragging and that sort of thing," Mason said.

"I see, I see," the detective said.

"So what brought you to the other end of the valley Mr. Owens?"

"Well there was shot down there too! Like maybe if a deer was running and someone missed and then someone else got it. That's what I figured anyways."

"How many shots?"

"Just one."

"Did that strike you as odd?"

"No, it came from Marty's area and it was only one so I figured for sure he must have got one."

"So knowing it was most likely Mr. Fischer, why not then send him a text and save yourself the walk over?" Mason did not answer. "Mr. Owens?"

"Because. Marty is like the guy who never texts. We give him crap all the time about it."

"When you say 'we' who exactly do you mean?"

"You know, the guys and me…Paul." At the mention of his name Mason's lip began to quiver again and he worked hard to hold back the tears. "As I was coming down the hill through the trees I saw Marty walking back towards his stand. At least I thought it was Marty. At that point I figure it was him that did the shooting but I didn't know why he was up by the trailer."

"What makes you think he was up by the trailer?"

"Cause that's where the first shots came from," Mason said.

"Why did you just tell me 'At least you thought it was Marty'?"

"Because I headed over there, and when I got there I seen him, laid out, all bloody." Mason once again was losing his composure. "And then my brother…murdered."

"Who did you see first Mr. Owens, Mr. Fischer or your brother?"

Mason paused before answering. "Neither. I saw Gordy. He was standing there like he just got caught."

"And then what did you do."

"It's all a blur. I think I rushed over to check on Marty but maybe that's when I saw the guy in the stand was Paul."

"Did your brother sit there often?"

"No, never. I saw he was tied up, I saw all the blood. I knew right there, I knew it." Again he sobbed.

"Knew what Mr. Owens?" the detective asked softly.

"I, I, I knew he was dead." Mason covered his face with his right hand and cried into it.

The beating of news helicopter rotors roared overhead. With mics drawn and cameras rolling reporters from local stations descended upon the scene.

"Okay, let's get you checked out, Mr. Owens. In case I didn't mention it earlier, you have my deepest condolences. I'm sending a few deputies to escort you. If by chance you think of anything else you can let them know and they can get ahold of me at any time. Just one more quick question though."

"Sure, sure, go ahead."

"Did you notice the clothes?"

"No, what clothes?"

"From what we can determine it appears as if they belonged to your brother. The killer appears to have taken the clothes off of Mr. Fischer and put them on your brother. Any idea why he might have done that?"

"No, I guess maybe he wanted the rest of us to think maybe Marty was still up there or something. I, I, I couldn't say," Mason said.

"Even more perplexing was the killer took the time to fold your brother's clothes and place them neatly out of the way. Does that make any sense to you?"

"I don't know, Gordy was kind of a neat freak. I was always bitching and moaning about the mess in the trailer you know? He killed my brother, he's fucking dead right? That's why he didn't answer you guys?"

"Yes, Mr. Ardent died as a result of his wounds. Alright Mr. Owens. That'll be all for now. We'll be in touch, get some rest and once again I'm very sorry." With that the detective stepped out of the ambulance and started closing the back doors.

Mason had a moment of panic. Had he said too much? How could he, he was just as much in the dark as anyone. "Wait! Wait detective!"

"Yes Mr. Owens."

"Don't you want to know what happened after that? After I saw Gordy standing there and then Tom got there?"

"Actually that won't be necessary Mr. Owens. And you can thank your brother. Somehow he managed to get ahold of his cell phone even though his hands were tied. Obviously he was not able to speak but he did manage to dial 911. His phone was recording the entire time. That's how we found you. Through the location service on his phone. If my hunch is correct your brother may actually be a hero. It's entirely possible that you and your party weren't the killer's first victims. Although there are some details to be worked out, we'll let you know. It looks to me like you're lucky to be alive. Take care Mr. Owens. Try to get some rest."

There was no thank you from Mason, no eruption of relief to be alive. Just a shocked stare. The closing rear doors of the ambulance seemed to him like the exclamation point on the end of his life punched into place by a sharp red pen.

CHAPTER 37

The mass shooting had gained national attention. Local authorities were under heavy pressure to produce a viable explanation for what happened. State and federal authorities were called in by the Governor to lend assistance and add credibility as well as fast-track a solid conclusion.

All evidence both solid and circumstantial pointed to Gordy. He had Mason's rifle when they found him. Ballistics showed that it was indeed the gun that fired the bullets that killed both Tomas Laseur and Paul Owens. He was at the scene according to a credible eyewitness and was seen standing over the body of one of the victims. As far as motive was concerned it was relatively simple.

Gordy never believed his brother committed suicide. He placed Paul in the tree stand for two reasons. First off, he was Gordy's prime suspect. He was admittedly the last person to see Barry alive and for all Gordy believed, he all but pulled the trigger. For that he wanted Paul to suffer. He wanted Paul to watch his own brother die. By taking Mason's rifle that morning and tossing the shells for the spare, he expected that Mason, who'd clearly drank too much the night before simply wouldn't go out. It was a mistake made in haste that he forgot to secure his own rifle, and it probably had not even occurred to him that they were of the same caliber. When he went back to the trailer and Mason was gone Gordy panicked and shot Paul early before Mason or anyone else could get to him. That explains the first shots. Three shells were ejected from Mason's rifle onto the ground in front of his vehicle.

The last shot it was determined had been from an accidental discharge of Marty's rifle which had been placed in or around the deer stand with Paul. Further testing showed the rifle must have been rigged to discharge as the malfunction could not be repeated using scientific means. The reason for this remained unclear. Without the evidence being conclusive as to where the rifle was or possibly how far it fell when it fired, it ceased to be a viable part of the equation. Nobody was there to argue the point.

For the pieces to fit, Gordy had to kill Marty first to keep Marty's elevated stand empty. Authorities surmised that he stove-in Marty's face with the butt of Marty's own rifle. Evidence that Marty knew and trusted the killer. Next Gordy would set his sights on Paul. Gordy, so consumed by revenge wanted Paul to see his brother walk into an ambush and be unable to warn him. Aided by the testimony of Mason Owens stating that Gordy did in fact consider Marty a suspect in Barry's death, authorities were able to make the revenge theory stick. Gordy had publicly declared that he thought Marty was involved simply because he was not present the weekend that Barry died. Once again, nobody was there to argue.

Poor Tom was just collateral damage. Authorities said that by chance alone he was the hero of the story, giving his own life for his friend and eventually making the shot that took down a vicious murderer.

The story had everything it needed, - antagonist, protagonist, heroes, and villains and of a lone survivor, the one spared by God to tell the tale. The media ate it up. The bad guy got his and the world goes back to normal. The state was also a fan of the tidy package and by law enforcement standards was wrapped-up unusually quickly.

For Mason it was not quite that easy. In the hospital that very night he had a severe mental breakdown. Uncontrollable crying mixed with fits of violent anger prompted authorities to commit him to an institution for his own safety and well-being.

"Who put Paul up there? Who killed Marty? Was it Gordy? No, I made the shot. Did he know? But why kill Marty? But he let me take the shot." His thoughts were consumed by questions he could never answer. Killing his own brother proved to be too much for Mason to coherently handle. Therapy and medication would have to work against the tide treating a man that could not admit what he had done for fear of self-incrimination. In the end he did get what he wanted. The land would be his. With his sister, Marty and Paul gone, he would own it all alone. A potentially quick sale would put him back in the money. At least a quarter of a million profit with no overhead. He never expected it would cost him his brother although the mental anguish became more bearable considering the unexpected ease of probate.

Three years and five days after Barry's suicide, Mason was finally given the green light to return to society. Before the general public really knew all the details, some of Marty's co-workers, as a nice gesture, put everything away at the trailer and closed the place up. A government looking late model fleet car bounced its way up the uncut field road to the front of the trailer. A case worker that faked at being a lawyer helped Mason unload some groceries, a duffel of clothes and one cardboard box roughly the size of a microwave oven. He did not have the patience or the care to wait for Mason to find the key, deciding instead that he had already gone above and beyond the call. He was not being paid to babysit.

Mason pried the trailer door open with a rusty tire iron that had been laying underneath the stairs for years. A bee's nest in the door jamb that had recently been abandoned crackled and broke like brittle paper. The inside was dank and musty. Even with all the media attention the place was pretty much left alone. People knew it belonged to a public victim. Although he did not want to, he knew he needed to be there. If for no other reason than to say he was sorry to his brother and goodbye to his friends. His fragile mind needed the closure. For him sadness took center stage in every view. If he had somewhere else to go, anywhere, he would have.

Most everything was removed for evidence and distributed to families, auctioned or destroyed. But not his bow. Years ago, when money was easy, he had the case monogrammed. The police must have realized it was his. He smiled at the thought of seeing it as well as having that sort of money again. "I'll see you in the morning brother," he said quietly while he stroked the case. He thought first of his bow then of his brother and intentionally referred to both.

He went to the cardboard box he had placed on the kitchen table, undid the flaps and removed a black plastic box with a small cross emboldened in silver on the cover. It was one of two.

He held his brother's remains reverently. "You'll be home in the morning."

He placed him on the table and then took Marty's ashes out of the cardboard box as well. "You too my friend, you too."

The next morning was cool and typical. The north breeze was a little heavier than he would have liked but then again hunting was not his primary focus. His old bow felt the same in his hands as the last day he used it more than three years ago when he drew back and missed that annoying squirrel. He was so far removed from the possibility of even seeing a deer that he did not even bother to get out to the stand before first light. In a small camo back pack he carried the two plastic bags of ashes that were nestled inside the decorative boxes.

It would be a short hunt anyways, more ceremonial than anything else. He needed a few minutes to spruce the place up. Wasting no time, he had scheduled a meeting with a realtor for later that morning. Her name was Jessica Lundeen, a greedy black widow type that he had consorted with years prior on various property sales. She agreed to help him out for half the standard commission because she owed him a favor.

Three years of no maintenance turned Paul's "questionable in the first place" tree stand into a virtual death trap. As he climbed, with every creak and groan Mason prepared for an eventual jump towards safety. This certain place in the woods seemed less sad to him as compared to where it all happened. He never really went over that way much and couldn't remember ever having sat in that stand before.

Divine intervention, he thought when he saw the buck approaching. The uncharacteristic reckless abandon to which it cruised the hillside was going to give Mason every chance in the world to get his bow up and come to full draw. It was going to be a fairy tale ending in the mind of a man that spent years convincing himself that it was all someone else's fault. He actually realized that Gordy may have been right all along. His theory became a man, and that man was death. He could be death again. He just had to make this one shot.

Mason moved clumsily as he readied his body for the shot. The old, damp plywood platform creaked and groaned under the stress of his shifting weight. The deer stand was a teenager, barely being kept in-line by weak and rusty parental nails.

A buck earns his antlers. The thickness of the base, every point added after another season of experience being the hunted. His alert was instant, his frozen stance fueled by dread and fear just as a person might be gravely unsettled by a sudden, unseen groan in their living room. Acting on instinct the buck swung his body perpendicular to the sound, offering less of a profile and obscuring himself behind multiple trees, hiding like eyes behind open stairs. He faced the sky, testing the air for any scent of danger. He hooved the ground and let out a loud, wheezy snort in an attempt to challenge the danger.

From a kneeling position barring unforeseen cramps Mason was in a good position to wait the buck out. He couldn't see the deer but could most certainly hear him. His heart raced at the anticipation. His hands shook from the adrenaline. The longer the buck took to make his next move the more Mason's body could absorb it, the calmer he would become. In the first twenty seconds of the stand-off Mason's come down was apparent as he was suddenly overcome with disappointment and regret with the grim realization that he may have blown his chance. *Come on baby.*

At that point for a hunter there is no past or future, only the now. In that sense he becomes more like the deer strengthening the ancient bond between predator and prey.

His eyes were wide and alert. He dare not move. Normally his patience was epic but this time it was different. This time he could feel something pulling him almost controlling every muscle. His face took on the expression of a man who was looking forward to solving a problem, intense with subdued enthusiasm and the underlying joy of a psychopathic clown. Fear and pain for a deer are basic but sudden disbelief and mortification are feelings that belong to men. Very carefully with great intent he chose soft steps forward keeping his body tight against the trees, nose down eyes up. He was aware of his antlers now, never having remembered remembering that they were even there. Mason's smell was apparent, his scent familiar. His silhouette against the skyline was obvious, hiding like a raven in a parakeet cage. His brazen attempt at an ambush was nothing less than an insult. The buck hated him. *Kill me again, it's your soul.* He offered himself as his only choice to feel vengeance. Chest out, head high he stepped into the open immediately locking eyes with Mason.

Mason was paralyzed. Frozen in place by the scene playing out in front of him, absorbing the shock of a familiar character playing a different role.

With a traditional bow the further the archer pulls the string, the more difficult it becomes to manage the potential energy stored in its limbs. Utilizing pulleys and cables a compound bow stacks up its potential energy in the beginning of the draw cycle allowing the archer to experience a let-off in pressure at full draw. At seventy pounds of draw weight, it is like pulling two cinder blocks across a desk and just when they are close someone removes the top block. At full draw it seems as if someone is half-heartedly trying to pull the bottom block back.

Mason struggled to pull the string. The atrophy of the last few years had taken their toll. *Just a little more.* He begged for the let-off. The buck waited, stoic in his resolve. Ten seconds of eternity.

The limbs of the bow are bolted to the riser, the place where an archer grips the bow. Those bolts, one on top and one on the bottom are sort of like a trailer hitch towing a tank uphill. Mason was the car behind it. When the top bolt gave way there was no warning, no creaks, no groans, just a sharp metallic snap. The limb flipped backward, burying itself perfectly horizontal to Mason's brow line just above his left eye. His body hit the ground before the ashes did. The buck's last dose of sentience came in the form of gratification, his instinct returned and with Mason's last heartbeat, he was gone.

Investigators would later determine that the factory installed bolts had been replaced, one of which had an obvious fault. Its integrity further weakened by rust, possibly from being left out in the rain.

Jessica Lundeen was nothing short of livid when Mason stood her up the first time. There was a significant amount of money to be made on this sale so begrudgingly she returned the next day. Things were as they had been the previous day, including an open door, the lights and the television. She left a note for Mason and returned later that same day. Again, there was no change. After her fifth visit on the fourth day in a row that she alerted authorities. Normally they would not put too much energy into the search for an ex-mental patient, but Mason's case and the media attention surrounding it was still relatively fresh in their memories.

Warden Ross Parent was taken slightly aback when he heard the name of the lost hunter come over the radio. He was more than familiar with the property. He had been there for Barry's suicide as well as his brother's revenge. He even remembered speaking with Mason in the Table Top during his search for a missing a hunter some weeks prior to the main event. Parent never fully bought into the tight little package that state investigators wrapped up with Mason's help. *Bad things just happen around this guy.*

"Wow I'm not sure I knew that place was even there," The Warden said to the pilot. The helicopter tipped slightly towards Blue Eyes' old cabin for a better view.

"Looks abandoned." Trees nearly completely obscured the log and moss roof from the air above. The overgrown road showed no sign of recent travel. They hovered over the cabin momentarily. The chopper whacked the air hard. "Owens' place is just over that next bluff. We can see pretty good with the leaves down. Can we get a little higher?"

"No problem."

The pilot steadily increased the aircraft's altitude and slowly advanced. Without warning he pulled back on the stick like he was reining in an aggressive horse. "Whoa! Are you seeing this Ross?" the pilot asked.

"There's no way that's coincidence," the Warden said.

The pilot banked the chopper and circled over a horseshoe valley below. It was the kind of thing that you cannot see until you see it. The rim was planted with a distorted outline of blue spruce trees forming a cloak like an old statue of the Virgin Mary. An older group of the same spruce growing side to side across the deep cut in the center formed a furled brow. The tall blue trees created a shadow over dark, indistinguishable eyes. The rest of the face was young, barely noticeable under the painted canopy of fall. The cheeks were flush red with maple as well as highlights above the brow. The mouth at the valley's deepest point was accented by a washout, covered in sunbaked stone that angled away howling into the small field below.

"You've gotta be kidding me," the pilot said as they circled. "It's like the emotion changes with the angle. I can't tell if it's sad, or scared, or angry, or whatever. But it's definitely dark man."

"Ok, let's get over there, we can come back to this," the warden said.

"Alright hold on," the pilot said as he snapped a few quick pictures with his cell phone. It did not take long for the men in the air to spot Mason. His body was barely beyond the southeast corner of the cloaked figure laying, prone below a tree stand. Volunteers were already on the ground with dogs that had picked up his scent and were tracking directly towards the body.

The pilot picked up the radio, "Ground rescue, ground rescue you're on the right track, subject is half a click northwest of your current location east of the ridgeline. Subject does not appear to be moving."

"Copy that air search, the dogs are locked and we will be on scene shortly." The chopper hovered over Mason's body until the ground crew arrived. "Suspect is deceased. Sherriff's office has been notified to report to the scene."

"Ten-four ground let us know if you need further assistance and FYI Molly is on the move." The pilot turned towards Warden Parent. "Let's take a better look at this thing. She's running right into it." Molly, the German shepherd who led rescuers to Mason's body uncharacteristically ran from the scene of Mason's demise ignoring pleas from the volunteers to stop who were afraid she was running away. Molly was an ex-military dog and her retired marine handler knew instantly that her behavior meant bad news. She stopped within sight of him and began to dig. She carved through the fresh dirt easily, as if it were loose fill. The small Colorado blue spruce began tip over as Molly cleared out the earth beneath the root ball. She bayed at the discovery of the bottom of Steven Resant's foot. For the men and women on the ground who were already drenched in shock nothing could have been worse than when Molly moved on to the next tree.

"My God, there she goes again. Oh my God!" one of the rescuers said as she turned towards the others in the group and started to cry. Molly continued to dig and find burial sites under blue spruces well into the night.

The detective watched as the five potted blue spruce trees outside of Mason's trailer were photographed and gathered for evidence. The scene was abuzz once again and appeared eerily familiar.

"The FBI is on their way, Ross," the detective said to Warden Parent who was back on scene. "This is big, bigger than we can handle. This is historical man." Parent nodded in agreement.

"Personally, I never thought the guy was that smart," the warden said.

The detective slowly turned and walked back towards the hastily erected command tent. The warden followed. "Looks like fate stepped in and did what we couldn't do," The detective said.

"I don't believe in fate."

Well-groomed TV front person types were doing their best trying to breach the lines of authorities in order to report anything real or contrived. Heavy equipment was brought in, and they worked through the night under the watchful eye of a media-blasted world unearthing a steady stream of human remains in various stages of decomposition.

The FBI report noted that the inside of the trailer was impeccably neat and clean. Kept tidy by the sort of man that took the extra time to fold his clothes.

CHAPTER 38

He left the jeep on foot, walking north up the Echo Trail in the blackness of sometime after midnight with only the barely distinguishable sky above the road to guide him. He packed heavy, light on provisions but heavy on equipment, with two long bows unstrung, tied vertically onto the back of his pack. The half a foot or so of snow on the ground was hard and crunchy, the victim of warmer daytime temperatures. New snow was lightly falling, exactly what The Hunter was waiting for. When the sky finally began to gather light, he stepped off the road into the forest that skirted the edge of a lake. The first cabin he found looked newer in relative terms. A steel garage that housed the summer's toys hissed under the falling snow. He pushed-on, flanking a gravel road that petered into a rocky trail.

The silver-bullet type travel trailer was forever grown into the surrounding forest. A dark water, swampy creek in front was forming ice on its banks, closing up like an old man's artery. It was a rarely used gateway to a million plus acres of reclaimed wilderness. A log hewn canoe rack stood between the trailer and the creek, a hitching post for the edge of canoe country. She sat askew, small trees pushing her off her foundation. The plywood screwed over the windows matched the aluminum shell, streaked black from exposure, frozen moss painted the edges. The stove pipe was dislodged but still attached bending back over the tin roof like a badly broken ankle.

One hard swing with his hatchet easily freed the door. Inside was like he remembered it, pale blonde paneling, homemade cedar bunks, a matching table, and a tiny wood stove. The propane furnace was removed and replaced with storage space for plastic totes. It smelled frozen damp like the inside of an old walk-in freezer. The effort to bear-proof her paid off.

The first thing he did was tear off the top bunk and the table and re-position them between the wall and the floor in order to create a level base. A few rounded granite rocks he managed to dislodge from the creek's edge he used to make a safe spot for the wood stove. The totes held a variety of freeze-dried foods and miscellaneous camping supplies including a near lifetime supply of waterproof matches which he immediately used to light the scrap and splinters left over from what he just destroyed. The food would provide the necessary vitamins that simply were no longer attainable in the winter landscape. Water was plentiful but he needed meat in order to sustain through the winter. Refrigeration in northern Minnesota was not a problem.

From his pack he removed a fresh bowstring and a hard-cased quiver that housed a dozed arrows and a plastic spool of heavy line. The string was secured to the bow by tension alone, looped into grooves on the ends of the limbs.

Placing one end on the ground with the string attached, he pulled up on the other using the back of his leg as a fulcrum, bending the limbs back until he could attach the other end of the string. He screwed the spool of line onto the front of the bow then finally threaded the heavy line through a hole in the knock of an arrow just as a person would thread a needle.

A thin beaver dam barely wide enough to keep a foot dry held the creek at an artificial level that would eventually step-up to the desired depth for the lodge. He stepped out and kicked the middle out of the dam adding the sound of trickling water to the perfectly picturesque winter landscape. As the water slowly drops eventually a resident beaver will show up to repair the breach. Meat, as they say, is meat.

Being there, in this place was as much accidental fate and circumstance as gravity. *Chance favors the prepared mind.* He was fond of that phrase, of the word "chance" really. It made him think, to delve ever deeper into what chance actually is or means. And he had all the time in the world to think about it. Here in this frozen prison that he created for himself so many years ago. He would wait, nothing more. He would wait until the days were longer and the snowpack receded.

A burly, middle-aged, and mostly filthy flatbed tow truck driver loosened the chains that secured the Jeep to the aluminum bed. "Truck looks too good to scrap."

"They couldn't send it to auction, it ain't legal. Someone popped off the plates, the VIN, stickers, even ground the numbers off the frame. So it's ours now," said Mike Fresco, general manager of the salvage yard just outside of Duluth. "Make a good plow truck anyways. It's a shame too, these jeep trucks are hard to find in good shape. Camo and nice big tires, it'd make a good hunting truck."

"It still could ya know?" the driver said with a wink and cigar-stained smile.

"Yeah, ya know what? Let's see how she runs and put her behind the shop for now."

"Probably stolen."

"Maybe, definitely abandoned at least. They found it just left on the side of the road. Echo Trail outside Ely I think he said, keys in it. I guess they kept it all winter. They couldn't find out if it was used in any crime and nobody reported it stolen so here she is. Picked her up for a song. Scrap dollars," Mike said.

CHAPTER 39

Ross could do little more than shake his head in disbelief. One of his favorite parts of the job was educating the public in regard to wildlife and natural resources. Sometimes though, there are those days. A call about a road-killed bald eagle had the warden on the highway early that morning. The turkey he found at the scene would have made Ben Franklin proud. According to the driver the bird came gliding in like an airplane on final approach and crashed into the fence on the side of the road, panicked and ran in front of her car. The chain-link fence was close to the road, ten feet high and topped with three strands of barbed wire angled towards any would-be trespassers. It encompassed 240 acres of the former Owens farm, paid for by federal disaster aid dollars. Remote cameras kept a watchful eye on the electric, coded entry gate. Ross did not like being there. Seeing it made him feel uncomfortable like he left for vacation and left the stove on.

As far as the world was concerned Gordon Ardent was circumstantially the worst mass-murderer in American history. Some authorities however disagreed. Some were actually quite certain that Mason Owens was behind the murders but as a few conspiracy theorists would find out, it's hard to kill a hero. Due to the difficulties identifying remains and potentially matching their last known locations with multiple suspect whereabouts, it would be years before the FBI completed the final report.

I would have known. Ross stared at the gate and replayed every meeting with Mason Owens over and over in his head. He recalled the fateful helicopter search that initially turned up the Midwest Nasco lines as some enterprising reporter coined it, referencing the huge ancient ground drawings in Peru that are only visible from the air. He thought about the cabin in the woods, a place he never knew existed. Reporters descended on it like flies for the typical "neighbor's take" but were as equally disappointed as the authorities who consequently blocked the access of what their title search would determine to be property abandoned and tax-forfeited decades earlier.

A dozed-up berm of gravely dirt topped with roadside weeds blocked what was quickly becoming more of a walking trail than a road. Ross parked in front of the berm and walked up the trail to the cabin. The heavy wood door was barred from the inside set-up to fall into place when the door was last closed. A test push with his shoulder proved fruitless. The inside looked relatively tidy from what he could see with his flashlight through the dirty, distorted glass. He moved towards the smokehouse. His gait staggered when he walked over the two shallow depressions in the soft ground next to the cabin. The encroaching forest had yet to consume the indentations in the ground where a vehicle had been parked. The air in the smokehouse was still dank and meaty, the wood forever saturated. Ross crouched down and pinched the ash wondering how after years of moisture and abandonment it could still have fluff. The windows of the cabin were too small for a man to climb through, so he half-heartedly took another shot at pushing open the door to once again no avail.

Inside the cabin tiny wood chips and sawdust billowed into view illuminated by sparse rays of sun. The chainsaw brought along its own thin light as it roared and ripped its way through the front door. Ross backed the saw out and this time easily pushed it open. He ran his finger over the wooden tabletop revealing an all too thin layer of dust. He tried the well pump, built with leather packings that should have dried out ions ago but still held prime after just a few strokes. The water quickly drained away into a rock-lined hole in the floor. A few dozen pieces of firewood were stacked next to the stove, concentrically laid across one another in small towers of like-sized pieces. On the flat, black top, two brass rifle casings stood out like the stones of Easter Island. A handful of others were scattered across the floor. Ross studied the casing, the caliber of which in the hunting world was anything but unusual. Millions like it were sold every year and have been for over a hundred more. Still as coincidence serves it was the caliber of the rifle Gordy used to shoot his hunting party.

Ross collected the spent casings and submitted them to the FBI for evidence. Initial firing pin marks proved beyond a reasonable doubt that in all likelihood the casings had been fired by Mason's rifle. But it did not prove when, or by whom or even where. For Ross it was another piece of evidence that did not add up.

Patches of snow still littered the rocky forest floor, kept cool in the shadows of boulders and dense stands of evergreen. The terrain was brutal. Black and White spruce boughs intertwined so thickly that a man could not pass through and steep, wet, granite cliffs cloaked in slippery lichen abruptly giving way to boot-sucking muddy marshes. Lakes and marshes of every size and shape littered the landscape, geographically intertwined like the nerves of one giant forest monster. For a man on foot, rats in mazes lead easy lives by comparison.

Progress was slow, hampered by all things deemed beautiful. Stripping to the waist or sometimes more in order to forge shallow water was taking a toll. The time needed to get dry, dress and recover seemed to increase with every crossing. Still, the angle of the sun was encouraging this time of year in the North Country even though days were still short and cold by southern comparison. Roaming beasts were busy recovering from the ravages of winter while the sleepers finally woke. Green plants sprouted from cracks in stone warmed by the sun. Still freezing nighttime temperatures kept retreating lake ice at bay. There was beauty in the revival of the living forest that seemed so dead and uninhabitable a few short months ago.

The sickly human call of a Raven he could never see gave voice to the spirit of the wilderness that was always with him. The grade steadily decreased until his feet fell upon an unnatural trail. Even his boots were disgusted. It was not the portage trail of French Voyageurs, men that had earned advantage through sweat and toil. It was not the portage of a tribe combed by the soft steps of moccasins. It was in fact the portage of a government park service. Volunteers that cut away deadfalls and over-aggressive brush. They dig and maneuver stones for makeshift stairs on steep grades so tens of thousands of undeserving weekend adventurists can get some mud on their synthetic boots and cross from lake to lake with greater ease. They made the veins bigger so the infection could run deeper. To a hunter, it was no more than a game trail.

Portage trails exist for a number of reasons. Creeks between lakes may be too shallow or rocky to paddle. Some may have dangerous rapids. Others circle small black mud swamps that don't hold enough water to float a canoe. Most often waters don't meet, and the trail is the only means of advancement, a short-cut more or less. This particular trail skirted the edge of a deep ravine. At the bottom a fast, rocky stream swelled with meltwater pushed class two rapids of ice-cold water past the point of passable. But still, he would not use the trail.

Perpendicular to the portage he crawled backwards to the edge of a cliff formed from one huge granite slab. The face was sheer, coated in wet, green moss. The bottom near the swollen creek disappeared in brush rooted over broken stone and miscellaneous deadfalls. As he hung there for a moment, he couldn't help but enjoy the musty stench of the moss, the greenest smell he could recall in his lifetime. The stone had a pitch, maybe a few degrees, just enough for gravity to keep his body glued to the face. The drop was no more than the height of an over-average, cornfield subdivision home. His chosen descent, the semi-controllable belly slide had just reached the speed of unmanageable when his feet finally found purchase on the rocks below. The water that had left the ice so peacefully from the lake on top roared with manic depression at the bank. The roughly ten-yard width of the rushing water held all the danger of a journey of a thousand miles. Long-dead cedars on both sides leaned over the stream like the swords of a red carpet military ceremony saluting occasional boulders that forged beneath, methodically pounding their way upstream. Their splash-soaked helmets of gray lichen provided no better footing than that of a ball of ice. With full pack he started up one of the larger cedars that reached well beyond the opposite bank. He hung upside down using his arms and legs to move along the trunk, his pack just a few feet above the torrent. The way a rabbit sees the talons of a hawk just before the strike he saw it. The branch, maybe about as thick as a man's arm stuck odds-perfect from a much larger log floated loose of the banks by the high water. It caught him with tremendous speed, hooking his pack and increasing its drag tenfold over the course of mere seconds. With the screaming growl of determination, he held on with all his might, which was slightly more than the base of the cedar could handle. The sudden, numbing-cold of the aerated water burned his sinuses like a chlorine pool.

CHAPTER 40

He came-to, shrouded in darkness so thick that it seemed to have mass. He may have been as cold as he could ever remember but only when he bothered to notice. He heard nothing, smelled nothing and was only aware of his own touch. He was annoyed, on the edge of angry once it occurred to him that this may be death, hardly the journey he had hoped for. A pinpoint of light caught his eye, flickering like a distant star, bright white but only visible to his peripheral. Focusing on the light meant it would disappear only to return seconds later, seemingly larger somewhere else on the furthest edge of his field of vision. It taunted him, mocking his hunter's senses, boiling his blood with the heat of the game. Seeing it required a different kind of focus, the kind a mother uses to keep watch over a rambunctious child. Then all at once, without further fanfare it was quite simply there, close enough to smell but just far enough away to see it in its entirety. It wreaked of rotten meat and fresh water. He was face to face with it, staring into eye sockets that were so empty and hollow he wondered how it could have ever been a threat. Beads of ice crystal-laden water trailed down its wooden face. Even at arm's reach the black form stayed shrouded in partial darkness, its cloak only noticeable on the tops of the creases while at the same time he was illuminated by his own light. The blackness around it eventually became more of a reflection of blackness, lacking depth with an almost silver tone.

He very slowly reached out to touch it even though it was just out of reach. The being mirrored his motion. Its flat, black hands met his as they touched fingertips eventually increasing pressure until they were palm to palm. Finally, their fingers intertwined like a prayer of desperation or the way a man's hands are arranged when he is laid in a coffin. That's when he knew.

He knew after all the years and all the torment the black form, the spirit he feared, the spirit he honored was not just with him, he now knew that it was him. He knew because he could feel it, because that was the exact moment he woke, firmly grasping his own left hand. He was warm again, wrapped in old horse-hair blankets laid out on a wooden bunk by a fieldstone hearth and a roaring fire in a small cabin somewhere along the Canadian border of Northern Minnesota.

"Mornin' sunshine. Fate is a funny thing. If I hadn't heard you yellin' I'da never known you was there. You're lucky to be here." I sat up abruptly, so fast that my vision grayed-out. I had to lay back down. My thoughts raced. I questioned my recent memories, where I was, what I was doing. I was crossing the creek because it was my last chance for miles. Miles that would have put me off course. The tree broke.

"Where's here?" I asked the old woman who woke me. My voice was raspy, I cleared my throat of the phlegm that gathers after a long sleep.

"Here is where you are no matter where you've been. Here is alive. Here is at my place and ain't nobody gonna find you here." She stepped around in front of me and rolled the blanket down that wrapped me so tightly. "Let me get a look at ya here." She placed her hand on my bare chest to feel my warmth. "Yea, you come out of it okay alright. You was wet and everything so I had to take your clothes but they're long dry by now. Name's Darlene."

"Darlene what?" I asked as she handed me my clothes.

"Last names don't matter a whole hell of a lot out here. Hell, names don't matter a hell of a lot out here. Names only matter if ya got someone to talk to. It's Hatchka though if you need to know." I sat back up more slowly this time. I flung the blankets to the side, stood, and put on my clothes. "I gotta say it's been a long while since I seen a man naked. Even longer since I did anything with it. It's a damn shame. A damn shame that it's been so long that is." I saw that she just made herself uncomfortable. I knew that because of that she was struggling with what to say next. I knew that the situation at the very least was not dire. "Say you haven't said a hell of a lot since you came to. Don't you want to know where you are? What happened? And I know you gotta be hungry."

"My pack. Were you able to retrieve my pack?"

"I did. It was stuck on a log that got caught-up in the rocks and rolled it right up in air, pretty as you please. And you're welcome by the way. You know, for saving your life and everything."

"You saved nothing," I said. She did jog my memory however and I remembered the last moment before I went into the water.

"Well my, my, ain't you a ray of sunshine. Fact is if I hadn't fished you out of that water you'd be dead. And even if you don't give a shit about your life you at least ought thank me for saving your gear. Hell if you were dead at least I could use it. So I saved something, something that has a use. How about you Mr. Happy? You got a use?" Darlene asked.

I sat back down on the bunk. I could feel the power return to my arms, my hands and I felt instantly strong again. "Well Darlene Hatchka, that which is saved is already possessed therefore it was never gone." The look in her eyes and her pause of concentration told me she understood.

"What about your soul? You want that saved don't you? Isn't that why you're out here in the first place? You know, the whole 'it's good for the soul' type thing? To get away from the ills of the civilized world?" she said mockingly.

"There is no civilized world and as far as I know there never was."

"I guess you got me there son." She laughed a few fake syllables just to accentuate the fact that she agreed with me. I never liked that about people. Saying it is enough. Fake words come from fake people.

"Well either way let me make the proper introduction since I already seen you naked." She walked over to me and held out her hand to shake. "Darlene, nice to meet ya." I took her large, callous, manly hand. She offered me a cup of coffee brewed from bark of bog evergreens black spruce and hemlock. "I got some smoked bear I'll get for ya here after a minute. He was a nice little one so he eats good." She sat down on the bunk cradling her tin cup in her large hands. "This is usually the part of an introduction where as you tell me your name."

She was never going to know my name, she had to know that. I thought I should choke her. I wasn't sure what she had access to on the counter. I stood, looking for utensils. She was close to the hot pot. I need to disable one arm. By the time I finished surveying the area I changed my mind, the initial surge of focused anger just ran out like the cup broke.

"I'm not sure." After the adrenaline surge of the past few moments, it was all I could muster.

"Not sure huh? Maybe it'll come back to ya. So tell me Mr. Not Sure, I seen your tools. I seen you ain't got no gun, no boat. I'm more than 70 years old and I been up in these woods close to over 50 years and I never seen a man come in like you. Oh I thought I seen it all, people with all kinds of kids, luggage, animals, people that had no business being out here. You though, you got some kind of business. Your hands are hard and you ain't the youngest man. So what's your business? You runnin' from something or to something?"

I took a long, hard sip of the bitter brew, "A man of will does not run away, he runs towards."

"Well okay then," Darlene chuckled, "What you runnin' towards?"

There was a long pause, only the sound of the crackling fire filled the dry air. "The end." I wasn't trying to be overly-cryptic with my answers beyond offering her as little as I could until I knew more than her.

"The end of what? Life? If that's the case maybe I shoulda left ya. But I don't think so. We all have a purpose. And who knows, maybe you done served yours already, maybe not. But all people are here for something. Yup that's the real truth whether you know it or not. Sometimes, most of the time we ain't even gonna know what it is, but it's there. Mine mighta been saving you. To think all these years out here just waiting for you to come along and fall in the drink." She chuckled. Finally, it seemed genuine.

"I doubt it," I mumbled into the hot cup.

"Hard to say. Maybe I served my purpose years ago. Maybe I ain't yet? It ain't up to me, or you. The Lord says what it is and he tells us at the end. Good or bad, stupid or smart, it don't make no difference. It's different for everybody. Might be so small of a thing you never thought about it, like a bird crappin' out a seed that grew into a tree. A tree that some damn fool tried to use to get across a river. Or maybe a flower. Heh, heh…it could go from crap to smellin' good in no real time at all. The trick is to not pick 'em. My Daddy used to scold me when I was a little girl. I'd get to pickin' the petals off the flowers, to smell 'em and rub 'em all soft on my face and such. He'd say 'Darlene leave those alone, let flowers be flowers.' I'd say, 'but Daddy these are weeds!' He'd stop what he was doin' and get all serious like and say 'Darlene honey I want you to listen real close like. Let flowers be flowers and weeds be weeds.' I never did pick no more, not that he would see anyways. And believe it or not I grew all the way up thinking about them words. I figure it was a one of them dual meaning type things. How about you, Not Sure? You a flower or a weed?"

I was looking through my pack taking inventory during her speech. It was obvious she hadn't had anyone to talk to in a while.

"You picked me Darlene Hatchka, so you tell me."

"I only pick what I need to survive, so I guess maybe that means you're here to help an old woman. Maybe that's your purpose. If you're feeling up to it, you can start by splittin' me up some wood, it's getting harder and harder for this old body to meet its needs. Every winter seems just a little longer than the last. Your coat ought be dry by now I guess. Them old army field jackets is tough to dry. You can grab us up some bear meat from the smokehouse when you're done. You'll find it easy enough."

She had turned the coat inside out and hung it on a peg next to the fireplace. I did not want to put it on too quickly. I did not want to let her know how anxious I was to get out of her sight, how her inquisitive eyes burned me.

I appreciated the construction of the door. A turnstile that pivoted in the center, made with vertical logs. It was innovative and difficult to make. It was more of a who moment than a why. It balanced well and opened easily. Outside I saw more than she could have told me. It was beautiful, all of it. Bob built the place into the cliff. He piped the smoke up towards the edge of the falls that fell into a thin, fast creek twenty paces from the door. He used granite slabs, moss and logs to build the pipe and it looks like it belongs there. All so smoke in the winter would look like steam. The whole place just melted into what was there, rock and trees. The log roof was covered in moss and deadfalls. It simply looked like forest floor. There were no windows. Darlene ambled out and confirmed what I had already known.

"Whataya think? Back in '65 they moved us all outta here. A designated wilderness area they said. We used to have a cabin over on Fourtown, my husband and I. They knocked it all down and turned it into a campsite. Well, we kinda said the hell with them so Bob and I moved back up in here. Bob was always good at building things so he made this place so that it couldn't be seen until you find it. We got water and plenty of room to grow things. I do miss the lake though. I go down there from time to time and watch the people paddle their canoes. Been known to happen into a campsite or two as well, fish catching equipment can be hard to replace out here. Them city folks ain't never gonna miss nothin'. I love combin' the portage trails after ice out, when I can float a canoe. Before they all come back. People are always leavin' things on the trails. That's how I come across you."

"What happened to Bob?" I asked her as I picked up the ax. I spun it in my hands.

"Oh he's dead now. Just gave up one day. I said some fine words and buried him under rock in a place he never liked to go. It's always wet in there and never really gets any kinda sun to speak of. He always liked his privacy and for sure ain't nobody goin' in there. It ain't hospitable and I guess, neither much was he. He was mine though, and I miss him still…always."

The lion's share of a thigh-thick cedar tree laid askew on the ground cut into sections with an antique two-handled logging saw. I stood one on end and laid into it with the ax. The two halves jumped apart, one nearly tumbling all the way down to the small but mighty spring creek. Darlene took a long, theatrical breath, "I love the smell of fresh cut wood. Don't matter what type of tree neither. As hard as you hit that it ain't gonna take you no time at all. There's an old saw layin' over there by that deadfall if you run outta pieces to split. That is, if you don't mind."

"Mind? Why would I mind?"

"Well I hope you remember your name before long although Not Sure ain't so bad. So I thank you Not Sure, I'm thankful that you're here." Her voice trailed off as she walked back inside.

CHAPTER 41

Splitting wood was easy for me. I had the back for it. It was mindless, just hard work. The ax wasn't what I expected. It was clean and brutally sharp. It was a temporary joy, a new toy at Christmas. Right then and there that ax was all I wanted, as simple as a man could get. The ax did not cause stress, it wasn't invasive. To me, it was no more or less an extension of my arms. My own cold steel hands cutting through the wood again and again. It was wet here nearly all the time, yet the head of the ax had no rust. All around was rock yet the blade was strangely unscarred. I'm that good. Next man up to polish my blade with your treasured grain as I split you open. I lined them up one at a time and there was little struggle besides their awkward stance. I wanted to be a pirate right then and there fighting on the deck of a ship.

I soon exhausted the supply of splitable wood. The saw could wait. Protein was of the essence. The smoke shack was built deep into the crevice of the rock that also made up the back side of the cabin. The door was made of logs loomed together with once-flexible roots and held in place by heavy posts wedged into the ground. The design was inconvenient. Maybe half a dozen roast-sized chunks of meat hung skewered on shaved cedar branches wedged between the rock walls. The meat was a rich brown, the aged color of carnivore. Almost every cut was boneless, all except one. On the bottom skewer there appeared to be a large turkey leg with saddle brown smoked skin and a large knuckle on the end of the exposed bone. I gave it careful study and consideration before replacing it and choosing instead one of the boneless cuts from the top rack. I brought it into the cabin and placed it on the table.

Darlene was fast asleep wrapped tightly into a bright blue nylon shell sleeping bag that had most obviously not yet stood the test of time. From my pack I removed a survival knife and a map. Now more than ever I needed to know exactly where I was. I moved out of there as quietly as possible. I wasn't about to eat the meat, but I left it for her regardless.

On the back side of the cabin deeper into the woods were two overturned canoes hidden under a pile of long-dead pine boughs, the aluminum so moss-covered and filthy that it provided its own camouflage. Neither appeared to have been moved in some time. I searched more, she had to have brought me back in a boat. I followed the creek until it dispersed into slack water at the head of a marsh. The boat was there, pulled ashore and stashed behind a large boulder under a makeshift lean-to. Cream colored Kevlar canoes are easy to see. The decal on the hull showed that it belonged to a local outfitter. The registration was current. The varnish on the paddles laid underneath the boat still shined. I kept on downstream but the edge along the creek turned to impassable marsh. I had to find a way to the top of the granite bluff behind the cabin for perspective. Against the map I could approximate my location.

It was like a mini mountain. Most of the base was huge chunks of granite splayed off the host, half stuck in the mud below and trees growing from the cracks. I circled it, looking for a way up. The woods grew dark here, buried in the shadow of rock under a canopy of ancient white pine. Moss grew thick on bases of light-deprived spruce trees as well as every exposed stone. Last season's brown ferns lay mashed on the ground under the weight of receded snow and ice. There was no recruitment of leafy ground cover or any deciduous trees. The way ahead was unobstructed and easy to see all the way to the dark crevasse that stood out like a black cathedral carved from a bald face of stone.

I approached slowly, almost reverently. It felt ancient and cold there. It did not matter from what direction a person came here, for the last few feet everyone followed the same path. The ground told the tale. Stones were piled carefully into the unmistakable form of a grave laid perpendicular to the entrance of the naturally formed cave. Inside rotten wood and pine branches served to hold down the smashed skulls and broken bones of animals that had been carved into edible meat. This was the dark place, the place the husband hated to be. The dumping ground of all non-usable parts besides wet entrails. I did not remember ever feeling stronger or ever concerned that it was not normal. There is a feeling to rot that is more than smell alone. It has a collective soul including fear and pain. It was Bob's duty to guard the entrance forever keeping vigil over the discarded bones and unrested spirits of the occasional camper on whose bodies and gear the couple survived. What a waste. Chickens, treated as no more than such when they died. They would have died anyways but most likely at least someone would have appreciated it. Most mourners do not know that they appreciate that it is not them when they look into a casket. I would have appreciated it.

I heard the metal clank of the rifle behind me. She came up on the moss through ferns. I was pleased with her stealth. People are not generally formidable. Lever action, no question probably holding at the hip.

"I knew it when you didn't eat no meat. Hell to tell ya the truth I actually been expecting ya."

I turned to face her slowly. So predictable, so sure of herself. That look of satisfaction on her face. Smiling at me without upper front teeth, I found it demeaning.

"I knew you was comin', the woods been tellin' me. I started to take notice of it this last winter being a special kind of dark. It loomed, stayed longer than is usual around here, seemed to move around sort of in patches like it was alive. And then there was the cold, the damn cold. You know when it's so damn cold your nose closes up if ya try and take a big whiff? Cold that if ya had your mouth open would burn your lungs? Cold, dead as hell air. That's the sort of cold I lived with my whole life out here. But this year was different, this year it had a smell to it. A sweet smell, like baked goods I remember from when I was a girl or even sometimes like flowers. Ain't many flowers out here Not Sure. Naw, it was death loomin'. The sweet smell of death comin' to get me for what was done. Cold air ain't got no smell. It was you I know as sure I'm standing here now. It was you I smelled comin'. You seen it, right there in my house. I heard ya. This place, these woods, they brought ya to it. They sent ya to me. Ain't nothing about no damn coincidence. And you and I both know what you gotta do but I got me this here rifle and we're gonna set some terms."

I stepped into the open onto the tomb, "And here lies Bob I assume? Did you eat him as well?"

"Ha, ha, hell no I didn't eat on old Bob. It's him that did the killin' anyways. I ain't never killed nobody," she said.

"Then how are you going to shoot me now?"

Darlene's glare tightened and her speech slowed to a crawl, "Survival is a hell of a thing, a woman might do just about anything."

I kicked one of the top stones of the grave over, exposing the underside. "There's no moss under any of these stones. You're not that careful and your meat is not that old."

Darlene laughed out loud. "I guess you got me young man. Like I said survival's a hell of a thing. Old woman like me has to hunt what's easy. I still didn't eat ole Bob though if that's what you're thinkin', he was a grissly son-of-a-bitch anyways."

She pulled the rifle up to her shoulder and took careful aim. "You just have seat right there on top of ole Bob's stones. You just sit down right there and listen to what I'm gonna tell ya." She had no reason to tell me anything at all. She sat down on a boulder and laid the rifle across her lap. "Them people didn't deserve to be here, this ain't their place, never was. This place offered them up as a temptation, like Eve pickin' the apple. So we picked, and picked, and picked. We put a lot of work in too, pickin' loaners from all parts near and far of these woods. As punishment for the killin' though the woods done took Bob from me. Awe sure Bob could build things but he ain't never had no idea on his own. Made a poor butcher too. Needed him though, needed his back mostly, much else I can't say he was good for. But I loved him I guess, and I miss him, I guess the way a woman would even miss a dog ya had to kick outta your way every so often. They made him pay for my sins. He died slow and painful. Tore up from the inside. Wasn't right, there weren't no reason for that, he was ignorant. Maybe that's why they done it though cause in the end he wouldn't hold no grudges cause he really wouldn't know no better, and they knew it would hurt me. He'd just figure that's the way it is. That way he could go on to a better place. Ya see? His dyin' that way plowed the road for me. In that way I figure Bob was sort of like my own personal Jesus, dying for the wrongs I done committed. And now they done sent you. I seen death in the eyes of people, I seen the fear, the pain. I guess I sort of gave that to 'em but I also took it away. My killin' 'em kinda healed 'em too. But I don't want that for me. For me, like the winter was, it has to be different. I don't want to see it comin' or feel it. And I want to be here, with him. Them that we killed they're part of us, they belong to us. It's up to Bob and me to watch over their souls in this dark place. It's the least we can do for them. And it's up to you to see that it happens in just that way. That place you're lookin' for is here. It's all ready for you. You done split your own wood today. I smelled your sweat comin', that peculiar scent of a flower, that's what was sweet in the air. It was your shadow I seen movin', you're the darkness. And now you're destined to live in this dark place, with us."

She took a long pause waiting for me to say anything at all, begging me to speak with her face. I gave her nothing.

"Now I'm gonna take a few steps back, I'm gonna lean this here gun up against a tree and walk away. After that I suspect you'll do what you was brought here to do."

CHAPTER 42

The operation was not exactly covert, but neither was it widely publicized besides the necessary legalities involving public notification. The fenced-in Owens farm was the perfect place for the Department of Natural Resources Forestry Division to study the forest regeneration rate in a controlled area sans whitetail deer. At least seven and as many as ten deer were known to live inside the fence. Federal sharpshooters would kill as many deer as possible in a two-week allotted time frame in what was called a special hunt. With the aid of corn piles and helicopters however it would be much more of an extermination than a hunt. Every one of the team of four men was capable of hitting a fast-moving target at over three hundred yards with nearly any common deer rifle. Predator populations would be monitored and addressed on a need-to basis. Ross met the men at the gate of the farm.

"Gentlemen, Ross Parent." He went through the progression of shaking hands. None of the men offered him a name instead greeting him with "pleased to meet you", "my pleasure" or a nod. Warden Ross Parent and men like him do the job for one reason, to protect what they love. The set of laws and regulations he is sworn to uphold help keep the playing field level as well as protect and preserve precious natural resources. These guys, as far as Ross was concerned, were professional poachers. And here, in this place his stress level peaked.

Spring turkey season was nearly over. Only one hunter was shot during what is the most dangerous season of the year. Wild turkeys see color quite well. Fully camouflaged hunters usually get shot sitting behind their own decoys. Anglers keeping more than allowed had been a plague so far this season with the hot shallow water crappie action. Earlier just after ice-out the walleye run on the rivers was also prolific, dangling easy multiple limits in front of a thousand guys that had been sitting in their trailered boats in garages drinking beer all winter. For a game warden, there's never a good time to take a vacation, but with game fish opener just wrapping up, now was as good of a time as any.

Ross opened the gate and handed the men a key. "There's only one spare, so please don't lose it. What are you guys planning on doing with the meat?" he asked.

"Generally we don't deal with that. We just shoot. Clean-up and disposal is handled by a different crew."

"Well where are those guys?" Ross asked.

"Can't be sure."

"So you're just going to leave em' lay?" None of the men answered. "Look, I'm sure I can round up a few guys that will come in and get it for the food shelf if..."

A different man cut Ross off mid-sentence, "Sorry Warden, this is federal operation. We will enter this gate, lock it behind us and complete the task at hand. It's been a pleasure to make your acquaintance." The man walked over and shook Ross' hand. "Rest assured we will take care of your key. Now if you'll excuse us we have to get to work."

Ross nodded his head and took the few steps back to the truck. He was going to leave without another word but he decided to stop and share a little piece of the last straw. "Gentlemen…thanks for helping me make up my mind. Drop the key off at the office when you're through. I will not be there." A little paperwork and a few phone calls later, Ross was eagerly ecstatic.

"Yes sir, I will sir." Ross said into the phone speaking to his Captain, "Yes sir, Ely sir, Vermillion Community College is where I earned my degree, that's right, fisheries and wildlife. See some old friends, that sort of thing…Thank you sir, you too."

And suddenly he was free.

"Who are 'They' Darlene? Who killed Bob?" I asked gently, quietly. I didn't bother to go for the rifle. She stopped and turned, smiling.

"You. You they." She stood there looking at me for a few moments. I don't think she expected a response but instead she stared for effect. I should have been more confused. With that she turned and slowly walked away.

I eventually found her standing at the creek's edge in front of her cabin, waiting. She was hoping it would come from behind, the sooner the better. She was ready. I watched her for a time feeling the thoughts of her memories. On the top edge of the next cool breeze, I chambered a round into the rifle that she had left for me. Trembling legs barely held her upright anticipating how it would feel to take a bullet to the back of her skull, like a person afraid of needles waiting for a shot to kill the pain.

"I don't wanna live no more. I'm ready." She started out strong but by the time she said she was ready her voice cracked off to an abrupt end.

"Living is easy. Dying is hard."

I gave that to her, I felt obligated. With the weapon shouldered, I was rock steady. It balanced well with open sights trained on the back of her brain. "Everything wants to live, it has to be alive to think so, but in between…that's where you have to be to know."

"Know? Know what?" she asked, I could tell she was crying.

"What you are. To truly know…that you are a weed." That was the end of my advice to her. She was fully expecting everything to be over right then and there. It was the logical end point.

In a way she was right. I did not shoot her. Instead, I took a few quick steps forward and planted the butt of the rifle into the back of her skull. I believe she may have been lights out before she even hit the water, but it was so fast there is really no telling what she felt first, the blow or the cold. In the cave I placed matches and candles strategically in anticipation that a person that awoke confused and scared in the dark may easily find them. I gave her meat as well, her very own personally smoked fare still on the skewer. Rainwater filtering through the rock chirped into a tin pot I placed at the very rear of the cave. It would have to be enough, otherwise she would die early. The rocky floor was littered with bones and pieces of meaty skulls. The shit-eating beetles would keep her company.

Eventually they will eat her body. It was her dark place too now. The stones I placed in front of the entrance were more than most men could handle.

"Damn you!" she yelled as loud as I think she could, "Damn you! We're the same!" She must have figured it out. "This ain't right, this ain't right!" She kept that up until her voice cracked and her pointless wail blended with the sound of bugs. I sat down and leaned against her tomb to listen awhile.

Ironically my face welcomed a long-lost smile of satisfaction. "Thank you," I said to her quietly and placed my hand lovingly on the stones. I liked Darlene as much as I had liked anyone in as long a time as I could remember. Even that moment as I sat there, I was feeling. When I was chopping wood, I felt for her. I almost wished I could have given her what she wanted, but that's the problem. Me almost wishing; me feeling. She caused that in me so for that she had to pay a penance. She was giving up her life anyway, so dying? Well, who cares? I gave her the gift of time, like Mason. I wouldn't expect her to be grateful yet because she did not know how precious time alive was. She had no respect for dying, for the end of life. Even the worst of times have their moments. And eventually she will still die. She just won't realize it when it happens. I gave her that too.

CHAPTER 43

The Mia-Shig-Wa Inn on the big lake just outside of Ely, MN had not changed much in the last twenty years. Accommodations included a single-story ten room motel with an attached office. Built in the sixties the harsh northern weather had taken its toll. Dirty, once peach-colored paint chips hung on window sashes like a bad sunburn. The chalky white vinyl siding, badly warped with the occasional hole was a cheap Band-Aid over the original hardboard the owners did not feel like painting anymore. Seven individual one-room, double loft cabins of various colors dotted the property's shoreline. A converted park shelter served as the common building that sold campfire wood and miscellaneous sundries. A dozen primitive campsites in the wooded area along the road sat empty. Each had a crushed gravel pad, a grassy tent site, a fire ring, a picnic table, and a short post with a covered electrical outlet. A pair of 40-foot-long floating docks were pulled up on shore resting on both sides of an 8 x 12 two-sink fish cleaning shack.

Ross remembered how the little house would reek of rotten fish in the warm months, attracting every bear in the neighborhood. *And the flies. God the flies.*

The road ahead of him narrowed. More numerous curves became ever increasingly blind and dangerous. It was a desolate and poorly maintained highway, the final leg of the journey north to the resort. After six hours behind the wheel, he appreciated the renewed focus on his old foe. He had been down this road before.

He spent four years working at the resort while he was in college. Not only did he work there, but as part of his salary he also lived there, in a fourteen-foot travel trailer on the least desirable campsite in the row. His duties loosely stretched from all-around repair guy to fishing guide and everything in-between. To the owners, Steve and Nancy Pendant his help was indispensable and after time he became like one of the family. They kept him busy year-round catering to the fishermen, hunters, and snowmobilers that came from every corner of everywhere. His duties there and his love for the place was also the reason it took him slightly more than three years to earn a two-year associate's degree. It is the last place he lived before he landed a job as a game warden with the Wisconsin Department of Natural Resources.

He walked into the office feeling like it he had just been there yesterday. The little bell on the top of the door as familiar as the sound of his own heartbeat. He tapped the counter bell purposely obnoxiously trying to rile whoever was in the office that was supposed to be manning the front counter.

"Okay, okay, hold your damn horses now," shouted Nancy from the side office, twisting the air with her thick northern accent. "I'm comin'." Her demeanor quickly changed from obviously irritated to over-joyed when she saw him, so much so that she actually sang his name.

"Rosssssssssssss!" She flipped up the hinged end of the counter and swung around for a hug. "Why didn't you phone us you were coming up?"

"Well it was sort of a last-minute decision. Plus I know you love surprises." Nancy contorted her face into a convincing "yeah right" look as she dug her chin into his shoulder.

"Well oh my God! Steve is goin' to be so excited! What brings ya up here? How long you goin' to be in town?"

"You know I just needed a vacation. Needed to get away for a while."

"Yaa I bet, we heard about all that stuff you were involved with that was goin' on down there. Scary stuff. Well it's so good to see ya and I'm glad you're here and like I said Steve is goin' to be ecstatic. So, how long ya say you were stayin' again?"

"Not sure. If the weather looks good I may paddle in for a few nights, fish a little, unwind, you know. Think Steve's up for a paddle?"

"Oh God no. He's too damn old for all that stuff now you know that."

"Well how about you hook me up with the presidential suite?"

"Oh you know it, absolutely," Nancy said.

"And let Steve know I'll be up after a little while for a cold one."

"Oh, I'm sure he's got a Schmidt with your name on it for ya. OK then, you're in cabin one, you know it's the best one we got, you remember that don't ya? Ok get settled in then and come on up," she rattled on excitedly.

"Thanks Nancy, I'll see you in a little while, you can get me up to date with all the latest gossip."

"Oh, there's plenty, Mr. Conspiracy is hard at it as usual. Anytime some poor guy or girl don't come back out of the bush ya know he thinks the boogy man got him or something or other. Oh you know how he is, just as much of a crazy nut as always. He'll love that you're up, I'm sure he'll tell ya all about it. See ya soon now."

Cabin One was the flagship cabin at the resort. A log building with a double loft over a common area in the center shrouded under the shadow of a huge elk-antler chandelier. It was cold, the temperature kept just warm enough not to freeze the pipes. The master bed and bath lived under one loft while a very north woodsy kitchen sporting a wall of windows that looked out over the lake was built under the other. Ross fed an ornate chrome-trimmed parlor stove parked in the middle of the common area some dry stock and lit a sturdy fire. He threw his oversized duffel over his shoulder and climbed the ladder to the loft. He enjoyed laying down at night looking out over the room. The space was soothing, a doorway to other spaces. The confines of a straight-walled bedroom would only force him to sleep, and this way there would be one less room for his host to clean.

"The hell you say. He is? Well why didn't you tell him to come up here?" Steve asked in an annoyed fashion when Nancy told him that Ross was there.

"Well of course you know I did! He's just puttin' some stuff away and then he's gonna be comin' right up," Nancy said. "I told him you'd have a beer ready for him."

"Of course I have a beer for him. He knows I have a beer for him. He doesn't need you to tell him that."

"Ugh! Why do you have to be so grumpy all the time? Honestly Steve."

"Because you say dumb things. It annoys me."

"Whatever. You need to get out more."

"More? When do I get out at all? Spend all winter holed up in here with you…" Steve's voice trailed off to an undiscernible grumble as he walked out and down the stairs. "Send him down when he gets here!" he yelled.

"Of course I'll send him down you old grumpy grump," she whispered to herself.

"Hey! Did you hear me? I said send him down when he gets here!" he yelled even louder from the bottom of the basement stairs. "Hello? Hey!"

"Ya! I got it!" she shrieked back. Over the yelling she nearly missed the light knock on the door. "Oh come in, come in here!"

Ross stepped in gingerly keeping a wry smile close to his vest. "I see nothing has changed up here," he said nearly laughing.

"Nope! Sure the heck hasn't! Same grumpy old man. He wants you to go downstairs by him."

"Hey! Is that Ross? Damnit I told you to send him down here!" Steve yelled. "Don't want you poisoning his mind."

"Poisoning my mind? What's he on about now?"

"You'd better just get down there and see for yourself. Oh it's so good to see ya. Do me a favor hon and try not to encourage him? You know how old hippies are," Nancy said as she hugged him one more time.

"There he is," Ross said as he entered the basement.

"Ross! I gotta say it's damn good to see you son! Damn good. Lemme' get a look at ya here." Steve moved towards him, grabbed ahold of his hand and pulled him into a hug.

Steve Pendant was as Nancy described him, an old hippie. An unapologetic level one conspiracy theorist, he was paranoid to the core, heavily discerning everything from television signals to packaged gum. His gray hair was long and thick. Most of the time he kept it pulled back into a ponytail held tight by hairbands made from cause ribbons. His style much like his ideology was constant. Thick, round, John Lennon style eyeglasses kept him from being functionally blind. After so many years and so many marches he still fancied tie dyed t-shirts but with the added north woods fashion sense and necessity of flannel. Even in the winter he wore sandals, unless of course he had to go out into the elements. In that case paraphrasing his own eloquence, he covered his feet "in joy and hypocrisy", donning the latest and greatest hi-tech footwear modern man could muster. Manufactured with every cancer causing, greenhouse gas emitting, un-environmentally friendly synthetic material ever designed to bring both joy and untimely death to their wearers. If only boots could be soul-less.

"Welcome back Kotter," Steve said jokingly referencing a 1970's television show.

Steve loved to speak in references whenever possible. One of many reasons that he had few friends. "Step into my lair my friend, I have got some shit to show you." His drawl was slow and gray. Steve pushed his palm against a joint in the wooden paneled wall. With the sound of a hard click the panel sprung open revealing a white room. Inside it was nearly antiseptic.

"Do me a favor my brother and kick off your shoes." He walked in a few steps, turned, and looked at Ross and broke out his best air guitar. "In the white room, with black curtains in the station!" he sang while he played. "Ha ha ha ha. Aww man, I love that one. That's why I had to put them short black curtains in even though there aren't any windows behind them to deserve it."

There were four black high-top tables like the ones in every high school science room in the world. The white bulletin board held a series of newspaper clippings, each with its own dossier pinned behind it. Steve took a packet down and handed it to Ross. "Feast your eyes on that my friend." He then reached into a small white refrigerator and pulled out two cold beers. "Heads up! He tossed one underhand to Ross.

"Just exactly what am I holding here? The Cliff Notes version?"

"I knew that woman. Her name was Mary Jane Redmond and let me tell you brother, she was loyal to the cause. She never come out of the bush and they never found nothing."

"She go in by herself?" Ross asked.

"Hell yeah she did. But she always did, that's the thing. That old girl was thin and wiry. You know the kind I mean. 95

pounds of pure muscle and sinew. Hell, she stayed out there half the year. She even rode out the big wind storm a few years back. They sent every swingin' dick they had for that one. Then here she come, paddled out without a scratch. Saw it comin' and sank her canoe. Then she crawled down in the crevasse of a truck-sized boulder by the shore on the windward side and rode it the hell out. Tied up her gear to bases of stumps. Never lost so much as a canteen. But here, here," Steve tapped his finger hard on the packet of paper Ross held in his hand. "Here, here my man, she was only headed out for a couple days and shazam! Gone. Not a trace. That wasn't her. I'm tellin' ya man, and that ain't all. Hold on man." Steve reached into a drawer and pulled out a joint. He lit the end and stole a huge drag muttering a few words through the held smoke. "All this man, all this that you see man." He exhaled concentric smoke rings out into the room suggesting years of practice.

"Are you really going to smoke that right in front of me?" Ross asked nearly laughing. "Ha, ha. Yeah man I know you're the fuzz and everything but you know I know that you my friend know that don't mean you gotta be the man as well. Look at it though, all these people on this board. Three, sometimes four a year. Sometimes they find gear, other times they don't. But they never found a body. Even if it was wolves, or less likely bears, they'd find something man. A coat, a pack. Hell, the boat."

"What's attached here?" Ross said paging through the papers.

"Profiles, you know whatever I could get off line, weather reports for the time they went missing, any other article or publication they were mentioned in either about their disappearance or anytime in their lives really. You know, just so I could get a better grasp on who they were. None of em' were green. Nobody goes out into the bush alone that's green."

Ross began to laugh a little. Steve bent his chin down to his chest and glared at him over the top of his glasses. "I'm as serious as a heart attack here my man. As…a…heart attack."

"Don't worry, I'm laughing because of fate and circumstance. Nancy said you were too old to go out anymore, but now you sort of have to because you're certainly not going to let me head out alone are you?" Ross took a long drink of his beer while still managing to keep the smile on his face.

"Head out? Well I guess what the hell else would you be up here for but head out? Ain't nothin' growin' yet. It's still colder than hell at night. What the hell you wanna head out now for?"

"The time is right. I just… I need to right now. I just have to clear things in my mind for a few days. No better place. Fishing should be good. So how about it? You in?"

"Hell no, I ain't in. One of the few things in this world that woman's ever been right about. Hey, speaking of…" Steve pulled open the door and yelled. "Nancy! Bring us down some more beer. Leave it outside the door." Nobody heard a thing. "Nancy!" Again, there was no response. "God damnit Nancy why is it every time I need something from you…" and suddenly she was there, six pack in hand.

"I brought it down here a few minutes ago if you would just open up your eyes," she said.

"Why wouldn't you just say you were putting them out there instead of being all sneaky? You're always sneaky."

"You're welcome dear," she said and just as quickly she was gone.

"See what I gotta deal with? Anyways, hell no I ain't in. And didn't you hear nothing I said? You fit the profile brother. You fit to a tee. The fishin' been slow anyways. Water is still too damn cold. You forget Old Man Winter stays late up here. Ice has only been out of the bay for a maybe a little more than a week."

"What better way to get to the bottom of it then?" Ross said.

Steve took a long drink of his beer. He smacked his lips a little and stared for a few silent moments into Ross' eyes. He began to nod his head affirmatively and pointed at Ross with his index finger of the hand that was holding the can.

"I know you're not serious when you say that but really you might be on to something here. Yeah, let me think here brother. Where are you thinking of heading in?"

"I'm sorry I said anything now. Let's just say I haven't quite decided yet," Ross said.

Steve's face lit up with a smile. "You and I both know that isn't true either. The man don't shit without a plan man," he said laughing. He scanned the desktop eventually finding a small black notebook stuffed like a pepper. He pushed it into

Ross' hand and closed Ross' fingers around it. "This is gonna get you through man. Like, there's maps, personal info, basically an abridged version of all these things hanging up here on the board. It's the cliff notes you were looking for man."

Steve's face turned grim, his glare was dark and serious. "It all fits man. The whole world. We're all in one big machine man. My wheels have been turnin' waiting for that clutch to go in and you're the gear man. You're gonna be what drives this. It's you man, like some sort of crazy destiny that nobody could ever see comin'. Yeah man, it has to be you. Someone has spoken man, someone has spoken."

CHAPTER 44

The stench of rot and methane filled the air with every scoop of marsh I cut with the spade. It was moving through me. Cold liquid mud filled the cavity instantly, each attempt preceded with a grotesque sucking sound. I pushed the last of Darlene's personal effects, a handful of clothes and a pair of yellow rubber boots bound tightly with roots down into the mire at the center of the hole. I repaired the sight as usual knowing that the spring green-up would hide it forever. I kept what was useful, a few boats, paddles and basic supplies.

Time for me now was only dictated by the rise and fall of daylight. Fortune good or bad led me to this place of strange darkness and peace. *You runnin' from something or to something?*

Darlene's question dripped through my mind. It all came to me faster than expected. I wasn't prepared to be settled until the next spring, maybe even summer. Now the time of day became free, even easy. So easy that I felt like I was only just going through the motions, like a tired motorist who suddenly realizes they have been driving for miles and cannot remember a thing. In the blackness of night, the world balanced. Most everything moved at night, safe from the world under the cover of darkness. Old owls are always asking me "who", but I cannot tell them. They guide me regardless because I think they know. I am not as much of a "who" as a "what" now. 'You a flower or a weed?' Again, a bit of Darlene's wit crept in. I wanted to tell her I was an Angel's Trumpet, poisonous, and I bloom at night, but for that I had to think too hard. It was a satisfying thought but hardly genuine.

Our senses lie. We try to feel so attuned but what we see isn't always what is there, what we smell brings memories so we can then lie to ourselves. For what we touch and what we taste we mostly rely on our lying eyes to determine and then sound which is different to everybody and to some even invisible.

The sound of distant thunder I thought at first. But it was too small, it didn't come with energy and the animals could not feel it. Distant canoes banging against rock piloted by fools. They didn't belong to the night. Fools that ask for trouble. Maybe it makes them feel alive but maybe they really do not want to be. Maybe that is why they have come, to feel good about themselves again, to face a refreshing danger of their own planning. No matter where I go there are weeds trying to crowd me out.

A few days after his arrival at the resort, thoroughly outfitted and leaning heavily on years of experience, Ross pushed off to calm seas at first light, alone. The few thick drops of water that flew off the paddle ahead of each stroke acted as ambassadors begging forgiveness for the disturbance to come.

He carried two packs, one personal and one for food, one extra paddle, and a plastic tube that protected his fishing poles. Ross felt stress from things he suspected would slip away as he took in the world around him. Docks along the lake disappeared and the shoreline soon became wild and untamed. Returning loons in flocks of three and four echoed their haunting calls above waterways he could not yet see. The sun peaked over towering white pines to the starboard side as he paddled dead north. His pace felt mighty, his stroke was divine. The cool air hovered barely above freezing but the heat of his muscles kept him warm.

There was one road yet to cross. One lonely two-lane rough blacktop that wound through the stony landscape. The last obvious sign of civilization however bleak. Before the sun set Ross expected to transverse seven lakes and haul gear over two miles of portages. There would be no more roads. The familiarity of the route removed anticipation. Pain slows time and makes miles seem longer. Without the anticipation there is only pain. Even that was familiar. A man's shoulders will grow weak from a thousand strokes before they go numb and he forgets about it. Then he will beg for the next chance to pull water after the cardiovascular purgatory of yet another treacherous portage. Hell would be saved for another time. In the bush, it can always get worse.

The cold evenings didn't bother me. I could not feel the vapor in the air, once upon a time cool against my skin. Those memories seemed distant. There was a time when I could almost taste it. Now the wet, marshy flavor was gone, replaced with the knowledge of sweet odor without the satisfaction. I thought for a moment of what I might have brought with me but just as quickly dismissed the need for anything at all. I felt a draw to the people. I needed to see them like I needed to look at my own wounds, how deep I was cut. Once I was out into the open water without a moon, I was invisible. I joined with the night, my boat just an empty vessel, a ghost canoe being propelled by will alone. I tapped into the energy of everything living around me. I felt peace and, for some reason, duty, like it was my calling to be there. I enjoyed a oneness of being with all living things around me, becoming a link in a chain of shared energy. It flowed like electric current through the chain, shorted only by the intervention of man.

Their fire burned through me. I wanted to take its air away. They were drunk and loud, deafened to all natural things by their own conversation. They discussed the many hardships in their little lives and told stories of their great adventures. So long I watched them. I felt them short circuiting the chain with every spoken word, destroyers of solitude. Other fires flickered in the distance; campsites crowded with all those who take. Every leaf on every tree gives back to the ground; these people gave nothing.

I no longer had to prove anything to the dark. Prove that it was or wasn't me to anyone. I did not need blue trees. Still, I longed to see their souls escape. To set them free for, as Jesus said, they know not what they do. I would be kind to them and let them keep their blood, and as payment, or more of a favor really, I only hoped to get a glimpse of their souls. If we trade these gifts, I offer them respect for their bodies. Every man so far has let me down compelling me to remove their body's dignity. They punished their families denying them closure and they themselves suffered as spirits who could not be heard saying goodbye. They still refuse to show themselves.

Their anger keeps them trapped between worlds. I could help them as well.

I stood feet away from their tent mired in dark shadow pretending like I was deciding. Playing the part of some sort of cosmic judge even though I had already made up my mind. Man one and man two were busy snoring off their drunk. Very carefully and very slowly I unzipped the tent matching the cadence of their foul tones then moved back into the shadows. I only want one at a time. It would need to happen this way. And so I waited till it was nearly light.

"What the?" Man one was up. "Who the hell left this open? Glenn you fuck." Man one zipped it back up and laid back in a huff.

"Might as well now, fuck it." He was getting up, Glenn had not moved. He took a few steps downhill and held his penis in his hand waiting for his tired, abused prostate to kick it into gear.

I used a round rock a little bigger than a soft ball. I wanted it to be that size so it would fit snugly between the top of his neck and cerebellum. I also did not want to break his head open, but I heard a slight crack when I hit him. Not sure if he was going to be useful anymore at that point. I watched him lay there for a ten count. Glenn was still snoring away unconscious to the world.

Sunrise was delayed by gray skies. I bound him in the parachute cord they were using as a clothesline, filled his mouth with thick, green moss and gagged him with a fishy smelling rag I found. Their camp was a mess. I carried him into the woods and laid him carefully under the watchful boughs of a large white pine. I did not care for Glenn. I did not give him credit to be up already. Must be an experienced drunk. He did not even bother to tie his shiny white sneakers. He just earned first chair.

"Kind of early to take a crap!" he yelled as he proceeded to do what men do, be invasive. "What the fuck did you eat? Hurry the hell up I gotta see the man!" He fished a little. He had a clicker on his reel, the kind that clicks repeatedly and obnoxiously with every turn of the crank.

I struck him with the same stone for the same reasons. He fell forward into the water. I was more careful this time, having earned a better feeling for the softness of their skulls compared to the stone I wielded. Glenn was out cold instantly. Not being able to use his hands to break the plane his face slapped an epic splashdown against hard water like a beaver that slaps his tail on the surface to claim territory. Beavers never want you there. I pulled him out quickly before he drowned.

I tied him much the same as I did man one using moss from the same stone. A bandana rolled into a headband hanging from a tackle bag served as the gag. One of them was kind enough to have left it there for me. Most likely Glenn, the pretentious one. He deserved to be hit harder.

Souls that have evaded me in the past may be more apparent to those whose company from which they care not depart. A theory to be sure but putting it to the test meant to keep them facing each other at all costs. Although each man was bound separately, I also tied them together, face to face. I bound them at the ankles and spun rope around them like the red stripes of a barber pole, a tribute to the original advertisement of blood. Their bindings were terminated at their necks, pulling their chins close enough together to taste each other's breath. I needed to know if other men who died at my hands could not avert their fate, then how their very essence could avoid my study.

The camp took time to clean, hanging the food pack, securing bedding and personal items. It needed to be set up correctly, neatly, respectfully. A strange reverence came to light once it was put together. Only the cancer of man could destroy it. Men were a disease here, begging to be cured. Let them fester otherwise in their Petri dish apartment buildings and clogged artery cities. Let them feed on each other instead of existing to the detriment of the trees. The trees that were awake now, mocking us, shaking their many fists at us in anger like an angry crowd, utilizing the power of morning winds.

Rooted in place they could only watch generations of brothers fall victim to the saw and the ax. Reverent corpses carried away to become shelter for vermin, limbs split in the daylight only to be unceremoniously burned at night. I carried their insignificant hatred on my shoulders as much as I carried the lives of the two men deeper into their midst. I absolve my guilt with their collective demise as I would in order, please myself at one time or another use them all.

Deeper in amongst the legs of trees a boulder set out of place by hands of ice two miles high ten thousand years prior kept its base together skewed from the top of the crevasse that split it down the center. The crack was wide enough to encompass the bodies of men at its top becoming increasingly narrowed as it tightened into a home for other vermin that belonged. Granite walls would hug them soundly, keeping them safe from threatening gray skies.

The trees would never dissuade their hatred for they were stubborn and long lived. Even hundreds of years from now the legends of those that came before would be passed on by the winds that blew harder with each passing moment. I would return under the cover of darkness as they slept, snoring away their many years on black breezes of stolen air, much like the men they despised. When the hour is late, trees only wake up in time to die.

CHAPTER 45

"The man don't do shit without a plan, man." Steve's witticism brought a smile to Ross' face as he hoofed the canoe on his shoulders over the first portage. Everything was wet making the jagged rock he walked on slippery and dangerous. The flawed footing slowed his pace. The water that rushed through a turn-of-the-century log jam next to the trail made a beautiful self-reflective noise. With the lightweight canoe he managed well in two trips.

Out from under the canopy at the edge of the relatively silent pond he noticed his morning sun was gone, the sky suddenly mired in gray. A light breeze came to life sounding hollow without fully fledged leaves to dull the sharp edge of the hiss. The music of the boreal forest is played in minor thanks to the evergreens that dominated the refrain. The direction of the wind could only be a guess at that point deceitfully swishing its way in and around granite valleys. The long portage in front of him would take over an hour, then there was big water to cross. A strong headwind could be a major concern. A tailwind on the other hand could make the long, open water paddle considerably easier. If a big blow came from either side, he could skirt the windward shoreline all the way up the lake. The latter would take many extra hours and thousands more strokes.

The clouds grew darker with each passing moment. Apprehended by their suffering victims they will be made to take the stand at their own trial. Brought up on trumped-up charges for killing the morning sun. All valid questions as to their intent would soon be answered as Mother Nature will force them to testify in their own defense.

He was old now, this newest and latest spring storm. Born in the Gulf he grew fat on tropical moisture and mid-continent meltwater. Spurred on by the sunlight of ever-lengthening days, his long and draining crawl up the plains left him short of breath and low on blood. The cold air over the boreal forest waited patiently, intent on wringing out every last drop. The old and powerful soul knew his fate and saved what he could for the end.

It never seemed to really get too light that day, it just stayed dark gray. Winds increased steadily throughout the morning as the temperature dropped. Ross had a long day in front of him. Soon came the rain. It was light at first, a mist barely noticeable, especially on the trails. On the open water it stung his face. It kept up like that until mid-afternoon when Ross began to notice tiny ice pellets bouncing off his rain gear. His face and hands were long numbed.

Well this bites. All day long he ground through small lakes and portage trails short and long. Some mired in mud, some wet, slippery rock and still others exposed, eroded roots that held black mud puddles like a stained-glass window. Finally at late afternoon, he dropped his gear at the foot of big water. The waves roared dark in the distance, the white caps pushing away. Not quite a tail wind he wanted; he could ride them anyway with a fair amount of work.

Only a few strokes from shore Ross could feel the effects of the wind. The shape of the lake slowly graduated like paddling into the bottom of a massive ice cream cone. At first the wind was his friend, moving him along effortlessly. The further he pushed into the cone the more strained their relationship became. By the time he got close to the ice cream, their friendship was officially over. Sharp gusts listed the boat.

"Whoa!"

Waves began to break at his side. The heading was not maintainable. If he turned with them he would have to ride them for miles to the east only to be pinned to the shoreline void of campsites. Against them he could be in calmer water in less than one excruciatingly difficult mile.

Choosing the latter, he stroked deep and painfully to turn the bow into the breaking waves. Perception in open water can be the enemy. He wondered at times if he was even moving. The rain was becoming more ice than rain. Eventually after an eternity the waves became manageable although the wind gusted on. Even tight against the shoreline the wind wanted to suck him back out into open water.

He dug through gear for a campsite map. Only one was feasible before dark. He had to hide against the western shoreline for almost two miles. With every stroke he would be getting further from his destination, but he could then make a sharp right turn and ride the waves another mile and a half into a narrow, assuming that he traveled in perfectly straight lines. There was a campsite where a warm fire and food awaited, just a few more hours of work, before it was too dark to travel.

He pushed off again, this time staying close to shore where the risk of striking bottom and damaging the boat is greater. Rocks and dead head logs just under the surface can be easily hidden by the tiny ripples from a strong gust of wind. Swamping the boat would be discouraging. He pressed on, managing to successfully avoid what he could see. At the turn he enjoyed the increase in speed. There was no longer any rain but instead ice that began to accumulate inside the boat. Finally out into the open lake, the experience became surreal.

The crash of the waves sounded like a raging river that could barely be heard under the torrent of falling ice. After three hours of hard paddling he finally reached the narrows. He was coming in hot into shallow waters. He desperately pushed against the water making sure not to spin the boat. Riding up on anything now would surely flip him. The canoe bounced off a log with the port stern riding one of the last big waves into the protected waters of a huge outcropping of boulders. It spun sideways into calm waters much to the relief of Ross' pounding heart which ironically was about to fall.

"Damn!" The site was taken. Even after that epic ride he felt defeated. With darkness setting in and clinically exhausted he had little choice but to paddle into the occupied campsite.

"Hello in camp!" Ross yelled as he drifted to the shore. "Hello in camp!" he shouted again.

He pulled the boat out of the water and tied off the bow. He continued to shout out to them as he walked up to the tent, assuming at that point that they had simply grown tired of the weather and went to bed. Ross knocked as best as a person can on a nylon tent, trying to at least make contact with the poles. Finally the cop inside got the best of him and he unzipped the tent.

Huh. Empty, with the sleeping bags rolled and tied tight and placed at the heads of perfectly aligned air mattresses. The clothes were neatly folded and stacked largest to smallest. He closed up the tent and took notice of camp.

Perfect. The food pack was hung and well-secured. There was no miscellaneous gear anywhere. There were two personal packs neatly folded and strapped to the bases of separate trees.

Firewood stacked like…

He had seen it once before, but exhaustion prevented him from remembering the exact reference. The boat was also there, pulled up into the woods, flipped and tied to a tree. The paddles leaned perfectly perpendicular against the hull. He unloaded his gear and pitched his small tent on an alternate pad further back in the woods. With his tiny camp stove he boiled enough water for a freeze dried meal and a full canteen before crawling into his bag for some well-deserved sleep. He brought a bear-proof food pack that amongst normal circumstances he would hang from a tree for added security. This night as it rested on the ground, he hoped the advertising would live up to its claims.

Maybe they're hikers. Ross pondered the location of his inadvertent hosts. *Hangin' out at a different site? A buddy or something?* Traveling in groups and staying at separate sights was not uncommon. *Guess I'll figure it out in the morning.* Normally after a day like this sleep would be instant, maybe even before his head hit his make-shift life jacket pillow. But tonight, rest would be fleeting.

CHAPTER 46

It was the fierce sniffing sound that brought Glenn back to consciousness. Heavy claws scratched against the lichen covered rock above him. He had no idea how long he was out although it was the better part of a day. The light was low, either impending night or early morning. From his position on the bottom, it was impossible to tell. Man One was still not awake after his blow to the skull. His breathing was shallow and occasionally his eyelids would flutter as if he was dreaming. Glenn was overcome with horror and fear. The weight of his friend on top of him had his back wedged into the stone. Above him the startled face of a black bear glared down at them; his black glassy eyes devoid of any potential emotion that may tip his hand as to his intent. Glenn could only watch him, straining his eyes to look straight up inadvertently smoothing his cheeks, paving the road for tears. He wanted so badly to scream through his gag, but the constriction of his lungs made it impossible. He was stuck there, like the worst of nightmares when a person is so overcome with fear that they cannot move, run away or even scream for help. He was powerless.

The bear began to act nervous. He pounced on the top of the boulder with his two front legs, snapping his jaws and clawing at the moss. Enormous amounts of drool created a suction when he opened his mouth, and it flew out to the sides of his cheeks in sick, sticky streams. He slammed his jaws closed and filled the dim air with the terror inducing sound of colliding skin covered bones. There was a moment of silence. For Glenn it was a moment of hope, for the bear it was a moment of decision. A decision that started with an innocent lick. Just a little taste of the dried blood on the back of Man One's head. He graduated to pulling out and eating tufts of hair and consequent attached swathes of scalp. He washed down his appetizers by intensively licking the weeping blood from the pink exposed flesh. That sound, that lapping of a raw roast sound. A heart that is barely pumping simply doesn't move much blood. The bear nibbled, pushing his snout into the head until his teeth could gain purchase. Man One's face pushed into Glenn's own making it difficult for him to breathe. The bear tore off thin strips of head meat and ate them like a sloppy child lacking manners. Glenn pleaded with God to take his friend before the bear ate him alive. The Lord it has been said, does work in mysterious ways. As if the closed back of a scissors was being pushed against his face, Glenn felt the smooth tops of the bear's claw slide down his forehead and press against his closed eyes. They dug and worked their way into Man One's facial cavities. The jolt was quick and powerful. So much so that it gave Glenn slight relief from the stone. The sound it made would make any potential mental recovery for Glenn impossible, like pulling a ten-pound knuckle off the end of a huge bone. The bear peeled the top of his skull open like a soup can and thoroughly embraced eating out of the bowl. A feat made easier by a well-cracked rear skull. His friend's blood burned in Glenn's tightly shut eyes. He did not want to look anyways. He was consumed by ultimate shock and panic. He was freezing cold and could barely breathe. His body shook with fear near to the point of convulsions. His only fortune was the sentience to pray. He prayed for it to be untrue, he prayed for lunacy, he prayed for everything besides being free. The thought of being free never crossed his mind. Such was the weight and the darkness of the overwhelming shadow of fear that overtook him. The bear gave a grunt and backed out of the crevasse.

I was not quite sure why the bear backed out as I wished but I was sure that he would. He did not go far but neither did I want him to. There was no emotion to seduce, no thoughts pouring from his eyes. He was just a bear doing only what he knows to do. I pulled the men free and cut them apart. I removed all restraints from the corpse and kicked it down over the side of the boulder.

"For you." I nodded to the bear. He moved in quickly and clutched the shoulder of the body in his jaws and dragged it off into the woods. Glenn was paralyzed, presumably from fear. As I carried him out of there, I was starting to get the feeling he was not going to answer me. I did not need to take him far. The windward shoreline was busy taking a beating from the storm. Glenn's body was cold, hypothermic. He might have been in the perfect state of mind.

I thought for a moment about being his savior, the hero that set him free. *How would that feel?* He would have an incredible story to tell, probably get famous and make a lot of money. I would be the temporary hero, worthy of much praise and admiration. Until somebody, somewhere figured it out. And it probably would not take long. I was growing angrier by the second thinking about the would-be stool pigeon who just could not mind his own business. I pictured a know-it-all type. The kind of guy that thinks he sees and knows more than everybody else in the room. He wore sweaters and extoled the virtues of craft beers and wines. Probably toted around some sort of liberal arts degree like a badge of courage. I wished it was him I dropped on the ground before me now. This one was weak, hypothermic, and dehydrated. He did not come prepared for the wilderness, prepared for me. Maybe his too smart for his own good, hipster buddy who could not keep his mouth shut should have considered the consequences of his actions.

"Tell me." I ordered him. He was free of all bonds now. Half-dressed from sleeping he rolled into the fetal position and stared up at me with terror in his eyes. Too cold to run and too frightened to even speak. "Did you see it?" I asked him again.

"Please," that's what he said to me. "Please, I, I, I."

He did not have any idea what he was asking for. Too far gone. Useless to the world in every way.

"I will save you," I told him. I wanted him to feel the irony, just for wasting my time, for being here and being the way he was, having the friends he had.

It was one massive cracking noise followed immediately by a series of smaller ones. I felt the violence in the ground beneath my feet. He probably could too. His body tensed in anticipation for what he could not yet see until I stepped aside.

The white pine behind me was old and weak in the knees. He broke one man high off his roots leaving a space underneath for a person to live through their crushing. I had met him earlier. He stood there for over a hundred years. A mere sprout when his fathers' fathers were taken for lumber to build the modern world. The same place all that time. I thought he might welcome death. Be free of the insects, from the birds, from the same old view. But he was pleased with all those things. He enjoyed the eagles that perched on him and knew them well. The bugs not as much but as long as he remained healthy, he was obliged to serve them. The squirrels, even more than intertwined roots he was closest with them. He had cracked in a storm weeks earlier and knew his time was limited. He could feel the pressure change, the slightest uptick in the wind. His view of the coming gray skies was unparalleled, and he was resided to the fact that this day would likely be his last. Then he met me. After everything that he would miss he was satisfied that upon his death he could also kill a man. That is why I knew exactly where he would break. He was not happy though. He was only satisfied. Trees do not get happy, or sad. They can appreciate and be pleased or be dissatisfied but never unhappy. Their emotions just cannot take them that far. They never love or never hate. If they did they would go insane. Simpletons, useful idiots is what they are but I never realized there was vengeance in their limbs.

The placement of the body was perfect. The trunk dropped right where he said it would. How would any of us live our lives if we knew exactly when and how we would die?

Glenn was still in the fetal position when the tree pinned him to the ground. The way his eyes bulged and his lips moved as he struggled to either speak or scream reminded me of one of those odd looking, googly-eyed goldfish. Being close to dying men never produced viable benefits for me so I stayed back, standing higher than his body on the trunk, towering over my subordinate from a bully pulpit. I was empowered by my pathetic congregation of two. One dead man and his soul. I needed only to pull them apart. His jaw finally extended almost comically wide open as he struggled to get one last breath. Why bother? Why would he want to live the last few hours anyway? I hoped it was to hold up his side of the bargain, to show me.

It was not anything a person could really see unless they already knew what they were looking for. I knew it stayed close to the ground. There were no edges, no mist or no ghostly apparition. Only an area of great feeling, so strong it nearly distorted the air. It separated into countless pieces and scattered, remnants passing into the ground and into the sky. Through anything, over everything. And then, just as suddenly they are gone.

Some of it passed into me. Hatred, anger, and fear walked through me as if they were three separate people. I met them all at that gate and I already knew them. They frowned at me, inside me. Then they left dissatisfied because only when they were free did they truly know me. Only then did they recognize me and know that they would not be able to stay. I know now that men are made of many and I steadfastly remain one.

CHAPTER 47

The wind blew steady through the night increasing at times. Sleep should have come easy save for the stress from the nearly drowned out sound of falling trees. Inside his tiny one-man tent he wormed his way into his rain suit, strapped on his boots and headed out into the storm. Choosing instead to be tired and cold instead of dead, Ross rode out the worst of the storm huddled behind a couple of large boulders on the windward shore of the lake. Safely free from the danger of falling trees and limbs.

Through hours of terrifying gusts and ice laden rain he tried to sleep, managing to doze off between nightmares. As the wee hours approached the force of the storm weakened enough that Ross felt safe returning to the tent. It was mid-morning by the time he emerged finally rested.

The old storm was dead now, leaving only a vacuumous hole in the atmosphere it used to call home. The winds that kept Ross pinned to the camp now were the result of the rest of the world trying to fill that hole. Mother Nature's giant hair dryer.

Still nobody huh? He went about boiling some water with his camp stove perched on the surprisingly level fire grate. *Somebody did this up pretty nice.* Flat rocks surrounded the fire pit stacked on end to make a windbreak, another flat stone to the side for a table. On the other side of the pit was the firewood, neatly stacked in concentric rows woven into small towers of like sized pieces.

Really? He recalled the cabin back in Wisconsin, the empty shells. That was the only other time he had seen wood stacked that way. After countless campsite visits in so many years, only once. Ross never met a coincidence that he liked. Too often they were simply the forgotten bread crumbs of a poorly covered trail. Now fully rested and squarely back in professional mode he drew connecting lines in his mind. Never had he seen a camp so neat, clean, and well-secured.

And those clothes. To Ross, that was the edge of the cliff. A place where after one more step turning back would no longer be an option. He could only fall or jump.

The option to break camp, brave the waves and take his chances loomed large in his mind. Just paddle away and forget everything he just saw. Embrace coincidence for once. Play the odds and assume everything will be just fine. Blame it all on a stressed-out subconscious that was inadvertently creating a crisis where there really was none. But he wouldn't be the man he was if he were to embrace apathetic logic. There was too much duty in his blood, an overwhelming desire for constant closure.

Where are you guys? Ross looked stoically to the forest searching for an answer. What he was given was not what he had hoped for as the manufacturer's praise of the subsequent indestructible durability of his bear-proof pack was about to be tested.

"Hey! Git bear!" Ross stood tall on the log he had been sitting on, waving his arms and trying to appear large and threatening. "Ya! Ya! Git!"

He never heard the bear coming, never even saw him. He was just, all of a sudden, there, staring like a statue with cold soulless eyes.

"Hey! Go! Git bear, git!" The bear was unaffected by Ross' pleas for departure. It pawed at the pack, almost playing with it like a cat plays with a ball of yarn. The bear picked it up with his teeth, tossing it around like it weighed virtually nothing. Ross slowly backed away to where the boats were tied. He picked up a paddle and banged it hard against the bottom of the overturned canoe. The booming, deep, carrying sound caused the bear to drop the pack and spring back, clearly startled. It turned to run but then abruptly stopped, picked something up off the ground in its teeth and then continued its retreat into the forest. A part of whatever prize he claimed fell away as he bounded.

What the hell did he grab? Before investigating any further Ross went into his personal gear pack to retrieve a hatchet thinking if it came down to it, that it might make a better defensive weapon than a knife alone. Inside he found a message written on the sort of little card that comes with gifted flowers. It was accompanied by a small red bow and attached with tape to the holster of a pistol.

"Thought you might need this buddy. Stay safe out there. Steve."

The holster housed an extra pre-loaded clip and underneath it was box of twenty fresh cartridges.

"You son of a…I thought she was a little heavy," Ross said to imaginary Steve. "But I have to say this time you most definitely done good."

He strapped up and went to where the bear was. The pack had lived up to its billing, a few holes in the outer material but the plastic bucket contained inside was virtually unscathed. There was also blood. Not fresh or bright red, but blood never-the-less. Based on its location Ross assumed it came from whatever it was that the bear ran off with. As there was no blood there previously, he also surmised that the bear must have brought whatever it was with him. He started down the trail where the bear ran off, pistol out and ready to fire. Ross had zero intention of shooting the bear but if he could spot him again and fire a shot, it would most likely scare the animal out of the area for good.

Discovery can be daunting. The side-bar riddle of the emerging situation was enhanced the moment Ross correctly determined that what the bear ran away with was a shoe. The color, the shape of it, all adding up in Ross' recall. The evidence was overwhelming as the final piece of the puzzle did not come with machine-rounded edges meant to be put back into place. That jagged piece that the bear dropped was the bitten-off at the ankle, still-socked foot that had inadvertently slipped out of the shoe. The bear in its haste left the candy and ran away with the wrapper.

It was a worst-case scenario as far as Ross was concerned. He was angry more at the situation than the bear. What were the odds? The chance that a warden would happen to be in this place at this time. A supposed time of introspection and leisure that has been stacked with drama and hardship nearly the moment it began. His focus now was on the bear. Damn the warning shots, a man eater had to be taken down. Bears can never be allowed to see people as food.

His heart raced as he slowly stepped forward. With two hands on the pistol, he scanned the brush side to side looking only where the gun was aimed. He kept to an obvious trail as long as he could before it disintegrated into thick underbrush of short juniper. He had to roll the dice now. Working the bear season in Wisconsin he was well aware of their habits and tendencies. Ross had to draw on every bit of his experience to be able to follow this bear. A stand of black spruce just ahead was thick enough to hide anything. Ross was barely inside the edge of spruce when the bear took off like a freight train out the other side. He resisted the urge to give chase. He knew he would never see it by the time he pushed through the boughs. It was better to stay still and listen. A frightened bear knows no stealth. Upon exiting the stand, hanging on one of the lower branches hung a dirty white sneaker, stained brown with dried blood and slobber.

The bear was headed towards the lake. Once there it could swim from point to point faster than Ross could ever hope to keep up through the woods. He had to hurry with the hopes of catching the bear in the water. He ran to the shoreline on the edge of a small bay. Still a few dozen strides from the shoreline he could see the bear was less than fifty yards offshore. Ross took careful aim. With only its head exposed the size of a bear can be deceiving when it is in the water. The first shot blew up the lake just behind and to the right of the target. Shot two echoed the dull, sickening thump of a bullet striking a skull. The bear rolled in the water making loud gasping noises before finally righting the ship and continuing on, blowing snot, chugging along like a broken tugboat. The next shot sounded different again, the bullet burying itself into the thick hide at the water line, just below the skull. The bear slowed; its head turned sideways in the water. Ross unloaded. A few rounds fell short, and a few went long but for the most part the lion's share buried themselves inside the bear's skull. Ross leaned back against a huge boulder to catch his breath through a few sighs of relief. He did not see the shirt at first, he was far too busy focusing on the bear. It lay strewn on top of the boulder, the blood-soaked sleeve hanging down into a crevasse from where the huge stone broke in two. Once he climbed up, he found more blood. Impossibly wedged at the bottom of the crack was the other shoe.

If you were stuck, where's your buddy?

CHAPTER 48

I found myself in the dark place when I heard the shots although I cannot recall a reason for being there. Their cadence told a story of anger and intent. I moved quickly, effortlessly through the forest of trees that lately were acting like rude friends you would rather not hang out with. Glenn had not changed much since we had last seen each other. I passed him by without any acknowledgement, a social faux pas back in the city. I choose not to risk small talk.

At the boulder I was aware of the spirit of the bear. It lived on top of the stone now, ever peering into the crevasse. When lightning and winds powered it, the spirit would draw enough energy to make noise, only to be drowned out by the movement of foliage and thunder. It could not tell me any more than it could have told while it was still alive. For a bear there is no knowledge gained in the next plane, just leftover energy destined to fade. Trapped here in this place of death by the negative emotions of the man that killed it.

The coal black fur barely broke the surface of the churning lake, camouflaged in the shadows of the waves. As long as the water remained cool the body would be preserved. It may not seem fair, but I will not avenge it for foolishly expediting its own demise. It was so much like a stupid person that changed everything because of greed.

The two stood side by side, each comedically unaware of the other's existence. The bear noticed me first, the advantage of unintelligible instinct seeing me through trees. The man eventually caught-on as well. He stared blankly in my general direction, but I doubt he knew why. Forced to use his eyes his vision was not as keen. His stress was thick, and it fed my resolve. Their attention to me was a diversion. I added noise to help the man understand, to reward him for his instinct. The cracking of thick branches would keep his attention focused on my direction. I thanked them as I moved away towards the camp. He would go there when fear and duty overpowered his weak anger. As I moved around him, I felt him on the wind and he was familiar.

From a kneeling position Ross loaded a fresh clip into the gun. The sharp crack of breaking wood across the small bay startled him. The possibility of another bear kept him on high alert, but a long wait turned up no more sign. It was the first real moment he had to slow down and assess the situation. Ideally, he could contact another camper while they paddled out and give them all the necessary information while he maintained the integrity of the scene. However, considering the weather this time of year recreationists are rare. His plan was to document the scene by journal and picture. He would then tear a page out and leave a note inside the tent as well as directions on what to do next should the missing camper return. Finally, he would pack up his gear and get out as soon as the wind allowed and contact the proper authorities.

Who knows? He stood up and holstered his gun dismissing the noise across the bay as a natural result of a windy day. He had to get back to camp before he could do anything else. On his way he found spots of blood he had walked by earlier without noticing. Every drop a constant reminder to be more vigilant and aware. Once there he immediately went to his pack and dug out the camera and his journal. His letter explained the potential evidence of an attack, careful not to deliver the worst of news. He included directions to leave immediately and relocate to the first available campsite across the lake and wait if possible. He gave a brief detail of his credentials as well in the hopes the person would not take it as a prank.

Every falling leaf or wind-blown branch earned his full attention on his way back to document the scene. Describing what happened with fresh recall aids in the validity of the report. He photographed the body of the bear and the place where he had shot it including the empty cartridges on the ground. His notes included captions with overall timing and a step-by-step depiction of events. As he worked through everything chronologically it occurred to him that he also needed to document the condition of the camp. He made a mental note to take pictures of it when he returned.

He did not see the woods in front of him. His mind was back at the little cabin next to the Owens farm, seeing the stacked wood. And then there was Mason's trailer. Everything so neat and clean and, of course, the clothes. He only now just remembered the clothes, folded and stacked. Just like missing hunters' gear they found when that whole business got started. Those men were all gone. The case closed. Ross could not help but wonder if there was one more. One more member of that hunting party that he had not known about. But what about the wood or even the shell he had found? Sure, Mason could have been in both places, which would explain everything except what was happening here and now. Where is the missing man? Who was the person who had just been killed by the bear? Without more remains the answer was impossible to determine. He needed to finish up and get out. He needed help.

When Ross saw that his food pack was gone, he traded his camera for a drawn gun, convinced now more than ever that there was another bear. He changed his mind in short notice but kept his gun out for other reasons. The most pressing was the fact that bears cannot paddle a canoe. Both boats, plus all the packs and paddles were missing. He raced to the shoreline outside of the protected harbor hoping to catch a glimpse of the thief on the open lake. There on the shore of a small island roughly a half a mile away were the two boats. Still fully loaded and pulled partially up on shore. Ross watched and waited but there was no sign of anybody. The person that did it must either still be there or paddled away in a different boat or boats directly away off the other side of the island. Even if that were the case, Ross would eventually be able to see them cross the open water. Longer still he waited and saw nothing.

Fear and mistrust, and frustration overtook him. He thought for a moment he would shoot at the island taking the opportunity to land a one in a million punishment shot. Maybe get lucky and offer someone the proper motivation to return the boats. Then the anger set in that would keep the spirit of the bear lingering, an unintentional poker tell to one who would be watching. Next to shore where the canoes were tied Ross found two life jackets that had not been there previously. Apparently, his hint to swim for it. The water was cold, hypothermia was a distinct possibility. His only chance would be to light a fire and change into dry clothes immediately if he made it. For the rest of the day, he would hold out hope that it was all just a cruel joke. Maybe they would give it up once it finally got dark. If not, he would make the swim just after the sun went down, wrapped tightly in his small nylon tent attempting to gain as much repellency and insulation as he could. If it was indeed a trap, then he could use the cover of darkness to his advantage.

Using the guy-out cords of the tent, he tied it tightly around his wrist and arms and then used a tight-fitting life jacket to keep it around his core. Every moment he could keep the cold water away from his skin would get him closer to the boats. The other jacket he would hold in front for greater buoyancy and aid in keeping his head out of the water. For propulsion he would kick his way over in the hopes that using his body's largest muscles and protecting his core he would generate enough heat for survival.

He moved quickly out into the water trying to gain an advantage with every second. He knew that if it took him anymore than an hour, he would not make it. The pain from the cold water sapped him mentally just as much as physically. His refusal to die, to dig down deep for the will and the energy he felt was nothing short of a miracle. The thought of someday telling the story of his survival helped keep him going. He thought about Steve, how with all his conspiratorial rhetoric he may have finally been right. He needed to live to tell him so. His death would be too much burden for his friend. One more kick, a few more feet, it all added up. The dark silhouette of the treetops on the island gave him hope. They were a black light at the end of the tunnel. He had forgotten why he entered the water in the first place, why he was swimming towards his own boat. He tried to recall falling overboard, when he last ate, who he last loved. When his foot struck the rocky bottom unexpectedly still far from shore, he thanked God for the shallow water. He was still shivering when he was finally able to lay down on the shoreline next to the boats. Time was of the essence. His hands refused to function from the cold. He cried as he struggled with the plastic buckles on his pack. Inside there was a lighter, dry clothes, and salvation. Even the breath he used to warm his hands was cold.

CHAPTER 49

Ross leaned into it, feeling like he was using every muscle in his body to release two small plastic clips. Finally getting it open was a small but important victory. He felt around with numb hands for his flashlight. A surreal struggle to push the button forward would have been comical had it not been so life threatening. Another small win emboldened his resolve. His hands trembled so hard the shaking light became disorienting.

"Lighter, lighter, please!" Ross begged. It was taking too long. He dumped the entire contents of his pack onto the ground. "Yes!" The latest of tears tasted of salvation. He pointed the light towards the woods across the large flat stone on which the boats sat, looking for anything to start a fast fire.

"What the?" Tinder in the form of a neat pyramid of red pine needles was carefully nested in the center of a small, now familiar stack of wood ready to burn. He was shaking now more than ever, a sign that blood was returning to his extremities. He thought about telling the tale of his miracle survival as motivation to actually make the lighter work. The fire came to life nearly instantly, but it would take much longer than Ross had anticipated to actually recover. Dry clothes were a priority. Every move was in slow motion. As he warmed, he began to shiver uncontrollably making it that much more difficult. A good sign that his body was back to doing its job surviving. He removed all the packs from the boats and used them to make a small wall behind the fire. He laid the canoes on their sides to form the other two sides of a triangle enclosing the fire. Once inside the reflected heat would cook him back into viability. He only needed to climb out occasionally to gather wood.

"Fuckin' Steve," Ross said as he stared at an old paddle. The finish had long been scarred off the blade. He used the stains and colors to imagine a creepy face much like finding shapes in the clouds. "And you're no Wilson either." He admonished the paddle for not being a better companion. A reference to a movie he had seen.

Steve would have appreciated that. He considered it an apology for blaming Steve for being right. This was no prank. He was lucky to be alive and he knew it. Ross had to admit he was behind the curve. That whoever it was out there was at least a step ahead of him, maybe more. The boats, the life jackets, finding a fire ready to go, it took planning and careful consideration. Plus he had to make it. For what? What if he didn't? What would be gained besides murder? The situation motivated him to take stock, to maintain his pistol and count rounds. They, he, or she would have heard the shots and known he was armed. That may be the very reason he had yet to see them.

A cool sunrise was met with a light northeast breeze. Choosing to travel light in the interest of speed, he loaded his canoe with only his personal pack, one extra paddle, and his life jacket. The rest of the gear he stowed under the other boat tied to a tree set back into the woods. He doused the coals of the fire that likely saved his life making a mental note to thank it for being there and pushed off.

Once back at the helm Ross regained a sense of control over the situation. His feet were cold from boots that had not had enough time to adequately dry but steady paddling would offer them warm, flowing blood. He looked back at where he was, at the morning mist wafting over the lake like smoke. In the fog, on the opposite shoreline back at the original campsite he was able to make out a man.

"Hey!" Ross yelled. "Hey! You on the shoreline! By the campsite! Hey!" There was no response, and the man did not move. Ross turned the boat towards the camp.

"Hey! Hey you by the camp! Can you hear me? By the camp! Hello!" He was able to get close enough to notice color. "Hey you in the red hat! Hey!"

Still the man did not move or respond. *Is he in his pajamas?* Because his boots were already wet, and he was clearly distracted it was the sound of sloshing water which first caught his attention.

"What the?" Ross' canoe was very suddenly filling up with water. He leaned forward and pulled the pack back towards him. Underneath it the lake wash pushing in through a separated keel. The more water that came in, the greater the pressure on the surface of the lake causing it to come in even faster. Ross turned back for the island, the closest piece of land. The moving water inside the boat made it terribly unstable. Soon his pack began to float inside the boat. The simple act of paddling alone caused it to dip to one side resulting in a complete swamping. Foam packed into the bow and stern should have kept the boat off the bottom which in their absence accepted the boat willingly. His pack was made of rubber and sealed tight by rolling the top down and clipping it in place. It even managed to hold some air which could keep it afloat depending on the weight of its contents. He towed it along slowly, expectedly becoming stiff and exhausted in the cold water. He considered letting it go but thought better not knowing what was inside the other packs. The only way he was going to survive was with fire and he knew what he had. He also knew he only needed to get to the shallow reef semi close to shore making the task of surviving slightly less daunting. The sight of a canoe in his peripheral gave him a burst of strength and hope. "Oh thank god!" He almost felt warm when his foot once again struck rock below the surface. Ross went as far as to nearly start a conversation with his rescuer until he noticed the boat was not coming any closer. With two feet firmly on the bottom he could focus now on the empty canoe that was quickly gaining speed on the ripples of a light breeze. He let go of his pack and lunged towards the boat, realizing instantly it was the same one he had tied up on shore earlier. It was moving way too fast. To go any further would surely result in death.

"Fuck!" Ross screamed at the top of his lungs. "Fuck me! What the fuck?" There was no more time to further his fit. He had to get back to shore. He made it with his pack in tow. He collapsed on the rocks, his face cold against bare granite. He reached for his pistol as he laid face down. Even though he was shaking far too much to offer aim it made him feel better to have it in his hands.

Splayed on the granite, soaking wet and freezing Ross could only muster a defeated laugh as the fire he doused earlier roared with addition of fresh, dry fuel and tinder. There were even a few extra pieces of wood available to burn, stacked neatly, familiarly next to the fire.

He crawled up next to it, trying to hang on to all the alertness that his hypothermic mind could muster. "I know you're here!" he yelled. "And… I will find you!" His threat trailed off into shivering as he stripped out of wet clothes. His muscles for the second time in so many days refused to cooperate reducing survival to a slow-motion affair. He changed back into the clothes he had dried by the fire the previous night, pleased that his pack had done its job. He tossed the rest of the wood on the fire and once again waited to warm and recover.

He was stranded, a realization that added some anger for warmth. His mind raced, trying to establish a motive for his tormentor. Initially he planned to stay alive because that is what people do. He could see all the packs that he had stashed under the canoe. Provisions for weeks if done correctly. Sooner or later another camper would happen by. He only needed to wait it out. Ross removed his gun from its holster and began to disassemble and clean each part.

"Rust and politicians." He chuckled out loud referring to a novelty sign he had seen in Steve's basement. "Your only enemies," he said to the gun. "And whoever it is out there." His voice trailed off.

Surviving would be easy, but as he laid out the parts to dry, he wondered if he would be allowed to. On the island, surrounded by ice cold water he was a sitting duck. He had to sleep, he had to eat. He would need fish to supplement his food supplies. All of these activities would leave him vulnerable. So far he was being played for a fool. It was all too perfect.

Something has to change. Ross gazed out over the water. The man on the other shoreline was gone. *Two steps ahead. Something has to change.*

CHAPTER 50

This one was different. I knew it. And I knew he would make it. I could smell the determination on him. That is what made him familiar. He moved offshore, back into the thick woods in the center of the island. A vantage point to see out but still hiding. A kettle of trees to stew in. I lit the fire, now it is just a matter of waiting for it to cook. What am I even making? Will the end result taste of worthy adversary? I wanted it to. I knew that now. His body belonged here, or he would not have survived. But it takes more than that. A woman was willing to eat men like him in order to survive. Easy prey. She had a strong body too, at least at first. It was deteriorating though, like his mind will. I am giving him my chance to know why I know him. He will use it to live, to survive and then I will know him.

Of course he's watching me, why wouldn't he be? Ross built a small lean-to in amongst the thickest stand of spruce. A place too thick to lay out even his small tent. He chose instead to use it as an interior liner for the roof. Boughs that he cut away for space would serve as bedding to keep his body off the cold ground. His fire would be kept small and necessary, using only the driest available wood in order to keep smoke to a minimum. Every camp item he used he made sure to quickly pack away. The organization aided the discipline he needed to stave off apathy.

So this is it then? Wait it out? Wait to die? Maybe someone comes along? Maybe he doesn't let them help. A simple thought of discouragement can lead to real and palpable defeat. So far, he had been made a fool of, and he knew it. It made him angry, and he unwittingly kept the soul of the bear alive. *C'mon man, you're better than this. What's the game here? Obviously, he doesn't want me dead, or I'd already be. Or they don't want me dead, either way. They could burn me out of here if they wanted to, just send me back into the water. Third times a charm, right? Why not? No, they want me here, right here, that's how they set it up. And I'm just going to sit here and take it. Be happy to survive, stay warm and fed, like a pet.*

"Like a fucking pet."

Ross was losing light. In a few hours the darkness would stack disadvantage against him. Add even the lightest of breezes and keen hearing becomes irrelevant. His island hideaway would be useless, possibly a hindrance. He stoked his small fire with green, smoky pine.

"Look at my nice warm fire." Ross had four packs that were airtight. He dumped the contents of them onto a pile for sorting. One change of clothes was distributed among the four, shirt in one, pants in another, undergarments, and a few disposable lighters. They were then blown full of air and sealed. The weapon as well as the rest of the shells he would keep on his person, along with whatever else his belt could hold. A knife, a canteen, a small leather pouch with miscellaneous gear. He still had a paddle. He girdled the branches off of six small pines with a hatchet and lashed them together as a frame, tying the inflated packs to each corner.

"I gotta make sure and bring you too," he said to the hatchet. The boughs from the trees he lashed tightly together and tied in the middle of the frame to form a seat.

It was many hours into the night before he finished the makeshift pontoon raft. He tossed more green pine branches on the fire. Thick, white smoke crackled off into the sky over the island. Ross took the boat to the shoreline that faced out over the open expanse of the lake. He had no intention of attempting the dangerous crossing. Being so close to death, so often in such a short amount of time demanded closure and not just for himself. He paddled around to the northern tip of the island under the cover of a moonless night. The light breeze at his back was good luck but the craft was growing weaker with every stroke. As he knelt atop the seat, he was getting progressively closer to the water. Lashings were wet and stretched, knots became loose and lost their worth. By the time he reached the opposite shoreline he was wet up to his thighs. The two front pontoons had splayed out like giant crab claws and his once stately raft was reduced to a pile of debris.

It would have never made the open expanse journey but as far as Ross was concerned it had made it far enough. The loose ropes untied easily and quickly. He concentrated all of the contents into one pack and rolled it tightly closed. The others he left empty.

Wanna play mind games with me? OK. He worked his way along the shoreline as quietly as possible, utilizing shallow submerged rocks to mask the sound of his approach. He approached the camp inches at a time, gun drawn, senses wire tight. *Of course*, Ross thought, referencing his general luck as of late. He found a seat to embrace temporary defeat on the log bench in front of the fire pit. He stared long and hard into the black burned-out coal. It gave him the idea that maybe he should have burned down the island. Surely a smoke plume of that size would be seen by the forest service. *They'd have to dispatch a helicopter or something.* He also knew that it takes just one spark to cross the bay. One spark that could lead to the destruction of half a million acres, especially at this time of year, before everything is greened-up. *Where are you, you son-of-a-bitch? On second thought don't worry about it. I'll find you.*

"Start with these." Ross dropped the three empty packs in the middle of the camp and retreated into the dark forest.

Water in a stream is never really as clean as it appears. Unless you are getting it right out of the ground you have to know there is a chance. Most of these people do not know. Ask Glenn. I had him laid in the fast, cool stream for days, away from crayfish and turtles or anything else that would appreciate slowly rotting meat. I used to think the soul cared about the body but now I know it is just a bag. A paper trash bag really, that nobody cares about or appreciates until it gets wet and rips. And when you are done with it, well…who cares? But still, despite his face Glenn was the only person I had spoken with in some time. I had grown tired of the high maintenance friendship. He was done giving although he had given me so much. If he was alive, he would probably be expecting a decent burial. That is the irony of it. What grand power would ingratiate me to bury a bag?

The smell of the smoke from the pine boughs was as pleasing a scent to Ross as it was confusing. The pieces that he added to the fire should have long burned out by now. The smoke was soon so pervasive that it started to burn his eyes. *The island.* His heart skipped as he tried to contain temporary panic. Burning down the forest was not on his agenda. Trying not to rush through the dark towards the shoreline the cracking of burning fresh boughs and the high light that followed froze him. Tall dancing flames gave ghost like movement to the shadow of a man that sat by the fire in the camp, shrouded in the white smoke of a different fire. Ross approached ever-so-slowly, his hand over his holster ready to draw.

"You in camp! Game Warden! Remain seated! Do not make any sudden movements!" Ross continued his approach. Even though the man sat next to a fire completely mired in smoke he did not cough, he did not hide his face. He was totally unaffected. Ross' mind had barely developed the question when the answer became obvious. He assumed at that point that the man with the crushed skull covered in dried blood and wearing dirty, wet pajamas had not breathed in some amount of time. The fire was not going to bother him at all.

The body had been propped so that it would appear to sit straight using a piece of wood tied perpendicular around its torso under its nightshirt and staked into the ground. As Ross stood there horrified and stunned, he realized that he had been baited.

How? There was no time to consider details. Illuminated against the night he was easy prey. His only hope was to return to the relative safety of complete darkness. It was a nightmare through which he had to move slowly and purposefully. Haste meant potential injury which undoubtedly and especially now meant death. Finally, when he felt far enough from camp he laid down and pulled his knees up towards his chest. He needed to absorb what had just happened, to wrap his mind around something he would never forget. He stared into the pitch black with eyes opened as wide as God would allow, like a child hiding from a thunderstorm under a thick blanket. It did not have to keep you safe, you only had to feel like you were safe.

CHAPTER 51

People say there are no coincidences but there are. These are the people that think there is a grand design for everything, that every little detail of your life is predetermined, and it just rolls out in front of you like a red carpet or roll of sod. They discredit chance, circumstance, and even luck. Once he said he was a warden it all clicked. Shame on me for not putting the taste with the smell earlier. What a little parasite, a black fly buzzing in my ear.

Back there he had honor, he served a purpose. We shared the commonality of cleaning up the trash. But here he was the trash, another paper cup covered in wax to prevent rotting. I will help him, he earned it by his works and who he was. Who he was should be his purpose.

He was half wet, curled up sleeping, barely. He shivered and twitched, probably traumatized by what I had shown him. He needed to see it though, to really appreciate that this is a dangerous place. Damn what he already knew. He knew how to buzz in my ear. That is what he knew. He knew how to be a cop. It was his sense of duty that made him a pawn, not his intelligence. Fear and anger were all that kept him from dying of exposure. I made them strong. They were all about me. I could keep them locked up inside him for as long as I wanted. They could not see me anyway, until they were free and then they would learn.

I pushed pine needles up against him very slowly. I wanted his body to become accustomed and comfortable with the support. To cover him I placed the needles one at a time, a thousand times a second as if they were being dropped in place by a directed wind. They would create a blanket that trapped the warmth of his body. A sign of safety that he will ignore. He will be threatened by good which makes him impartial, and I wanted that. All I have done is useless unless others know more than nothing.

Ross woke up startled, eyes wide open from nightmare level fears. He stretched out his legs, dislodging and crumbling his pine needle comforter.

What the? He jumped back out of them, never taking his eyes off of the needles as if they were to blame. A small flock of chickadees greeted the sun on the light breezes of a beautiful morning. He stood fully and brushed himself off. Taking stock, he was surprised to still have his gun that he held at the ready on his way back to the camp, to the man by the fire.

The body was how he last saw it in the dark the night before. The tiniest waft of smoke escaped from the otherwise dead fire. It was as grizzly a sight as Ross could ever remember and one he would surely never forget. He took a sleeping bag that was still neatly folded inside what he now assumed was the man's tent and wrapped his body tightly inside. He then placed the stones that surrounded the fire over the body, getting as many extra from the shoreline as needed to complete the grave.

The damn clothes. Ross laughed the laugh of a snapped man.

"Of course!" he yelled. "It's you! Has been all along, hasn't it? What? You didn't want to bury this one? Huh? Answer me! I know you're out there you son of a bitch! Answer me!"

Ross' voice was going hoarse. He fell to his knees and hovered at the edge of crying. He murmured quietly to himself, "no, no, you are not going to get me too. No, no way, you're breaking me down. Fuck that, fuck this, you're so mine. I'm so coming for you."

He sprang to his feet, renewed with strength and purpose.

"You hear that?" he screamed into the woods. "You hear that you son-of-a-bitch? I'm comin' for ya. That's right. Comin'!"

A post-tirade pause one would assume a result of so much emotion was actually a direct reflection of not knowing how to go about it.

Ross picked over every inch of the camp, searching for clues, a trail, anything. All the while being vigilant of what was happening in the forest around him. The packs that he dropped there earlier were gone. He found the place where the body had been propped-up along the shore as a scarecrow to steal his attention away from a porous boat. He found a rainbow-colored sock there, soaking wet and filthy that he prayed was empty, possibly belonging to the unwitting accomplice. The rest of camp was still immaculate, not even an old cigarette butt.

The bastard probably even cleaned up old garbage. How'd he miss the sock?

The only trail out led back to the bear rock, back where he had first discovered what he thought was the sight of the kill. With his recent epiphany removing chance from the equation, he moved down the trail to what he was now convinced was a crime scene.

Things were different for Ross now. His purpose was beyond survival. He carried a stout cocktail of emotions mixed with more sense of duty and less anger, less fear but with added portions of vengeance and vigilante justice. He even moved differently, slightly crouched with his hands off to his sides as if he needed to hold his balance. At the rock nothing had changed, the body of the bear was on the bottom of the shallow water up against the shore. The brush was thick near the muddy shoreline. There was no obvious route forward besides a game trail made thin by beavers and pine squirrels.

There's no way a man goes through here and leaves no prints. Ross recalled the sound of cracking branches he had heard after dispatching the bear. *Gotta be another trail.*

His hunch was rewarded not with the boot prints he longed for but with another distinct trail that followed the water's edge. An occasional spot of brown blood dotted the ground, a sign that donor was already dead. Slowly following along he could not shake the feeling that it was all going just a little too easy. Eventually he came to a freshly fallen tree with a large area of blood-stained rock below it. The sibling of the rainbow sock he found back at camp was snagged on the bark of the trunk. He pulled it free and studied closely.

"That's it all right." He looked out into the forest. "You left it for me. Could have had me again," he said to himself in the slightest of whisper. Upon further inspection on the bark above the blood stain, he found a small piece of the victim's scalp with accompanying, still attached disheveled hair. *This one you crushed, the other guy you fed to the bear. Me, you tried to drown.* There was little more he could do and although he had yet to discover any sign or remnants of a moving man, he continued on down the trail.

There was no more blood to be found, no more socks. No broken branches or boot prints. Every stone looked as if it had been laying there undisturbed forever. The width of the path covered with fallen, brown pine needles gave way to sandy mud and then finally slabs of rock that in ancient times flowed as liquid. He came to the face of another bay. A much larger finger pointing deep into the western skyline, the end shrouded in the spring-browned greens of a distant marsh. Big enough to be another lake in and of itself. Ross noticed the paddle first, leaned against a pile of boulders another dozen steps down the shoreline. Behind them was a boat, flipped over and tied to a tree trunk just a few feet from the water.

What? He looked the canoe over carefully, checking for holes or cracks in the hull. *He left this for me. He had to.* He stood and stared at it for some time, his mind raging with inner debate. *Unless he's scared. Maybe he just wants me to go home, get out of his hair. But more than likely it's just another trap. It's him steering me. The socks, the blood trail, everything.*

Deep in the bay there was a loud thud reminiscent of thunder. On a clear day that could mean only one thing, a canoe. *Or maybe he's running, and he just ran out of time.*

Hurriedly Ross untied the boat, flipped it right, pushed off and paddled hard towards the noise in the back of the bay. By the markings he determined it was an outfitter's canoe, very light, made of Kevlar and fast. He knelt slightly back from center careful not to bang the sides with the paddle and give away his location. Another boom, another breadcrumb.

He's tired, he's runnin'. I'm comin'.

CHAPTER 52

The bay eventually narrowed to the width of the distance between the trees of a four-lane highway. At its head the bay terminated in a shallow, muddy swamp strewn with stumps and beaver chewings. The shoreline was tall marsh grass, stiff and brown from winter. A beaver hut fortified with fresh poplar stood sentinel. Ross paddled straight for it with the intention of using it for a vantage point. His canoe scratched and whined through sticks and rocky mud. The top greeted him with discovery.

"There's more water." At first it appeared to simply be a swampy pond, but it too narrowed on its western end, the dead grass exposing its hidden inlet.

If he came this way… Ross looked over the area carefully but again found no sign of man. The hut was a wall as well as a doorway. On the backside, facing the pond he found a smooth crease. About two inches wide and narrowing at the top it extended up the side of the beaver hut only a half a dozen inches, but also continued into the mud under the shallow water. It was the footprint, of a canoe. The angle and the depth told the story of a boat that had been traveling from the west.

I'm betting you went back that way too. The inlet was indeed a feeder that seemingly wound on forever. At times it was only slightly wider than the canoe. Ross pushed his paddle against the boggy shore in order to advance. It opened up again to an area three boats wide and as long as a couple of city lots. It had been nearly an hour since he crossed over the beaver hut and found the creek. The water was deeper here and although still barely, moved noticeably faster than when he first put in.

There, underwater grasses bent from flow were the only indication that the water moved at all. Ross pushed-on to the very end. He had come too far not to make sure. The air was still. Ahead, out of sight from where the marsh grass and stumps ended and green pine trees began, the forest whispered the never-ending "push" of running water. A dogleg to the north carried yet faster water through a thinner bed. It was deeper, scoured to hard sand by the increased flow. Finally into the trees, the creek was becoming increasingly rocky and shallow. At the point of impassable was a boulder and a muddy landing off to his left. There was a canoe flipped behind the boulder. It was a short and stubby, old aluminum boat nearly black from moss and mold stains. More like a skiff than a canoe. A splintered paddle wreaking of the same old age leaned up against the overturned hull.

Ross pulled his boat up next to the other. He was pleased with himself. He had been careful to remain stealthy despite his exuberance. Dried indentations from human feet beat down a path next to the creek. He followed it with the slow intention of ambush. At its end, where the water turns white and goes up into rocky bluffs, he found a cabin. A dwelling unlike any other he had ever seen. A roof of forest floor and walls of rock. If not for the door a man might bump into it before he noticed it was even there. Another small door was built over a crevasse on the side of the cliff. Gray wood chips from former ax work littered the forest floor the area of a large car next to the cabin. The ax was lodged into the grain of a white cedar log. A rusty relic left to stand tall until its firm host gives way to inevitable rot.

"Hello inside? Game Warden." He pounded twice on the door and moved to the side out of the line of fire. "Hello inside! Game Warden." Entering the dwelling was now his only option. He drew his pistol and attempted the door which opened surprisingly easy.

Inside was devoid of light besides what Ross allowed through the open door. He made out an oil lantern hanging from the ceiling by the door. *And this is why we bring lighters.* He was able to reach it while keeping the door open with his foot. He took the lantern back outside. The reservoir was still full of oil, although it was unlike any Ross had seen before. White and thicker than normal lamp oil it nearly smelled rotten, with a faint hint of petroleum. Once lit he re-entered the building.

"Hello inside. Game Warden. Is anybody in here?" He found another lantern and lit that one as well and placed it next to the fireplace. The counter was covered with camping supplies laid out like a high-end department store. Perfect rows of utensils, folded clothes, canteens, and everything in between. Ross drew in closer with the lamp. Ross felt his stomach drop like a roller coaster ride when he saw not just any camping equipment, but more specifically his camping equipment.

Everything he left behind, from food to blue jeans along with what he assumed were the supplies of the men from the camp. And every empty pack, the same packs he dropped at the campsite to prove his point after escaping from the island. A cold shroud of terror overcame him. *Where is he?*

Ross trained his sidearm at the sound of a solid thump at the door. He waited nervously but nobody entered, nor were there any additional sounds. He tried to push it open, to test it for a mechanical answer. The door was completely immobile, heavily barred from the outside it was no more moveable than the walls that surrounded it. He walked the inside perimeter searching for another way out. The flame of the lantern by the hearth began to flicker down quickly extinguishing itself altogether. His vision started to cloud, and simple movement was becoming more difficult almost as if he was drunk. Ross staggered to the door in a desperate attempt to get outside into fresh air. The lantern he carried in hand also dimmed and in short order was totally snuffed as Ross looked on closely through the curved glass. In moments he found himself on his knees, totally shrouded in darkness and gasping for air. In the very next moment, he was passed-out on the floor.

Ross was awoken by a cool, ashy breeze. He was still dizzy, his head throbbed, and he was nauseous. It took him a little while to realize where he was, that he was still inside the cabin. His mind toiled to recall the series of events that brought him there. It was all coming back to him coasting on the oxygen of fresh air from the chimney flu. Feeling his way, he searched for the first lantern that had gone out, but it did not seem to be where he thought it was. He crawled the dark floor, arms flailing hoping to accidentally bump one.

"They're not there." At that moment I could have said anything, and he would have stopped looking. I knew what he was looking for. Light would have to be the first step of his own salvation. He spent the next few seconds wondering if he really heard me say anything at all. The tense moments were pleasing. The anticipation just hung there, tangible, laughable.

"Hello?" he said timidly probably not sure if really wanted an answer. I did not respond, content with having all the time in the world. "Is someone in here with me?"

That was a good question. I was not used to good questions or any questions at all for that matter. He made his way blindly to the door, jarring it a few times, checking to see if it was still locked. That was ironic to me because here, now in the darkness he knew where he stood. He was still, unsure, afraid. I heard his hand fumble with the snap on his holster.

"That's not there either," I said quietly attempting to sooth him with my inflection. I did not want him to panic. Startled he jumped back into the counter, disrupting what I had so carefully arranged. "I took you for the type of man to be calmer, more careful," I told him. "The type of man who could control a situation, or at least die trying."

"I'm not trying to die today," he said. His voice was collected, instantly living up to my expectations although I hoped it was not the result of suggestion. "Who the hell are you?" he asked angrily. My respect for him went in and out. At times when I carried a bit of reverence for who he was or what he did I would have wanted to tell him. Other times when he was my mouse, he did not deserve to hear my voice unless he got away with the cheese. Then I was back on board. He would never know anyway. As if anyone could give an immediate answer. Livestock people will tell you they are what their job is, even if they are unemployed. That is how conditioned they are to doing what they are told. They do not even know who is telling them. Hell rang out though, I hadn't thought much about it. *The hell, who the hell.* Even the dramatic pause between the words echoed in my mind. "You might have a point. About the hell I mean."

"You need to open that door and let me out of here immediately." He was in police mode, trying to scare me into submission. I am sure it works on the livestock. I could hear him moving ultra-slowly towards the sound of my voice.

"You know that you don't have your gun so you must therefore assume that I have it, yet you try to apprehend me in the darkness."

"I'm willing to take my chances. Night vision? Is that it? I have to be honest, it isn't all that magical or scary man. That's movie shit. Nothing we couldn't do with the lights on. Guys like you can't compete on even ground."

"Have you ever met a guy like me?"

"I don't know. I guess I haven't really met you yet but I'd sure like to though." He was threatening, clearly angry but other than that he was playing his cards close to his chest. There was so much more he wanted to say. I wanted to give him the chance but what he wanted was communication, trust. He wanted me to believe in him and buy his box of candy. He was not being a person yet so I did not want to talk to him anymore. No more than a few minutes passed before he started asking for me.

"Attempted murder", "I am a police officer" and other random catch phrases that are probably on page four of the manual were loosely included in his multiple matter of fact speeches. I slept warm wrapped in the tension my silence created. For hours I would hear him move, feel his intentions by the words he spoke. He was probing, remembering, getting the feel of the lay of the room in case he got a chance. He was not breaking, not yet. He was still working, wasting my time, disappointing me.

He could not be like the others, like prey. Petulant children that always think they know better even before they learn their ABC's. One too stupid to know when it is being insulted but yet positive it is brilliant. He needed to become people before them, before they did. I could see their eyes when they finally shed their personas, their paperback covers. It was too late. A person is not weak because they show their desire to give everything. Instead, those that would not only prove that their stubbornness and strong will let them die needlessly. By the time I took them it was already too late, or they would have never been there in the first place.

"Hey, if you're here can I get some water?" It had been some time since he had spoken, or even moved.

"Everybody uses the water. They have to you know or else they would die. Water from when they are born. Water to be baptized and to bathe. Water to drink. It sustains life, it takes lives. It's so important but yet we can't breathe it. Doesn't seem fair does it. Men like us take care of water. Be the man that needs it, try to breathe it. Take it from the air like it's all yours man! You have to stop being what you do if you'll ever earn it."

"I came pretty close to breathing water a few times because of you. You get your jollies? Huh? You satisfied being the game master?" He swept more gear off the counter in a mini childish fit of rage.

"What force besides your own will brought you to these moments?"

"My own will? My own will? You left me no choice. I swam to survive. With the means you left me to play your sick game. And those other two men. Your fingerprints are all over that camp. You and your excessive compulsive psychosis."

"Men are gerbils. Take them from their cages, off their wheels away from the feeders and they become prey to the wilderness which I do not control. I am part of it, as you could be too. But instead, you're my gerbil, scurrying in its cage searching for water and grain. I thought more of you, of course as I have learned you are a highly trained officer of the law." I mocked him, trying to draw out his anger.

"Fuck you! Fuck you! You want the man? Well here's the man, man," he carried out his last syllable theatrically, most likely trying to mock me as well. "I came here to take you down. Not sure who I was going to find but I know who you are, where you've been. I was there. I saw the bodies of the people you buried, on the Owens farm. It wasn't Mason at all, it wasn't any of them. It was you, somehow, I haven't put all the details together yet but I know it was you. God help me. If I can't level justice, I pray he will." His voice cracked from the stress of his confession. He cleared his throat and tightened his resolve. "And you haven't killed me yet so as far I'm concerned nothing has changed."

"It has because you are thirsty." I released the log that pinned the door closed. It was dark out now. I had spent the day with him. I slipped out ahead of him exposing faint starlight. If there had been a moon, I feel the effect of my silhouette would have been greater.

I watched him feel his way forward to the creek's edge. Most men would have stepped in it before they knew they were there. He was tuned-up, hardened by his ordeal. It made him sharp. He had me to thank. He knelt down just at the edge and put his lips directly into the water to drink. If I dropped a large stone on him now, he would die. I saw it happen in my mind but I chose against the notion. I gave him too much to waste.

He would paddle the dark creek if I let him. I left him no option save for flight. Run gerbil, run down your tube. I wanted him to roll over and refuse, to realize that he was being told to run for the food, for the bait. He stayed along the water line searching for the path to the boats. The telltale sound of impact, of a body losing its wind accentuated his hard fall. It was quiet as once again he struggled to breathe.

"The more men come here the more men die," I told him. I was on the path this time careful to let him make out my shape against the black sky. He got up quickly, lunging at me most likely trying to kill me with his bare hands. I stepped aside and provided the necessary pressure to send him tumbling into the creek.

He reported with the sound of an injured man, twisting his ankle between a series of rocks and opening his head on another. "What the hell do you want from me?" he yelled, his anger and frustration finally boiling over.

"Isn't it obvious? I want you to run. You're welcome to spend the night, however. Dry off, rest. The lanterns are just outside the door, the hearth full. There is adequate equipment to feed yourself as well. I want you to run down your tube and tell people of the bears, of the wind and the trees. Tell them how the water is unfit to breathe, and that death thinks of everything that they do not." He dragged himself from the creek but remained on hands and knees. "Instead, you'll come back, with men and equipment. You as a man will not be able to let it go and that's exactly why I chose you. And even this you will not understand. Now go, you will not see me again. Let the ax be your keel. If it strikes bottom you will take on water."

CHAPTER 53

Ross crawled inside and lit a fire. He could have paddled out in the dark but the realization that if this man wanted him dead, he would be already was a sobering lesson in survival. Soon he was dry and warm enough to find a lantern and raid the camping supplies on the counter for food and comfort. He savored every bite, as thankful as he was confused that he was alive. He was mentally exhausted. After eating he laid down on a pad and sleeping bag that was in with the equipment. As tired as he was, he could not sleep. Logic told him that he was safe, but fear is irrational.

He drifted in and out over the course of the night, at times waking, not sure if he had even slept. Usually, a person closes the door to feel secure. Not for Ross. On this night he chose to avoid the surprise.

The first robins of spring kept his attention about an hour before sunrise. He packed one pack with basic necessities, this time tossing in some food as well. He even spoiled himself with freeze dried coffee and a canteen cup full of oatmeal. It was light enough to make his way when he headed down the trail to the place where he tied up the boat. His canoe, the fast one was gone. Left in its place at the ready was the stubby, old aluminum skiff. He found it hard to be angry as a moment of realization overtook him. Many times, over the long, previous night, he labored over the man's strange words. In the stern of the boat the ax he had noticed when he first arrived on the scene was wedged halfway through the bottom of the boat. For it to not take-on water it would have to stay in place.

The old boat paddled poorly. It scratched through the water laboriously over a skin of filth and a shape not conducive to speed or agility. He zig-zagged his way wasting half of every stroke that pushed him off center. Whenever the threat of striking bottom arose, he stepped out, often into mud, to walk the boat over the obstacle assuring that the wet and cold would sap him even more.

It was mid-morning by the time he reached the beaver dam at the edge of the lake. There was no way he would make it out before dark and he was already overdue. The average breeze lent the trip above-average difficulty, his progress a mere fraction of what it would normally be. Finally reaching the open mouth of the bay the main lake body greeted him with near-breaking waves and the defeated feeling of making no ground. By late afternoon he had forged more than three quarters of the lake. In both mind and body, he was defeated. He rode the wind to closest shore to set up camp.

He packed no tent instead choosing to use the canoe for cover against the elements. His decision to bring food was paramount especially considering he did so before he knew the condition of the boat. Ross gathered wood knowing that he needed three times more than he wanted to keep the fire lit through the night.

As the fire crackled, he prepared a place to lay down, once again using cut balsam boughs to keep his body somewhat insulated from the heat-sucking ground. It was not quite dark yet when Ross noticed a canoe with a single paddler out on the lake. Very slowly he moved closer to the shoreline for a closer look.

"Is that you, you bastard? Checking up on me? Making sure I carry out your effed-up mission? Well come on in, you son-of-a-bitch, come on in." Ross ducked down and made his way back to the canoe which he turned away from the water. He donned a piece of firewood, a beaver chewing wrist-thick about three feet long and stepped back into the shadows.

The paddler was almost to the shore. He wore a camouflage hoodie and cheap, black gloves available at any gas station. Once up on shore and close to the fire he said nothing. Ross bolted from the brush ready to strike the man with all the force he could muster. The man turned and saw him a split second before Ross swung. They both screamed in terror. Ross fell to his knees, dropped the log, and sobbed relief.

"Steve!" Ross said, his crying turning to laughter. "Steven! My friend!" he yelled at the top of his voice.

"Ross man? What the hell happened to you? We got worried when you didn't come out. Figured I better come in and find ya. This your camp? Where's your tent? All your gear?"

Ross just continued to split time between laughing and sobbing on the ground.

"Something happened to you out here, didn't it? Here man, let's get you up and right. You alright?"

With tears running down his cheeks Ross smiled at Steve, took him by the shoulder and quietly asked, "Where you been man?" before finally embracing him. Ross laughed at his own response. "Thank you, thank you."

"Look my friend I don't know what went down out here but you definitely ain't you," Steve said.

Ross sat back by the fire and leaned up against the canoe. "Oh I'm me alright, I'm just a different me."

"Now what the hell is that supposed to mean?"

"My friend you won't believe what I'm about to tell you." Ross filled Steve in on the finer points and details from his ordeal in Wisconsin. He tied it to the stacked wood, the folded clothes and the body that he found. He told him about his swim and the sinking boat. "It's the same man."

"Sounds like kind of a one-in-a million type thing to me," Steve said.

"No wait, it gets better. I got on my horse and found this guy. Then I let myself get trapped in his cabin. I mean it's pitch black. I can't see anything, and this is after he somehow sucked all the air out of the room and I passed out, I, I, I hit the ground. Well I wake up, like I said it's pitch black, my gun is gone. Thank you very much for that, by the way, I may not be here today without it. Anyways he starts talkin' to me. I can't find him, can't quite get a fix on him in there then he disappears. For hours! I don't know if he's still in there or not but I keep talkin to him regardless. Then I ask him for water. Sure as hell he's in there. He gives me some sort of convoluted speech and then opens the door and lets me out. Tells me he's out of there, I'm free to go and that he knows I'm coming back for him with more men. And on top of that I told him I knew about Wisconsin and he didn't bother to deny it."

"Well they say crazies like that always really want to get caught even though they don't know it," Steve said.

"This guy will be long gone by the time we can get back. No way he waits for me, uh uh, no way."

"I'm tellin' ya I knew shit like this was goin' down man. I told you! Everybody thought I was crazy," Steve said.

"That thought definitely crossed my mind. For a while I was even on board until I realized who this guy was. He would have had to have traveled. I didn't think he would but I since I met him I wouldn't put anything past him," Ross said.

"We gotta worry about this dude tonight?" Steve asked.

"I don't think so, I don't know with you here maybe. Him and us don't have the same things in our heads."

"You say you met him? You already knew by that point he was a mass murderer and all and you didn't try and take him down? Or did ya? I noticed your face is a little busted up. He must have got away, huh? Or else I'd guess you'd be dead."

"No!" Ross yelled, annoyed and quick-snap angry. "No! Yes, he could have killed me. Yes, I tried to get him. I'm telling you it was just impossible from the position I was in.

He had me. He always had me. At every turn. Every decision I made played straight into his hands. He told me to run down the tube. Out on the lake today paddling that piece of crap canoe I finally got it. You know I had to think back to what he said but I got it. Run down the tube like a gerbil."

"Well my friend he don't have ya no more and you ain't nobody's gerbil. Let me get the tent up, we'll get some rest and get you the hell out of here at first light. Here." Steve tossed a .22 revolver and a small box of rounds onto Ross' lap. "Load that up just in case, huh?"

Ross laughed. "A lot of good a gun did me last time against this guy. This thing won't even kill a bear."

"It don't have to kill a bear, man."

CHAPTER 54

Steve had only been out of the bush for the last couple of years, but his gear was old enough to make retro look new. The straps of his tattered canvas Duluth pack were serrated into strings. His trusty nylon tent had faded to a robin's egg from dark blue and in areas was nearly transparent. Two aluminum break-down poles held either end of the simple triangle erect.

"I can't believe you still have that old tent." Ross said.

"She's rusty but trusty. And it's a hell of a lot better than what you got right now. You could give me a hand ya know. Instead of just sittin' there."

"Yeah?" Ross got up, picked-up a softball sized stone and walked over to Steve. "How's this?" He raised the stone high above his head. Steve who was knelt over attempting to push tent stakes into the rocky ground instinctively jolted into a defensive posture. Ross just opened up his hand and theatrically let the stone fall at Steve's side.

"I'm not really sure what the hell that was all about but thanks, I guess."

"Yeah. Well you said you needed help so that should help." Ross turned back towards the fire and took a few slow steps away. "I've been up against it the last few days ya know? Makes a man think. I mean, this guy. What are the odds? We just keep ending up in the same place? People end up dead?"

"Sure does," Steve said while he bent down to unzip the tent door.

"Sure does what?"

"Makes a man think." Steve went about bringing his gear inside preparing to turn in for the night. "No doubt you've been through it man. You need some good, solid rest and I promise your head will be clearer in the morning. We'll get the hell out of here and then we'll have all the time in the world to think about it."

Ross brushed the dirt and debris off his thin sleeping bag and climbed inside the tent. "My head is already clear and I'm thinkin'. Trust me." He zipped the tent closed and laid back onto the damp beadroll. "Clear as a bell."

"If you say so," Steve said as he rolled onto his side and went to sleep.

The beeping alarm cut the early morning air at 4:30 sharp according to Steve's vintage digital watch. The dim 1980's technology gave a warm, green hue to the inside of the old tent. Its hypnotic chirp took Ross back to younger days as he tried desperately to ease himself to sleep with comforting memories.

"Ok that's enough, shut it off," he said quietly.

"Steve!" he said louder. "Steve!" Ross reached over and pushed the button on the side of the watch to turn off the alarm. "What the hell, I'm not sleeping anyways."

From what transpired over the last few days Ross' body was not used to being fully hydrated. Hurriedly he unzipped the tent, took two quick steps and nearly broke into dance as he fumbled with his fly.

"Whew!" he said aloud, pleased with the steady stream. His suddenly emptied bladder made him shiver in the cool, morning air. The fire still smoked from all that was left of the butt of a once wet log. Ross scooped a handful of pine needles and forest litter from under the nearest tree and tossed them onto the coals. The smoke grew exponentially and with a few added breaths soon erupted into steady flame. He took some of the sticks he had collected earlier and threw them in as well. He crunched down close to get warm as the flame grew. The pleasing scent of smoldering pine began to burn his eyes until it smelled acrylic and harsh.

"What the?" Steve woke up coughing, panicked, and screaming. "Ahaeeee! Fire!" He dove out of the still unzipped door through a cloud of black smoke as the old nylon tent went up in flames like a dried Christmas tree. With middle tension gone the tent collapsed in on itself and rendered to a black burning goo.

"Oh my God!" Ross rushed to help Steve who was on his hands and knees coughing in front of the total loss.

"What the hell happened?" Steve said managing a few words between coughs.

"I don't know! I was…" Ross pointed towards the fire as he helped Steve to his feet but did not say it.

"You were what?" Steve asked, "by the fire?" Steve shrugged Ross' hands off of him and stepped to the side. "This yours? You drop this?"

Steve bent down and picked up very new-looking disposable cigarette lighter semi-stepped into the dirt. "I mean, it ain't mine and it's not like this was a regular campsite or anything."

Ross instantly recognized it as his. He had only just recently used it to light the lanterns in the stone cabin. "OK, he's here. Keep your eyes open, shh, get down."

"What? Nobody is here man! Just us. Just you, me, and your lighter."

"No, I must have left it back at his place. Yeah it's mine but not anymore ya know?" Ross explained.

"You trying to tell me he snuck up here and lit the tent on fire at the same time you just happened to be out here making a fire? Well?" Steve threw his hands in the air. "Where the hell is he then, man? You see him? Hear him? Anything? You were out here man!"

"Listen I know how this looks but I'm telling you this is how this guy works. He's like a ghost, always two steps ahead, trust me. It's him. Shh."

Both men stood as quietly as possible, listening. Steve still battled the occasional muffled cough.

I wanted to make the sound of an owl or a wolf. A reward for their trial and a dose of fake circumstance to keep them thinking, to maybe move them along. After listening to their sooshing and whispering I decided their minds would do a fine job of building unreasonable terror on their own.

A flashlight danced around the camp, presumably searching for me. The little friend who was never part of my plans thought he could find me in the light. His ignorance combined with what he knew was perfect. I could not have hoped for better.

"I don't hear anything Ross. Not a hoot owl, nothin'. Nothin' but the crackin' of the fire."

"Shh."

"Listen, don't shoosh me again. I don't know what happened but I sure as hell don't hear anything." Even after his little speech Steve gave quiet time a few more minutes before finally giving up for good. "That's it. We're up now. Let's get some food in us and get the hell out of here at first light. I'll get some water and get the stove goin'. You be a sweetheart and get the food pack down. Try not to light anything on fire."

"I didn't burn the tent, Steve. Look you may not believe me but he's out there, right now. Watching, listening to every word we say, planning God knows what."

Steve turned and walked up the rocks from the shoreline with a tin full of fresh lake water. "Hey man I know you say you've been through a lot but you're talkin' about the boogie man here, brother."

"Say? Say I've been? You think I made this up? You think I'm like some guy that maybe got caught hunting out of season and now I have to make things up?" Ross said agitated.

"No, ah no man. It's not like that. I mean, it would have to be a hell of a lot bigger deal than that, right?"

"What? What do you mean?"

"You know man, well…I meant there ain't no bigger deal than almost get killed like that."

"Yeah, exactly. And I'm telling you he could do us at any time. We're sitting ducks out here," Ross said.

"Well all the more reason to get some grub and hit the water as soon as we can," Steve said doing his best to calm the tense situation. They went about their own camp business, one cooking while the other packed. They sat next to each other and ate oatmeal and powdered eggs the whole time neither speaking a word. Ross was still angry about not being fully believed and Steve was still angry about the tent incident as well as the newfound feeling of wariness around his old friend.

After eating, cleaning camp and putting out the fire they flipped Ross' boat over into the woods minus the ax. They both pushed off in Steve's canoe just before first light. Ross was in the bow seat paddling hard.

"Whoa say man, cool you're jets a little. I know you want to get out of here, but I'm supposed to be rescuing you remember? You're switching too much, making it hard to steer," Steve said.

"Yeah, sorry about that," Ross said taking his paddle from the water laying it across his lap. "I guess I'm just used to that other boat. All day I pushed that thing side to side."

"Well slow her down some. We're too close to shore now. Gotta turn out." Steve paddled the port side trying to take the boat out further into the open lake while Ross dipped his paddle into the starboard water. "Other side man, we're too close to shore."

"I know it. Getting your foot on a rock or a ledge might be the only thing that gets you back alive you know? Trust me. And a life jacket. Always wear it," Ross said.

"I've been totin' the same life jacket around for I don't know how long. Makes a good seat pad anyways. Hey switch it up. I don't like being this close, can't see shit yet. Ross. Ross!" Steve yelled.

The initial bump has a tendency to raise the bow slightly giving the canoe a split second of lift. Depending on speed and the shape of the obstacle the boat may slide over the top, come to a screeching halt or even list sideways and swamp. No matter how or when it happens and most especially in the dark water it is an instantaneous moment of panic for the paddler.

"Damn it, I told you!" Steve yelled from the stern. The boat listed sideways dipping the starboard side quickly beneath the surface. In the blink of an eye the canoe was half full of water. It was due to the luck of experience that both men managed to counter the sloshing weight and level the boat. The gunwale was just above the water line.

"Shit that's cold. How could you not see that thing? Hell it's sticking out of the damn water!" Steve yelled.

"Like you said its dark, okay? We have to dump this out or we're never going to make it."

"I know, I know. Try not to lean. If you lean or paddle hard we're going over. I'm serious here. I already can't feel my legs."

CHAPTER 55

"You know I'm finding it harder and harder to believe that you couldn't see that rock man. You gotta get your head into the game. Careful, careful! Look for a sandy spot, easy, easy." The boat came to rest in shallow rocks a few yards from shore. The men unloaded their gear, dumped the water out of the canoe, carried it up on shore and flipped it. "I'm going to get into something dry. Feet will still be wet though. Thanks for that. Beats drowning I guess."

"I wouldn't hit anything on purpose. I just didn't see it," Ross said.

"Well, by my count that's twice in the last twelve hours you tried to kill me," Steve said jokingly. He glanced towards Ross so that Ross could see that he was smiling, that Ross would know it was good-natured ribbing. Ross was not amused. Such was the look on his face that Steve doused his smile and turned back towards digging out dry clothes.

Steve thought to apologize but decided to let it pass believing that anything he would say might just throw fuel on the fire. He had never seen Ross like this before, this angry. The look on Ross' face gave him grave concern, even fear. It is not what he knew about Ross that scared him but what he didn't know. He farmed his own seeds of doubt. He never was one to let a good conspiracy theory go to waste. "A fire?"

"I don't have any extra clothes, besides you can dry your boots some."

"You and your fire again. Glad I ain't sleepin'." The fact that Ross ignored him only added to Steve's concern. *He ain't arguing.* "I say we just get the hell on down the road. I mean, if we hit it hard we could be out by the end of the day."

"Easy for you to say, you're dry. It's cold out. I've come close enough to hypothermia this week. Why push it?"

"Why push it? Didn't you tell me there is an unstoppable madman in the woods? Following us? Lighting our tent on fire? I'd say that's a pretty good reason to push," Steve said.

"We're doing what he wants. If he wanted to kill us, he would have."

"Maybe you. You weren't in the damn tent. Don't light it man, I don't wanna stay out here one minute longer than I have to with you."

"With me?" Ross asked.

"You know what I mean. And besides, hell yeah with you. If it wasn't for your deep, soul-searching boat ride I wouldn't be out here right now."

"I didn't ask you to come."

"That's bullshit and you know it because first of all you did ask me to come. Second of all someone had to save your ass."

Ross' anger had passed. "Yeah, the more I think about that I think it might just be the other way around."

"What is? You haven't made any sense since I found you."

"Well, maybe you're still alive because of me. Because you're with me. Like I said he let me go but he didn't let you go." Ross lit the carefully arranged tinder he had gathered. "Let's get some heat on the subject." He swung the ax hard and often sending wood chips flying in all directions.

"All the more reason to beat feet man. C'mon man we don't need all that," Steve said nearly begging. Ross kept chopping as if he never heard him speak at all. "See that's what I'm talkin' about. You just are not hearing me. We gotta go!"

Ross stopped working and took a deep breath. "Fine!" He yelled as he threw the ax end over end sticking it into the trunk of a large tree. "Sorry old guy, people just don't know when to quit."

Steve looked at the ax in the tree and then back at Ross. "Were, I mean are you talkin' to me or the tree, man?" Ross did not answer.

"C'mon, pack it in. You put the fire out," Ross said as he took a few steps towards the overturned canoe. He flipped it over harshly, and quickly without care, banging the hull on the rocks. "Gimme a hand," he said bending into position to launch the boat onto his shoulders.

Normally one man will bend towards the center of the boat and the other towards the bow. Both will swing the boat up into the air together. The man in front holds the upside-down canoe steady while the other positions himself under the yoke.

"We can just grab it. I mean there's no need really…" Steve said sheepishly. Meaning that each man could grab the handle on either end and walk it because it was already close to the water.

"I got it!" Ross said choosing to hoist it up by himself like an angry child. Steve never saw it coming. Just before Ross managed to get under the yoke he lost his grip forcing him to abandon the lift. The stern swung around fast. The point of the canoe smashed into the side of Steve's face. He was out before he hit the ground. Steve's right leg was between two rocks. As his body fell the leg stayed in place effectively snapping his bone just below the knee.

When Steve opened his eyes he was under the boat, tucked in his sleeping bag next to a tall fire. It was dark. He also woke up to the pain as he tried to sit up.

"Ahhh God!" He reached down, felt the splint made from his own paddle and laid back down quickly. He rolled onto his side, dry heaving from the pain, nearly passing out.

"Mornin' sunshine," Ross said exuberantly. "I've been trying to keep you out of shock all day."

"Jesus Christ man? What the hell happened?" Steve asked through labored breaths.

"When you fell your leg got twisted up in the rocks, the bone looks broke through."

Steve could barely speak. "Get me out of here man. Get me out of here."

"I don't think that would be a very good idea. That leg is pretty bad. One good jar and it might even come apart, rupture a blood vessel. No, either we wait till you can travel or I go out and get help, send in a chopper or something."

Steve clenched his teeth tight as he tried to answer, "Fuck you. You're not leaving me here." The combination of stress and pain taxed his consciousness causing him to finally succumb and pass out.

"That's OK, we can talk about in the morning," Ross said.

Steve woke to the drum beat sound of a canoe being man-handled on rocky ground. His pack was behind him deflecting heat from the well-tended fire. He sat up, his head throbbing. As he put his hand against his forehead, he felt the dried blood from the initial impact. He felt the swelling in his face. He was dizzy and had to lay back down. Ross was nearly ready to go. "Hey man, you can't leave me here." Ross did not answer. "Hey man! I'll die!" Steve pleaded.

Ross put the boat in the water and placed his gear inside. Amidst Steve's pleas he stomped angrily up to where he laid. "Look, you can't be moved. If I move you, you could die. At least here you've got a fighting chance. I left food, water, plenty of wood." He pointed towards six small towers of firewood stacked next to the pit. Sorted by size each stick was stacked perpendicularly with space between. "I should be out by the end of the day. Who knows, maybe they'll mobilize yet tonight. If not, I'm sure it'll be first thing in the morning."

"You gotta get me out of here man, I can take it."

Ross very lightly jarred Steve's leg with his foot causing him to scream. "No way." With that Ross turned to leave, climbed into the boat and struck paddle to water.

"Wait! Wait," Steve yelled. "At least give me the gun!" He threw his head back, crying to himself, "At least give me the gun…"

Ross stopped himself mid-stroke and backed up towards shore. He walked back up by Steve and dropped the revolver and box of shells in his lap just as Steve had done for him the day before. "It won't do you any good against him you know."

Steve broke the chamber open to see if the gun was loaded. He closed it with snap of his wrist and pointed it directly at Ross. "I'm not using it against him. Or am I?" He pulled the hammer back as he sat up. "Real careful now, you're going to get me the hell out of here."

CHAPTER 56

"Think about what you're doing here Steve," Ross said calmly. "There's no way you can keep that gun on me the whole time."

"Oh yeah? Watch me brother. Just watch me. This is how this is gonna work. You very carefully put my shit in the boat and I'm going to drag my ass down there." Steve paused to absorb pain. "I'm gonna face you and you are going to paddle us the fuck out of here. Got me? And I swear to God

I'll shoot you if I have to. Like you said, got nothin' to lose, gonna die either way."

Steve dragged himself, sleeping bag and all to the canoe being careful to demand Ross stay close enough to shoot but not close enough to be a threat. His screams of pain from getting himself in the boat he used as focus on Ross, channeling it into hate and anger.

"Now you!" he screamed, exhausted from the ordeal. "Wait, gimme my life jacket."

Ross stepped into the back with Steve towards the bow facing backwards. "Don't think about ramming us into nothin' because I swear I'll shoot you before I hit the water," Steve threatened.

Ross simply followed directions, remaining calm and silent until they were well underway. "Sure are anxious to shoot me, aren't you? A man you know?"

"Bullshit man, I did know you but I sure as hell don't know you. Man, I seen the wood, through all that you're fine, not a scratch? Look at me man. Look at me!" Steve screamed once again combining his pain and anger. "Probably got those fuckin' people back home too. Uh, uh, you're not doing me like that brother. You just paddle, shut the fuck up."

Steve fought hard against the normally unnoticeable smacking of rippled waves against the side of the canoe. The miles of water sapped his very being, he thought about death and Jesus. For the first time in his life, he questioned whether it was smart to have denied him and how hypocritical it would be for him to call on him now. From the corner of his eye after so much open sky he finally caught sight of a shoreline. "Thank God."

"We're coming up the rocky pullover," Ross told him.

"OK. Water was flowing through there a few days ago. You're gonna hop out and pull me through."

"We'll bottom out. No way I'll be able to get through there."

"There's no way you won't try."

"What's the point? After that we have the pond, and there's no way I pull you up the next one, what are we going to do on the portage?"

"We'll cross that bridge when we come to it. Slow up, come in slow," Steve said as they coasted to the mouth of the creek. "Now spin us around and pull from that end."

Ross did as he was told, walking the shallow, rocky water literally dragging the boat over the bottom. Steve braced himself against the jarring pain of bouncing off boulders that Ross gave no effort to avoid. A grueling ten rods (a unit of measure usually 16.5 feet) later Ross reached the end that opened up into a large spill pond, dug by the whitewater creek that entered on the other side. When the water was deep enough to float the canoe, he let go of the bow, grabbed the ax and dove into the deeper water ahead. Momentum sent the boat drifting into the open water, a helpless victim of current.

"Damn you!" Steve fired twice, off balance he missed Ross as he slipped back into the trees. "Damn! Damn you!"

The canoe continued to float backwards towards a small eddy. The flow carved out a mini-bay the size of a passenger van. Logs and litter that washed down the creek ended up here before the water broke the corner and spread out into the pond. The majority fed the main lake while the rest trickled off into a weedy backwater. Steve struggled to turn his body, to see what was coming. In the back of the tiny bay Ross was there, holding the ax in both hands staring down at the water. He made no attempt to flee.

"Put it down man! Put the fuckin' ax down man or I swear!" Steve demanded. "Hey! What is that? My God! You son of a bitch!" Steve fired the pistol four more times, using every round at his disposal. After the first hit, Ross looked at him, utterly stunned but with roughly a second between each next corresponding hit he did not have enough time to answer.

At times what is right seems so right. Just a little push and it is as if divinity takes over. Something capable of pulling strings on marionettes, on men and you are moving in its shadow. I must have broken Ross. The strong man I made would never otherwise stand still and allow himself to be taken down so easily. To be shot by another broken man. And now what? He will wait for help, someone will eventually come over this portage, just as I once did. It was a long time since I was this close. The broken fool wept as his boat spun in the current.

I moved in closer. Ross' bullet-riddled body laid on the shore with one leg in the water. It was cold water, fed by multiple springs and stored in a deep, sheltered pond. He laid shoe-deep behind a handful of floating logs and requisite raft of rapids-driven foam.

The water was still here offering little movement. Only the strongest of winds might touch it while motion generated waves were blocked by what once was alive but now had fallen. I noticed the coat first, a camouflage field jacket, army issued back in 1980's. The sound of the water washed out nearly everything with its violence but yet there it was in front of me, so still and so very reflective.

It had been some time since I had seen myself. I couldn't recall for anyone's life in all the years the last time I looked in a mirror. I should have been more confused looking back. My bloated body laying just below the surface of the calm pool, gray and pathetic. I still had the pack on my back. It filled with water and sank with me, the pressure from the branch tore the strap free on one side leaving a hole. It pulled me down like an anchor.

A back-lit glimmer of sun gifted an appropriate accent through my black cloaked, semitransparent reflection. I could not feel its warmth. In fact, I felt nothing. Not hot nor cold, not hunger or pain. There was no drive to go forward, no remorse to revisit the past. There was not even satisfaction from knowing who I was or what I had become. I did not hate what I was looking at because I knew now that I had never loved it.

The broken man in the boat dropped all of his shells while feverishly trying to reload his gun. Our eyes met, he froze, "My God!" he said.

"Not even close." I heard myself think it.

A chorus of pond lilies sprouted from the mud between the rocks on the bottom where my body lay. Invasive people cut them down to make way for boat passages and swimming beaches considering them a nuisance, weeds. Maybe it is because they take up as much space as possible, to gather sunlight and to feed. Their sole purpose to spread their seeds and reproduce, to sacrifice themselves for the flowers.

THE END

The author would like to thank the individuals who supported the development of this work. Some read a few pages and others the entire work. Your feedback as a reader and friend was helpful in shaping the story.

ABOUT THE AUTHOR

Daniel Rehm became a full-time writer after a long career in the paint and industrial coatings industry. Dan wrote this work, *Let Flowers Be Flowers*, between 2008 and 2011 and launched Rudbeckia Productions, LLC in 2020 to publish his work. Dan has since consisted on a diet of plain bologna sandwiches on white bread, water, and whatever was growing behind the homeless shelter as few writers can make a living in a spiraling world of illiterate, angry, political junkies.

In 2020, he wrote the series *The Adventures of Philippine Maximine, PI* in an effort to capture the essence of some of the characters found in *Flowers*. It is in *Philippine Maximine* where you first meet Darlene and Bob, The Hunter, as well as others from the *Flowers* hunting party.

Dan's writing includes various landscapes he knows very well – from the coulee area of western Wisconsin to the boreal forest of the Boundary Waters Canoe Area. He has enjoyed writing *Let Flowers Be Flowers* because he was able to explore both character development and bringing to life the various relationships among men and their families. In addition, exploring the sociopathic nature of a killer – what motivates a killer, what haunts a killer, and what purpose that killer believes he has in his life.

The Hunter's story continues in Dan's current work – as of yet titled – and expected to be published in 2023.

Dan can be reached at contact@DanRehm.com

Rudbeckia
PRODUCTIONS